THE WEIGHT OF HONOR

(KINGS AND SORCERERS—BOOK 3)

MORGAN RICE

D1490609

Books by Morgan Rice

KINGS AND SORCERERS
RISE OF THE DRAGONS
RISE OF THE VALIANT
THE WEIGHT OF HONOR

THE SORCERER'S RING
A QUEST OF HEROES
A MARCH OF KINGS
A FATE OF DRAGONS
A CRY OF HONOR
A VOW OF GLORY
A CHARGE OF VALOR
A RITE OF SWORDS
A GRANT OF ARMS
A SKY OF SPELLS
A SEA OF SHIELDS
A REIGN OF STEEL
A LAND OF FIRE
A RULE OF QUEENS
AN OATH OF BROTHERS
A DREAM OF MORTALS

THE SURVIVAL TRILOGY
ARENA ONE (Book #1)
ARENA TWO (Book #2)

the Vampire Journals
turned (book #1)
loved (book #2)
betrayed (book #3)
destined (book #4)
desired (book #5)
betrothed (book #6)
vowed (book #7)
found (book #8)
resurrected (book #9)
craved (book #10)
fated (book #11)

"If I lose mine honor,
I lose myself."

--William Shakespeare
Antony and Cleopatra

CHAPTER ONE

Theos dove for the countryside, filled with a fury he could no longer contain. He no longer cared what his target was—he would make the entire human race, the entire land of Escalon, pay for the loss of his egg. He would destroy the entire world until he found what he was looking for.

Theos was torn by the irony of it all. He had fled his homeland to shelter his egg, to spare his child the wrath of all the other dragons, all threatened by his offspring, by the prophecy that his son would become Master of All Dragons. They had all wished to destroy him, and that, Theos could never allow. He had fought off his fellow dragons, had received a grievous wound in the battle, and flown, wounded, thousands of miles across many great seas, until he had come here, to this island of humans, this place where the other dragons would never look for him, all for safe harbor for his egg.

Yet when Theos had landed, had placed his egg on the remote forest floor, it had left him vulnerable. He had paid for it dearly, receiving fresh wounds from the Pandesian soldiers, and losing sight of his egg as he'd fled in haste, his life spared only by that human, Kyra. On that confusing night, amidst the snowstorm and raging winds, he had never been able to find his egg again, buried in the snow, despite circling, returning again and again. It was a mistake for which he hated himself, a mistake for which he blamed the human race, and for which he would never, ever forgive.

Theos dove ever faster, opened his jaws wide, roared in rage, a roar that shook the very trees, and breathed a stream of flame so hot that even he recoiled from it. It was a massive stream, powerful enough to wipe out an entire city, and it rained down on his haphazard target: a small country village unlucky enough to lie in his path. Down below, several hundred humans, spread across farms and vineyards, had no idea of the death about to greet them.

They looked up, faces frozen in horror as the flames descended—but it was too late. They shrieked and ran for their lives, but the cloud of flame caught them. The flames spared no one—men, women, children, farmers, warriors, all those who ran, and all those who stood frozen. Theos flapped his great wings and

8

set them all aflame, set their houses aflame, their weapons, their livestock, their possessions. They would all, every single last one of them, pay.

When Theos finally swooped back up, nothing remained. Where the village once stood was now a great conflagration, fires which would soon reduce it to ash. Fitting, Theos thought: from ashes humans came, and to ashes they would return.

Theos did not slow. He continued to fly, staying low to the ground, roaring as he hacked away at trees, clawed off branches in a single swipe, tore leaves to shreds. He flew along the treetops, carving out a path, still breathing flame. He left a great trail of flame as he went, a scar upon the land, a roadway of fire for Escalon to always remember him. He set aflame great swaths of the Wood of Thorns, knowing it wouldn't grow back for thousands of years, knowing he would leave this scab upon the land and gaining some satisfaction at the thought. He realized, even as he breathed, that his flames might find and burn his own egg. Yet, overwhelmed with rage and frustration, he could not stop himself.

As he flew, gradually, the landscape changed beneath him. Woods and fields were replaced by stone buildings, and Theos peered down and saw he flew over a sprawling garrison, packed with thousands of soldiers in blue and yellow armor. Pandesians. The soldiers scanned the skies in panic and wonder, armor glistening. Some, the smart ones, fled; the brave ones stood their ground and as he neared, they threw spears and javelins his way.

Theos breathed and burned all the weapons in midair, sending them raining back to the earth as piles of ash. His flames continued down until they reached the now-fleeing soldiers, burning them alive, trapped in their shiny suits of metal. Soon, Theos knew, all those suits of metal would be rusting husks on the ground, a memento of his visit here. He did not stop until he burned every last soldier, leaving the garrison one giant cauldron of flame.

Theos flew on, flying north, unable to stop himself. The landscape changed, and changed again, and he did not slow even when he spotted a curious sight: there, far below, appeared a massive creature, a giant, emerging from a tunnel in the ground. It was a creature unlike any Theos had ever seen, a powerful creature. Yet Theos felt no fear; on the contrary, he felt anger. Anger for its being in his path.

The beast looked up and its grotesque face collapsed in fear as Theos dove down low. It, too, turned and fled, back for its hole— but Theos would not let it go so easily. If he could not find his child, then he would destroy them all, man and beast alike. And he would not stop until everyone and everything in Escalon was no more.

CHAPTER TWO

Vesuvius stood in the tunnel and looked up at the shafts of sunlight pouring down on him, sunlight from Escalon, and he basked in the sweetest feeling of his life. That hole high above, those rays shining down upon him, represented a victory greater than any he could dream, the completion of the tunnel that he had imagined his entire life. Others had said it could not be built, and Vesuvius knew he had achieved what his father and his father before him could not, had created a pathway for the entire nation of Marda to invade Escalon.

Dust still swirled in the light, debris still filling the air from where the giant had punched a hole through the ceiling, and as Vesuvius stared through it, he knew that hole high above represented his destiny. His entire nation would follow on his heels; soon all of Escalon would be his. He grinned wide, already imagining the rape and torture and destruction awaiting him. It would be a blood fest. He would create a nation of slaves, and the nation of Marda would double in size—and territory.

"NATION OF MARDA, ADVANCE!" he shouted.

There arose a great shout behind him as the hundreds of trolls crammed in the tunnel raised their halberds and charged with him. He led the way, charging up the tunnel, slipping and sliding on the dirt and rock, as he made his way toward the opening, toward conquest. With Escalon in sight, he trembled with excitement as the ground shook beneath him, tremors from the giant's screeching up above, the beast, too, clearly thrilled to be free. Vesuvius imagined the damage the giant would do up there, let loose on a rampage, terrorizing the countryside—and he smiled wider. It would have its fun, and when Vesuvius tired of it, he would kill it. In the meantime, it was a valuable asset in his rampage of terror.

Vesuvius looked up and blinked in confusion as he saw the sky suddenly darken up above, and he felt a great wave of heat come his way. He was baffled to see a wall of flame descending, suddenly covering the countryside. He could not understand what was happening as a horrific wave of heat came at him, scalding his face, followed by the roar of the giant—and then, a tremendous shriek of agony. The giant stomped, clearly hurt by something, and Vesuvius looked up in terror as it inexplicably turned back around. Its face half-burned, it charged back into the tunnel, underground—and right for him.

Vesuvius stared, but could not comprehend the nightmare unfolding before him. Why would the giant turn back around? What was the source of heat? What had burned his face?

Vesuvius then heard a flapping of wings, a shriek even more horrific than that of the giant—and he knew. He felt a shudder as he realized that up there, flying by, was something even more terrifying than a giant. It was something Vesuvius had never thought he'd encounter in his lifetime: a dragon.

Vesuvius stood there, frozen in fear for the first time in his life, his entire army of trolls frozen behind him—all of them trapped. The unthinkable had happened: the giant was running scared from something even greater than itself. Burned, in agony, panicked, the giant swung its huge fists as it descended, swiped with its vicious claws, and Vesuvius watched in terror as all around him his trolls were swatted. Whatever lay in its wrathful path was crushed by its feet, cut in half by its claws, smashed by its fists.

And then, before he could get out of its way, Vesuvius felt his own ribs cracking as the giant scooped him up and threw him in the air.

He felt himself airborne, tumbling end over end, the world spinning—and the next thing he knew his head was smashing into rock, the awful pain ripping through his body, as he impacted a stone wall. As he began to plummet to the ground, to lose consciousness, the final thing he saw was the giant, destroying everything, undoing all his plans, all he had worked for, and he realized he would die here, far beneath the earth, but feet away from the dream he almost had.

CHAPTER THREE

Duncan felt the air rush past him as he slid down the rope at sunset, scaling down the majestic peaks of Kos, holding on for dear life as he slid faster than he'd imagined possible. All around him the men slid, too—Anvin and Arthfael, Seavig, Kavos, Bramthos, and thousands of others, Duncan's, Seavig's, and Kavos's men joining together as one army, all sliding down the ice in rows, a well-disciplined army leapfrogging over each other, all of them desperate to reach the bottom before they were detected. As Duncan's feet touched the ice, he immediately pushed off again, repelling downward, his hands spared from being torn to shreds only by the thick gloves Kavos had given him.

Duncan marveled at how fast his army moved, all in a near free fall down the cliff. When he had been atop Kos, he'd had no idea how Kavos had planned on getting an army this size down so quickly without losing men; he hadn't realized they'd had such an intricate array of ropes and picks that could get them down so smoothly. These were men made for the ice, and for them, this lightning-fast descent was like a casual hike. He finally understood what they'd meant when they'd said the men of Kos were not trapped up here—but rather, the Pandesians, down below, were the ones who were trapped.

Kavos suddenly came to an abrupt stop, landing with both feet on a wide and broad plateau protruding from the mountain, and Duncan stopped beside him, as did all the men, momentarily pausing halfway down the mountain face. Kavos walked over to the edge and Duncan joined him, leaning over, seeing the ropes dangling far beneath; through them, far below, through the mist and final rays of the sun, Duncan could see at the mountain's base a sprawling, stone Pandesian garrison, teeming with thousands of soldiers.

Duncan looked over at Kavos, and Kavos looked back, delight in his eyes. It was a delight Duncan recognized, one he had seen many times in his life: the ecstasy of a true warrior about to go to war. It was what men like Kavos lived for. Duncan felt it himself, he had to admit, that tingling in his veins, that tightness in his gut. The sight of those Pandesians made him as excited for the thrill of battle as the next man.

"You could have descended anywhere," Duncan said, examining the landscape below. "Most of it is empty. We could have avoided confrontation, and moved on to the capital. Yet you chose the spot where the Pandesians are strongest."

Kavos smiled broadly.

"I did," he replied. "The men of Kavos do not look to avoid confrontation—we seek it out." He grinned wider. "Besides," he added, "an early battle will warm us for our march on the capital. And I want to make these Pandesians think twice the next time they decide to surround the base of our mountain."

Kavos turned and nodded to his commander, Bramthos, and Bramthos rallied their men and joined Kavos as they all rushed for a massive ice boulder perched at the edge of the cliff. They all, as one, leaned their shoulders into it.

Duncan, realizing what they were doing, nodded to Anvin and Arthfael, who rallied their men, too. Seavig and his men joined them, and as one, they all pushed.

Duncan dug his feet into the ice and pushed, straining under the weight of it, slipping, pushing with all he had. They all groaned, and slowly, the massive boulder began to roll.

"A welcoming present?" Duncan asked, smiling, grunting beside Kavos.

Kavos grinned back.

"Just a little something to announce our arrival."

A moment later Duncan felt a great release, heard a cracking of ice, and he leaned over and watched in awe as the boulder rolled over the edge of the plateau. He stepped back quickly with the others and watched as the boulder hurled down at full speed, rolling, bouncing off the ice wall, gaining speed. The massive boulder, with a diameter of at least thirty feet, fell straight down, rushing like an angel of death for the Pandesian fortress below. Duncan braced himself for the explosion to follow, all of those soldiers below unwitting, waiting targets.

The boulder struck the center of the stone garrison, and the crash was greater than anything Duncan had heard in his life. It was as if a comet had struck Escalon, a boom echoing so loudly he had to cover his ears, the ground shaking beneath him, making him stumble. An enormous cloud of stone and ice rose up, dozens of feet high, and the air, even from up here, became audible with the terrified shouts and cries of men. Half the stone garrison was destroyed on impact, and the boulder continued to roll, crushing men, flattening buildings, leaving a wake of destruction and chaos.

"MEN OF KOS!" shouted Kavos. "Who has dared approach our mountain?"

There came a great shout as his thousands of warriors suddenly charged forward and leapt off the edge of the cliff, following Kavos, all grabbing ropes and rappelling so fast, they were practically free-falling down the mountain. Duncan followed, his men behind him, all jumping, too, grabbing onto the ropes and descending so fast he could barely breathe; he felt certain he would break his neck upon impact.

Seconds later he found himself landing hard at the base, hundreds of feet below, descending into a huge cloud of ice and dust, the rumble still echoing from the rolling boulder. All the men turned and faced the garrison and they all let out a great battle cry as they drew their swords and charged, rushing headlong into the chaos of the Pandesian camp.

The Pandesian soldiers, still reeling from the explosion, turned with shocked faces to see the army charging; clearly, they had not expected this. Dazed, caught off guard, several of their commanders lying there dead, crushed by the boulder, they seemed too disoriented to even think straight. As Duncan and Kavos and their men bore down on them, some began to turn and run. Others reached for swords—but Duncan and his men descended upon them like locusts and stabbed them before they even had a chance to draw.

Duncan and the men rushed through the camp, never hesitating, knowing time was of the essence, and they felled the recovering soldiers on every side, following the trail of destruction left by the boulder. Duncan slashed every which way, stabbing one soldier in the chest, smashing another in the face with the hilt of his sword, kicking one who charged him, and ducking and laying his shoulder into another as the man swung an axe at his head. Duncan did not pause, felling everyone in his path, breathing hard, knowing they were still outnumbered and that he had to kill as many as he could as quickly as he could.

Beside him, Anvin, Arthfael, and his men joined him, all watching each other's backs, all rushing forward and slashing and defending in every direction as the clangs of warfare filled the garrison. Embroiled in a full-scale battle, Duncan knew it would have been wiser to have conserved his men's energy, to have avoided this confrontation and marched to Andros. But he also knew that honor compelled the men of Kos to fight this battle, and he understood how they felt; the wisest course of action was not always what moved men's hearts.

They moved through the camp with speed and discipline, the Pandesians in such disarray that they were barely able to put up an organized defense. Every time a commander surfaced, or a company formed, Duncan and his men hacked them down.

Duncan and his men rushed through the garrison like a storm, and hardly an hour had passed when Duncan finally stood there, at the end of the fort, turning every which way, and realized, blood-spattered, that there was no one left to kill. He stood there, breathing hard as twilight fell, a mist settling over the mountains, all uncannily silent.

The fort was theirs.

The men, realizing, let out a spontaneous cheer, and Duncan stood there, Anvin, Arthfael, Seavig, Kavos, and Bramthos coming up beside him, wiping blood from his sword, his armor, and taking it all in. He noticed a wound on Kavos's arm, seeping blood.

"You're wounded," he pointed out to Kavos, who didn't seem to notice.

Kavos looked down at it and shrugged. He then smiled.

"A beauty scratch," he replied.

Duncan surveyed the battlefield, so many man dead, mostly Pandesians and few his own men. He then looked up and saw the ice peaks of Kos towering over them, disappearing in the clouds, and he was in awe at how high they had climbed, and how fast they had descended. It had been a lightning attack—like death raining down from the sky—and it had worked. The Pandesian garrison, seeming so indomitable but hours ago, was now theirs, nothing but a flattened ruin, all its men lying in pools of blood, dead beneath the twilight sky. It was surreal. The warriors of Kos spared no one, took no mercy, and had been an unstoppable force. Duncan had a fresh respect for them. They would be crucial partners in liberating Escalon.

Kavos surveyed the corpses, breathing hard, too.

"That is what I call an exit plan," he said.

Duncan saw him grinning as he surveyed the enemy bodies, watching their men stripping the dead of their weapons.

Duncan nodded.

"And a fine exit it was," he replied.

Duncan turned and looked west, past the fort, into the setting sun, and motion caught his eye. He squinted and saw a sight which filled his heart with warmth, a sight which somehow he had expected to see. There, on the horizon, stood his warhorse, standing proudly before the herd, hundreds of warhorses behind him. He had, as always, sensed where Duncan would be, and was there, loyally awaiting him. Duncan's heart lifted, knowing his old friend would bring his army the rest of the way to the capital.

Duncan whistled, and as he did, his horse turned and ran for him. The other horses followed, and there came a great rumble in the twilight, as the herd galloped through the snowy plain, heading right for them.

Kavos nodded in admiration beside him.

"Horses," Kavos remarked, watching them approach. "I myself would have walked to Andros."

Duncan grinned.

"I am sure you would have, my friend."

Duncan stepped forward as his horse approached, and caressed his old friend's mane. He mounted him, and as he did, all his men mounted with him, thousands of them, an army on horseback. They sat there, fully armed, staring into the twilight, nothing before them now but the snowy plains leading to the capital.

Duncan felt a rush of excitement as he felt, finally, that they were on the brink. He could feel it, could smell victory in the air. Kavos had gotten them down the mountain; now it was *his* show.

Duncan raised his sword, feeling the eyes of all the men, all the armies, upon him.

"MEN!" he called out. "To Andros!"

They all let out a great battle cry and charged with him, into the night, across the snowy plains, all prepared to stop at nothing until they had reached the capital and waged the greatest war of their lives.

CHAPTER FOUR

Kyra looked up into the breaking dawn and saw a figure standing over her, a silhouette against the rising sun, a man she knew could only be her uncle. She blinked in disbelief as he stepped into view. Here, finally, was the man she had traveled across Escalon to meet, the man that would reveal her destiny, the man who would train her. Here was her mother's brother, the only link she had to the mother she never knew.

Her heart slammed with anticipation as he stepped forward out of the light and she saw his face.

Kyra was amazed: he looked startlingly like her. She had never met anyone who bore her resemblance—not even her father, as much as she hoped. She had always felt like a stranger in this world, disconnected to any true lineage—but now, seeing this man's face, his high, chiseled cheekbones, his flashing gray eyes, a man who stood tall and proud, with broad shoulders, muscular, dressed in shining gold chain-mail armor, with light brown hair that went down to his chin, unshaven, in his forties, perhaps, she realized he was special. And by extension, that made her special. For the first time in her life, she really felt it. For the first time, she felt connected to someone, to a powerful bloodline, to something greater than herself. She felt a sense of belonging in the world.

This man was clearly different. He was obviously a warrior, proud and noble, yet he did not carry any swords, any shields, weapons of any sort. To her amazement and delight, he carried only a single item: a golden staff. A *staff*. He was just like her.

"Kyra," he said.

His voice resounded through her, a voice so familiar, so much like hers. Hearing him speak, she felt not only a connection to him, but even more exciting, to her mother. Here stood her mother's brother. Here was the man who knew who her mother was. Finally, she would get the truth—there would be no more secrets in her life. Soon enough she would know everything about the woman she had always longed to know.

He lowered a hand, and she reached up and took it, standing, her legs stiff from the long night of sitting before the tower. It was a strong hand, muscular, yet surprisingly smooth, and he helped her to her feet. Leo and Andor stepped toward him and Kyra was surprised they did not snarl as usual. Instead, they walked forward and licked the man's hand, as if they had known him forever.

Then, to Kyra's amazement, Leo and Andor stood at attention, as if the man had silently commanded them. Kyra had never seen anything like it. What powers did this man have?

Kyra didn't even need to ask if he was her uncle—she sensed it with every ounce of her body. He was powerful, proud, everything she had hoped he would be. There was something else in him, too, something she could not quite grasp. It was a mystical energy radiating off of him, an aura of calm, yet also of strength.

"Uncle," she said. She liked the sound of that word.

"You may call me Kolva," he replied.

Kolva. Somehow, it was a name that felt familiar.

"I crossed Escalon to see you," she said, nervous, not knowing what else to say. The morning silence swallowed her words, the barren plains filled only with the sound of the distant crashing of the ocean. "My father sent me."

He smiled back. It was a warm smile, the lines in his face bunching up as if he had lived a thousand years.

"It was not your father who sent you," he replied. "But something far greater."

He suddenly, without warning, turned his back and began to walk, using his staff, away from the tower.

Kyra watched him go, stunned, not understanding; had she offended him?

She hurried to catch up, Leo and Andor at her side.

"The tower," she said, confused. "Are we not going inside?"

He smiled.

"Some other time, perhaps," he replied.

"But I thought I had to reach the tower."

"You did," he replied. "But not enter it."

She struggled to understand as he hiked quickly, entering the woodline, and she hurried to catch up. His staff clicked on the dirt and leaves, as hers did, too.

"Then where shall we train?" she asked.

"You shall train where all the great warriors train," he replied. He looked ahead. "In the woods beyond the tower."

He entered the woods, moving so quickly Kyra nearly had to run to keep up with him, even though he seemed to be walking at a slow pace. The mystery around him deepened, as a million questions raced through her mind.

"Is my mother alive?" she asked in a rush, unable to contain her curiosity. "Is she here? Have you met her?"

The man merely smiled and shook his head as he continued to walk.

"So many questions," he replied. He hiked for a long time, the forest filled with the sound of odd creatures, then finally added, "Questions, you will come to find, have little meaning here. Answers have even less. You must learn to find your own answers. The *source* of your answers. And even greater—the source of your questions."

Kyra was confused as they hiked through the forest, the trees a bright green, seeming to glow all around her in this mysterious place. She soon lost sight of the tower, and the crashing of the waves grew quieter now. She struggled to keep up as the trail wound every which way.

She was burning with questions, and finally, could no longer contain her silence.

"Where are you taking me?" she asked. "Is this where you will train me?"

The man continued hiking, over a running creek, twisting and turning between ancient trees, their bark glowing a luminescent green, as she followed on his heels.

"I shall not train you," he said. "Your uncle shall."

Kyra was baffled.

"My *uncle*?" she asked. "I thought you were my uncle."

"I am," he replied. "And you have another."

"Another?" she asked.

Finally, he burst into a clearing in the woods, stopping at its edge, and she, out of breath, stopped beside him. She looked out before her and was stunned at what she saw.

On the opposite side of the clearing sat an immense tree, the largest she had ever seen, ancient, its branches stretching everywhere, shimmering with purple leaves, its trunk thirty feet wide. The branches twisted and intersected with one another, creating a small tree house, perhaps ten feet off the ground, looking as if it had sat there forever. A small light came from inside the branches, and Kyra looked up and saw a sole figure sitting on the edge of the branches, looking as if he were in a state of meditation, staring down at them.

"He is your uncle, too," said Kolva.

Kyra's heart slammed in her chest, not understanding any of this. She looked up at the man he said was her uncle and wondered if he were playing a trick on her. Her other uncle appeared to be a boy, perhaps ten years old. He sat perfectly straight, as if in meditation, staring straight ahead, not really looking at her, his eyes glowing blue. His boyish face was lined, is if he were a thousand years old, his skin a darkish brown, covered in age spots. He could have been hardly more than four feet tall. It was as if he were a boy with an aging disease.

She did not know what to make of it.

"Kyra," he said, "meet Alva."

CHAPTER FIVE

Merk entered the Tower of Ur, walking through the tall, golden doors he never thought to pass through, the light shining so brightly inside it nearly blinded him. He raised a hand, shielding his eyes, and as he did, he was in awe at what he saw before him.

There, standing opposite him, was a real Watcher, his yellow eyes piercing as he stared back at Merk, the same eyes that had haunted Merk from behind the slot in the door. He wore a yellow, flowing robe, his arms and legs concealed, and the little flesh he showed pale. He was surprisingly short, his jaw elongated, his cheeks sunken, and as he stared back, Merk felt uncomfortable. Light shone from the short golden staff he held before him.

The Watcher studied him silently, and Merk felt a draft behind him as the doors suddenly slammed shut, trapping him in the tower. The hollow sounded echoed off the walls, and he involuntarily flinched. He realized how on edge he was from not sleeping all these days, from nights of troubled dreams, from his obsession over entering here. Standing inside now, he felt a strange sense of belonging, as if he had finally entered his new home.

Merk expected the Watcher to welcome him, to explain where he was. But instead, he turned wordlessly and walked away, leaving Merk standing there alone, wondering. He had no idea whether to follow.

The Watcher crossed to a spiral, ivory staircase at the far end of the chamber and, to Merk's surprise, he headed not up but down. He quickly descended and disappeared from view.

Merk stood there in the silence, stumped, not knowing what was expected of him.

"Shall I follow you?" he finally called out.

Merk's voice rang and echoed back at him, off the walls, as if mocking him.

Merk looked around, examining the inside of the tower. He saw the walls, shining, were made of solid gold; saw a floor made of an ancient black marble, streaked with gold. The place was dim, lit only by the mysterious glow coming off its walls. He looked up and saw the ancient staircase, carved of ivory; he stepped forward and cranked his neck and, at its very top, he spied a golden dome, at least a hundred feet high, sunlight filtering down. He saw all the levels above, all the different landings and floors, and he wondered what lay up there.

He looked down and, even more curious, he saw the steps continuing down below, to subterranean floors, where the Watcher had gone, and he wondered. The beautiful ivory stairs, like a work of art, twisted and turned mysteriously in both directions, as if rising up to heaven and down to the lowest levels of hell. Merk wondered, most of all, if the legendary Sword of Flames, the sword guarding all of Escalon, lay within these walls. He felt a rush just thinking about it. Where could it be? Up or down? What other relics and treasures were stored here?

Suddenly, a hidden door opened out of the side wall and Merk turned to see a stern-faced warrior emerge, a man roughly Merk's size, wearing chain mail, his skin pale from too many years of not seeing sunlight. He walked toward Merk, a human, a sword on his waist with a prominent insignia, the same symbol Merk had seen etched outside the tower walls: an ivory staircase rising to the sky.

"Only Watchers descend," the man said, his voice dark, rough. "And you, my friend, are no Watcher. Not yet, at least."

The man stopped before him and stared him up and down, laying his hands on his hips.

"Well," he continued, "I suppose if they let you in, there must be a reason."

He sighed.

"Follow me."

With that, the abrupt warrior turned and ascended the staircase. Merk's heart pounded as he hurried to catch up, his head swimming with questions, the mystery of this place deepening with each step.

"Do your job and do it well," the man spoke, his back to Merk, his voice dark and echoing off the walls, "and you shall be allowed to serve here. Guarding the tower is the highest calling Escalon has to offer. You must be more than a mere warrior."

They stopped at the next level, and the man stopped and stared into Merk's eyes, as if sensing some deep truth about him. It made Merk uncomfortable.

"We all have dark pasts," the man said. "That is what drove us here. What virtue lies in your darkness? Are you ready to be born again?"

23

He paused, and Merk stood there, trying to comprehend his words, unsure how to reply.

"Respect is hard won here," he continued. "We are, each of us, the best Escalon has to offer. Earn it, and one day, you may be accepted into our brotherhood. If not, you will be asked to leave. Remembers: those doors which opened to let you in, can just as easily let you out."

Merk's heart sank at the thought.

"How can I serve?" Merk asked, feeling the sense of purpose he had always craved to feel.

The warrior stood there for a long time, then finally turned and began ascending the next flight. As Merk watched him go, it was dawning on him that there were many things forbidden here in this tower, many secrets he might not ever get to know.

Merk went to follow, but suddenly, a large beefy hand slapped him in the chest, stopping him. He looked over to see another warrior appear, exiting another hidden door, while the first warrior continued on, disappearing into the upper levels. The new warrior towered over Merk, wearing the same golden chain mail.

"You'll serve on this level," he said, gruff, "with the rest of them. I am your commander. Vicor."

His new commander, a thin man with a face as hard as stone, looked as if he should not be crossed. Vicor turned and gestured to an open door in the wall, and Merk entered cautiously, wondering what this place was as he twisted and turned down narrow stone halls. They walked in silence, passing through open arches carved of stone door, and the hall opened into an expansive room with a high tapered ceiling, stone floors and walls, and lit by sunlight filtering in through narrow, tapered windows. Merk was startled to see dozens of faces staring back at him, faces of warriors, some thin, some muscular, all with hard, unflinching eyes, all alight with a sense of duty, of purpose. They were all spread throughout the room, each stationed before a window, and they all, wearing the golden chainmail, turned and looked out at the stranger entering their room.

Merk felt self-conscious and he stared back at the men in the awkward silence.

Beside him, Vicor cleared his throat.

"The brothers don't trust you," he said to Merk. "They might never trust you. And you might never trust them. Respect is not handed out here, and there are no second chances."

"What is it that I am to do?" Merk asked, baffled.

"The same as these men," Vicor replied gruffly. "You will watch."

Merk scanned the curved stone room and at the far end, perhaps fifty feet away, he saw an open window at which sat no warrior. Vicor walked slowly toward it and Merk followed, passing the warriors, all watching as he went, then turning back to their windows. It was a strange feeling to be among these men, yet to not be a part of them. Not yet. Merk had always fought alone, and he did not know what it was like to belong to a group.

As he passed and surveyed them, he felt these were all, like he, broken men, men with nowhere else to go, with no other life purpose. Men who had made this stone tower home. Men like him.

As he neared his station, Merk noticed the final man he passed looked different than the others. He appeared to be a boy, perhaps eighteen, with the smoothest and fairest skin Merk had ever seen, and with long, fine blond hair down to his waist. He was thinner than the others, with little muscle, and he looked as if he had never been in battle. Yet, still, he had a proud look to him, and Merk was surprised to see him stare back with the same fierce, yellow eyes as the Watcher. The boy almost looked too frail to be here, too sensitive—yet at the same time, something in his look set Merk on edge.

"Do not underestimate Kyle," Vicor said, looking over as Kyle turned back to his window. "He is the strongest among us, and the only true Watcher here. They sent him here to protect us."

Merk found it hard to believe.

Merk reached his post and sat beside the tall window and looked out. There was a stone ledge to sit upon, and as he leaned forward and looked through the window, he was afforded a sweeping view of the landscape below. He saw the barren peninsula of Ur, the treetops of the distant forest, and beyond that, the ocean and sky. He felt as if he could see all of Escalon here.

"Is that all?" Merk asked, surprised. "I just sit here and watch?"

Vicor grinned.

"Your duties have not even begun."

25

Merk frowned, disappointed.

"I have not come all this way to sit in a tower," Merk said, to the looks of some others. "How am I to defend from up here? Can I not patrol on the ground?"

Vicor smirked.

"You see far more up here than you can below," he replied.

"And if I see something?" Merk asked.

"Sound the bell," he said.

He nodded and Merk saw a bell perched beside the window.

"There have been many attacks against our tower over the centuries," Vicor continued. "All have failed—because of us. We are the Watchers, the last line of defense. All of Escalon needs us—and there are many ways to defend a tower."

Merk watched him go, and as he settled into his station, in the silence, he wondered: just what had he signed himself up for?

CHAPTER SIX

Duncan led his men as they galloped through the moonlit night, across the snowy plains of Escalon, hour passing hour as they charged, somewhere on the horizon, for Andros. The night ride brought back memories, of past battles, of his time in Andros, of serving the old King; he found himself getting lost in thoughts, memories blending with the present blending with fantasies for the future, until he no longer knew what was real. As usual, his thoughts drifted to his daughter.

Kyra. Where are you? he wondered.

Duncan prayed she was safe, that she was advancing in her training, and that they would soon reunite for good. Would she be able to summon Theos again? he wondered. If not, he did not know if they could win this war that she had begun.

The incessant sound of horses, of armor, filled the night, Duncan barely feeling the cold, his heart warm from their victory, from their momentum, from the growing army behind him, and from anticipation. Finally, after all these years, he felt the tide turning his way again. He knew Andros would be heavily guarded with a sitting, professional army, that they would be vastly outnumbered, that the capital would be fortified, and that they did not have the manpower to stage a siege. He knew that the battle of his life awaited him, one that would determine the fate of Escalon. Yet that was the weight of honor.

Duncan also knew that he and his men had cause on his side, had desire, purpose—and most of all, speed and the power of surprise. The Pandesians would never expect an attack on the capital, not by a subjugated people, and certainly not at night.

Finally, as the first traces of dawn began to break, the sky still a bluish haze, Duncan saw in the distance, just beginning to appear, the familiar contours of the capital. It was a sight he had not expected to see again in his lifetime—and one that made his heart beat faster. Memories rushed back, of all the years he had lived there, had served the King and the land loyally. He recalled Escalon in the height of its glory, a proud, free nation, one that had seemed undefeatable.

Yet seeing it also brought back bitter memories: the weak King's betrayal of his people, his surrendering of the capital, of Escalon. He recalled he and all the great warlords dispersing, being forced to leave in shame, all exiled to their own strongholds, all across Escalon. Seeing the majestic contours of the city brought rushing back to him longing and nostalgia and fear and hope all at the same moment. Those were the contours that had shaped his life, the outline of the most magnificent city in Escalon, ruled by kings for centuries, stretching so far it was hard to see where they ended. Duncan breathed deep as he saw the familiar parapets and domes and spires, all of which were deeply ingrained in his soul. In some ways, it was like returning home—except Duncan was not the defeated, loyal commander he had once been. Now he was stronger, willing to answer to no one, and he had an army in tow.

In the breaking dawn the city was still lit by torches, the remnant of the night's watch, just beginning to shake off the long night in the morning mist, and as Duncan neared, another sight came into view which made his heart churn: the blue and yellow banners of Pandesia, flying proudly over the battlements of Andros. It made him sick—and gave him a fresh wave of determination.

Duncan immediately scanned the gates, and his heart soared to see it was guarded by only a skeleton crew. He breathed a sigh of relief. If the Pandesians knew they were coming, thousands of soldiers would be guarding it—and Duncan and his men would stand no chance. But that told him they did not know. The thousands of Pandesian soldiers stationed there must still be asleep. Duncan and his men, luckily, had advanced quickly enough to just have a chance.

This element of surprise, Duncan knew, would be their only advantage, the only thing giving them a chance to take the massive capital, with its layers of battlements, designed to withstand an army. That—and Duncan's insider knowledge of its fortifications and weak points. Battles, he knew, had been won with less. Duncan studied the city's entrance, and he knew where he'd have to attack first if they stood any chance of victory.

"Whoever controls those gates controls the capital!" Duncan shouted to Kavos and his other commanders. "They must not close—we cannot let them close, whatever it costs. If they do, we shall be sealed out for good. I will take a small force with me and make with all speed for the gates. You," he said, gesturing to Kavos, Bramthos and Seavig, "lead the rest of our men to the garrisons and protect our flank against the soldiers as they emerge."

Kavos shook his head.

"Charging those gates with a small force is reckless," he shouted. "You'll be surrounded, and if I am fighting the garrisons, I cannot protect your back. It's suicide."

Duncan smiled.

"And that is why I chose this task for myself."

Duncan kicked his horse and rode out before the others, heading for the gates, while Anvin, Arthfael and a dozen of his closest commanders, men who knew Andros as well as he, men he had fought with his entire life, rode to follow him, as he knew they would. They all veered for the city gates at full speed, while behind them, Duncan saw, out of the corner of his eye, Kavos, Bramthos, Seavig, and the bulk of their army veer off for the Pandesian garrisons.

Duncan, heart slamming, knowing he had to reach the gate before it was too late, lowered his head and urged his horse faster. They galloped down the center of the road, over King's Bridge, the hooves clopping on the wood, and Duncan felt the thrill of battle drawing near. As dawn broke, Duncan saw the startled face of the first Pandesian to spot them, a young soldier standing guard sleepily on the bridge, blinking, looking out, his face spreading with terror. Duncan closed the gap, reached him, brought down his sword, and in one swift move slashed him before he could raise his shield.

The battle had begun.

Anvin, Arthfael, and the others hurled spears, felling a half-dozen Pandesian soldiers who turned their way. They all continued to gallop, none of them pausing, all of them knowing it meant their life. They raced over the bridge just like that, all charging for the wide-open gates to Andros.

Still a good hundred yards away, Duncan looked up at the legendary gates of Andros, a hundred feet high, carved of gold, ten feet thick, and he knew that, if sealed, the city would be impregnable. It would take professional siege equipment, none of which he had, and many months, and many men pounding at the gates—which he did not have, either. Those gates had never given, despite centuries of assaults. If he did not reach them in time, all was lost.

Duncan surveyed the mere dozen Pandesian soldiers guarding it, the guard duty light, the men sleepy at dawn and none expecting an attack, and he urged his horse faster, knowing his time was limited. He had to reach them before they spotted him; he needed but one more minute to assure his survival.

Suddenly, though, a great horn sounded, and Duncan's heart dropped as he looked up to see, high atop the parapets, a Pandesian watchman staring down, sounding a horn of warning again and again. The sound echoed throughout the city walls, and Duncan's heart sank as he knew that any advantage he may have had was lost. He had underestimated the enemy.

The Pandesian soldiers at the gate broke into action. They rushed forward and put their shoulders into the gates, six men on each side, pushing with all their might to close them. At the same time, four more soldiers turned massive cranks on either side, while four more pulled at chains, two on each side. With a great creaking, the bars began to shut. Duncan watched with desperation, feeling as if they were shutting a coffin on his heart.

"FASTER!" he urged his horse.

They all picked up speed, in one final, mad dash. As they neared, a few of his men hurled spears at the men at the gate in a desperate effort—but they were still too far, and the spears fell short.

Duncan urged his horse like never before, riding out recklessly before the others, and as he neared the closing gates, he suddenly felt something whiz by him. He realized it was a javelin and he looked up to see soldiers atop the parapets hurling them downward. Duncan heard a cry and looked over to see one of his men, a brave warrior he had fought beside for years, impaled and go flying backwards off his horse, dead.

Duncan pushed harder, throwing caution to the wind as he aimed for the closing doors. He was perhaps twenty yards away and the doors were just feet away from closing forever. No matter what, even if it meant his own death, he could not let that happen.

In a final suicide charge, Duncan threw himself off his horse, diving for the open crack just as the gates were closing. He reached out with his sword as he did and thrust it forward, and he managed to jam it in the crack just before it closed. His sword bent—but did not break. That slice of steel, Duncan knew, was the only thing keeping those gates from closing for good, the only thing keeping the capital open, the only thing keeping all of Escalon from being lost.

The shocked Pandesian soldiers, realizing their gate wasn't closing, looked down at Duncan's sword, amazed. They charged, all rushing for it, and Duncan knew that, even it cost his life, he could not let that happen.

Still winded from his fall from his horse, his ribs aching, Duncan tried to roll out of the way of the first soldier pouncing for him, but he could not move quickly enough. He saw the raised sword behind him and braced himself for the deadly blow—when suddenly, the soldier cried out and Duncan turned, puzzled, as he heard a neighing and saw his warhorse leaning back and kicking his foe in the chest, right before he could stab Duncan. The soldier went flying back, ribs cracking, and landed on his back, unconscious. Duncan looked up at his horse with gratitude, realizing that he had, once again, saved his life.

Given the time he needed, Duncan rolled to his feet, drew his spare sword, and prepared as the group of soldiers descended upon him. The first soldier slashed down at him with his sword and Duncan blocked it overhead, spun around, and slashed him across the back of the shoulder, sending him to the ground. Duncan stepped forward and stabbed the next soldier in the gut before he could reach him, then jumped over his falling body and with both feet kicked the next one in the chest, knocking him to his back. He ducked as another soldier swung for him, then spun around and slashed him in the back.

Duncan, distracted by his attackers, spun as he sensed motion behind him and saw a Pandesian grabbing the sword wedged between the gates and yanking it out by its hilt. Realizing there was no time, Duncan turned, took aim, and threw his sword. It spun end over end and lodged itself in the man's throat, right before he could extract his long sword. He had saved the gate—but it had left him defenseless.

Duncan charged for the gate, hoping to widen the crack—but as he did, a soldier tackled him from behind and drove him down to the ground. His back exposed, Duncan knew he was in danger.

There was little he could do as the Pandesian behind him raised a spear high to impale his back.

A shout filled the air as Duncan saw, out of the corner of his eye, Anvin rush forward, swing his mace and smash the soldier on his wrist, knocking the spear from his hand just before it impaled Duncan. Anvin then jumped off his horse and tackled the man down to the ground—and at the same time, Arthfael and the others arrived, attacking the other group of soldiers heading for Duncan.

Freed up, Duncan took stock and saw the soldiers guarding the gate were dead, the gate barely being kept open by his sword, and as he saw, out of the corner of his eye, hundreds of Pandesian soldiers beginning to emerge from the barracks in the dawn and rush out to fight Kavos, Bramthos, Seavig, and their men. He knew time was short. Even with Kavos and his men engaging them, enough would slip through and make their way for the gate, and if Duncan did not control these gates soon, all of his men would be finished.

Duncan dodged as yet another spear was hailed down upon him from the parapets. He rushed over and grabbed a bow and arrow from a felled soldier, leaned back, took aim, and fired at a Pandesian high at the top as he leaned over and looked down with a spear. The boy shrieked and fell, impaled by the arrow, clearly not expecting that. He plummeted down to earth and landed beside Duncan with a crash, Duncan stepping out of the way so as not to be killed by the body. Duncan took particular satisfaction to see this boy was the hornblower.

"THE GATES!" Duncan shouted to his men, as they finished felling the remaining soldiers.

His men rallied, dismounting, rushing up beside him and helping him yank open the massive gates. They yanked with all their might—yet they barely budged. More of his men joined in, and as they all yanked together, slowly, one began to move. One inch at a time, it opened, and soon there was enough space for Duncan to put his foot in the gap.

Duncan squeezed his shoulders in the gap, and he pushed with all his might, grunting, arms shaking. Sweat poured down his face, despite the morning cold, as he looked out and saw the flood of soldiers streaming out of the garrison. Most faced off with Kavos, Bramthos and their men, but enough skirted around them and headed his way. A sudden shriek rang through the dawn and Duncan saw one of his men beside him, a good commander, a loyal man, fall to the ground. He saw a spear in his back, and he looked up to see the Pandesians were in throwing range.

More Pandesians raised spears to hurl their way, and Duncan braced himself, realizing they were not going to make it through the gate in time—when suddenly, to his surprise, the soldiers stumbled and fell, face-first. He looked up to see arrows and swords in their backs, and he felt a rush of gratitude to see Bramthos and Seavig leading a hundred men, forking off from Kavos, who faced off with the garrison, and turning back to aid him.

Duncan redoubled his efforts, pushing with all his might as Anvin and Arthfael squeezed in beside him, knowing he had to get the gap wide enough for his men to charge through. Finally, as more of his men squeezed in, they dug their feet into the snowy ground and began to walk. Duncan took step after step, until finally, with a groaning, the gates opened halfway.

There came a victorious shout behind him and Duncan turned to see Bramthos and Seavig leading the hundred men forward on horseback, all of them rushing for the open gate. Duncan retrieved his sword, raised it high and charged, leading the men through the open gates, stepping foot inside the capital, throwing all caution to the wind.

With spears and arrows still raining down on them, Duncan knew at once that they had to gain control of the parapets, which were also equipped with catapults which could do unlimited damage to his men below. He looked up at the battlements, debating the best way to ascend, when suddenly he heard another shout and looked ahead to see a large force of Pandesian soldiers rallying from within the city and charging their way.

Duncan faced them boldly.

"MEN OF ESCALON, WHO HAS INHABITED OUR PRECIOUS CAPITAL!?" he shouted.

His men all shouted and charged behind him as Duncan remounted his horse and led them to greet the soldiers.

There followed a great clash of arms as soldier met soldier, horse met horse, and Duncan and his hundred men attacked the hundred Pandesian soldiers. Duncan sensed that the Pandesians were caught off guard in the dawn, had smelled blood in the water when they had spotted Duncan and his few men—but had not expected such a huge number of reinforcements behind Duncan. He could see their eyes widen at the sight of Bramthos, Seavig, and all their men pouring through the city gates.

Duncan raised his sword and blocked a sword slash, stabbed a soldier in the gut, spun, and bashed another in the head with his shield, then grabbed the spear from his harness and hurled it at another. He cut a path fearlessly through the crowd, felling men left and right, as all around him, Anvin, Arthfael, Bramthos, Seavig, and their men did the same. It felt good to be back inside the capital again, these streets he once knew so well—and it felt even better to be ridding it of Pandesians.

Soon dozens of Pandesians piled up at their feet, all unable to stop the tide of Duncan and his men, like at wave crashing through the capital at dawn. Duncan and his men had too much at stake, had come too far, and these men guarding these streets were far from home, demoralized, their cause weak, their leaders far away, and unprepared. After all, they had never met in battle the true warriors of Escalon. As the tide turned, the Pandesian soldiers who remained turned and fled, giving up—and Duncan and his men rode faster, hunting them down, felling them with arrows and spears until there were none left.

With the path into the capital cleared, and with arrows and spears still hailing down, Duncan turned and focused again on the parapets, as another one of his men fell from his horse, an arrow through his shoulder. They needed the parapets, the high ground, not only to stop the arrows, but to aid Kavos; after all, Kavos was still outnumbered out there, beyond the walls, and he would need Duncan's help at the parapets, with the catapults, if he were to stand any chance of surviving.

"TO THE HEIGHTS!" Duncan shouted.

Duncan's men cheered and followed as he signaled to them, forking off, half following him and half following Bramthos and Seavig to the far side of the courtyard, to ascend from the other side. Duncan headed for the stone steps that lined the side walls, leading to the upper parapets. Guarding them were a dozen soldiers, and they looked up, wide-eyed, at the coming assault. Duncan bore down on them and he and his men hurled spears, killing them all

34

before they could even raise their shields. There was no time left to waste.

They reached the steps and Duncan dismounted and led the charge, single file, up the steps. He looked up with a start to see Pandesian soldiers running down to greet him, spears raised high, ready to throw; he knew they would have the advantage, racing downward, and, not wanting to waste time in hand-to-hand combat as spears were hailing down upon him, he thought quick.

"ARROWS!" Duncan commanded the men behind him.

Duncan ducked, hitting the ground, and a moment later he felt arrows whiz overhead as his men followed his command, stepping forward and firing. Duncan looked up and watched in satisfaction as the group of soldiers racing down the narrow stone staircase stumbled and fell off the side of the steps, crying out as they plummeted and landed on the stone courtyard far below.

Duncan continued running up the steps, tackling a soldier as more came charging and knocking him over the edge. He spun around and bashed another with his shield, sending him flying, too, then came straight up with his sword and stabbed another through the chin.

But that left Duncan vulnerable on the narrow staircase, and a Pandesian jumped him from behind and dragged him to the edge. Duncan held on for dear life, clawing at the stone, unable to grab hold and about to fall over—when suddenly the man atop him went limp and slumped over his shoulder, over the edge, dead. Duncan saw a sword in his back, and he turned to see Arthfael lifting him back to his feet.

Duncan continued charging, grateful to have his men at his back, and he ascended level after level, avoiding spears and arrows, blocking some with his shield, until finally he reached the parapets. At the top sat a broad, stone plateau, perhaps ten yards wide, spanning the top of the gates, and it was packed with Pandesian soldiers, shoulder to shoulder, all armed with arrows, spears, javelins, and all in the midst of raining down weapons on Kavos's men below. As Duncan arrived with his men, they stopped attacking Kavos, and instead turned to fight him. At the same time, Seavig and the other contingent of men finished scaling the steps on the far side of the courtyard, and attacked the soldiers from the far end. They were sandwiching them in, with nowhere to go.

The fighting was thick, hand-to-hand, as men on all sides fought for every precious inch. Duncan raised his shield and his sword, and as clanging filled the air, the fighting bloody, hand to hand, he hacked through one man at a time. Duncan dodged, avoiding slashes, and lowered his shoulder and shoved more than one man over the edge, shrieking to his death far below, knowing that sometimes, one's best weapons were one's hands.

He cried out in pain as he received a slash in the stomach, but luckily he twisted and it grazed him. As the soldier came in for a death blow, Duncan, with no room to maneuver, headbutted him, making him drop his sword. He then kneed him, reached over, grabbed hold of him, and threw him over the edge.

Duncan fought and fought, every foot hard won, as the sun rose higher and the sweat stung his eyes. His men grunted and cried out in pain on all sides, as Duncan's shoulders grew tired with killing.

As he gasped for breath, covered in his foe's blood, Duncan took one final step forward and raised his sword—and was shocked to see Bramthos and Seavig and their men facing him. He turned and surveyed all the dead bodies and realized, amazed, that they had done it—they had cleared the parapets.

There arose a shout of victory as all their men met in the middle.

Yet Duncan knew the situation was still urgent.

"ARROWS!" he shouted.

He immediately looked down at Kavos's men and saw a great battle being waged below, in the courtyard, as thousands more Pandesian soldiers rushed out of the garrisons to meet them. Kavos was slowly being surrounded on all sides.

Duncan's men raised bows from the fallen, took aim over the walls, and fired down at the Pandesians, Duncan joining in. The Pandesians never expected to be fired upon from the capital, and they fell by the dozens, dropping to the ground, Kavos's men spared from deathly blows. Pandesians began to drop all around Kavos, and soon a great panic ensued, as they realized Duncan controlled the heights. Sandwiched between Duncan and Kavos, they had nowhere left to flee.

Duncan would not give them time to regroup.

"SPEARS!" he commanded.

Duncan grabbed one himself and hurled it down, then another, and another, raiding the huge reserve of weapons left here atop the parapets, designed to fend off invaders of Andros.

As the Pandesians began to waver, Duncan knew he had to do something definitive to finish them off.

"CATAPULTS!" he yelled.

His men rushed to the catapults left atop these battlements and pulled on the great ropes, turning cranks as they got them into position. They placed the boulders inside and awaited his command. Duncan walked up and down the line and adjusted positions so that the boulders would miss Kavos's men and find the perfect target.

"FIRE!" he called out.

Dozens of boulders flew through the air, and Duncan watched with satisfaction as they plummeted down and battered the stone garrisons, killing dozens of Pandesians at a time as they poured out, like ants, to fight Kavos's men. The sounds echoed throughout the courtyard, stunning the Pandesians and increasing their panic. As clouds of dust and debris arose, they turned and turned, unsure which way to fight.

Kavos, veteran warrior that he was, took advantage of their hesitation. He rallied his men and charged forward with a new momentum, and while the Pandesians wavered, he hacked his way through their ranks.

Bodies fell left and right, the Pandesian camp in disarray, and soon they turned and fled in every direction. Kavos hunted each and every one down. It was a slaughter.

By the time the sun had fully risen, all the Pandesians lay on the ground, lifeless.

As silence fell, Duncan looked out, stunned, filled with a dawning sense of victory, as he began to realize that they had done it. They had taken the capital.

As his men shouted all around him, clasping his shoulders, cheering and embracing, Duncan wiped sweat from his eyes, still breathing hard, and began to let it sink in: Andros was free.

The capital was theirs.

CHAPTER SEVEN

Alec craned his neck and looked up, dazzled, as he passed through the soaring arched gates of Ur, jostled by mobs of people on all sides. He marched through, Marco beside him, their faces still covered in dirt from their endless trek through the Plain of Thorns, and he stared up at the soaring marble arch, appearing to be a hundred feet high. He looked at the ancient, granite temple walls on either side of him, and it amazed him that he was walking through a cutout in a temple, serving also as the city entrance. Alec saw many worshippers kneeling before its walls, a strange mix with all the hustle and bustle of commerce here, and it caused him to reflect. He had once prayed to the gods of Escalon—but now he prayed to none. What living god, he wondered, could have allowed his family to die? The only god he could serve now was the god of vengeance—and it was a god he was determined to serve with all his heart.

Alec, overwhelmed by the stimulation all around him, saw right away that this city was unlike any place he had ever been, so unlike the tiny village where he had been raised. For the first time since the death of his family, he felt himself being jolted back to life. This place was so startling, so alive, it was hard to enter and not be distracted. He felt a stirring of purpose as he realized, inside these gates, were others like him, like-minded friends of Marco, set on vengeance against Pandesia. He looked up at it all in wonder, all the people of different garb and manner and race, all rushing in every direction. It was a true cosmopolitan city.

"Keep your head down," Marco hissed to him, as they passed through the eastern gate, merging into the mobs.

Marco nudged him.

"There." Marco nodded to a group of Pandesian soldiers. "They're checking faces. I am sure they search for ours."

Alec reflexively tightened his grip on his dagger, and Marco reached over and grabbed his wrist firmly.

"Not here, my friend," Marco cautioned. "This is no country village but a city of war. Kill two Pandesians at the gate, and an army will follow."

Marco stared at him with intensity.

"Would you rather kill two?" he pressed. "Or two thousand?"

Alec, realizing the wisdom in his friend's words, released his grip on his dagger, summoning all his will to quell his passion for vengeance.

"There will be many chances, my friend," Marco said, as they pressed on through the crowd, heads lowered. "My friends are here, and the resistance is strong."

They merged with the throng passing through the gate, and Alec lowered his eyes so the Pandesians would not see them.

"Hey you!" a Pandesian barked. Alec felt his heart pounding as he kept his head down.

They rushed his way, and he tightened his grip on his dagger, preparing. But they stopped a boy beside him, instead, roughly grabbing his shoulder and checking his face. Alec breathed deep, relieved it was not him, and he passed through the gate quickly, undetected.

They finally entered the city square, and as Alec pulled back his hood and looked inside the city, he was in awe at the sight before him. There, before him, stretched all the architectural magnificence and bustle of Ur. The city seemed to be alive, pulsing, shining in the sun, seeming to actually sparkle. At first Alec could not understand why, and then he realized: the water. Everywhere was water, the city laced with canals, blue water sparkling in the morning sun, making the city feel as if it were one with the sea. The canals were filled with every manner of vessel—rowboats, canoes, sailing boats—even sleek black warships sailing the yellow and blue banners of Pandesia. The canals were bordered by cobblestone streets, ancient stone, worn smooth, being tread on by thousands of people in every manner of wardrobe. Alec saw knights, soldiers, civilians, traders, peasants, beggars, jugglers, merchants, farmers and many other folk, all mingling together. Many wore colors Marco had never seen, clearly visitors from across the sea, visitors from around the world who were visiting Ur, Escalon's international port. Indeed, bright, foreign colors and insignias were flown by all the different ships cramming the canal, as if the whole world had come together at one place.

"The cliffs surrounding Escalon are so high, they are what keep our land impregnable," Marco explained as they walked. "Ur has the only beach, the only harbor for large vessels wishing to beach. Escalon has other harbors, but none as easy to access. So when they wish to visit us, they all come here," he added with a wave of his hand, looking out at all the people, all the ships.

"It is both a good and a bad thing," he continued. "It brings us trade and commerce from all four corners of the kingdom."

"And the bad?" Alec asked, as they squeezed their way through the crowd and Marco stopped to purchase a stick of meat.

"It leaves Ur prone to attack by sea," he replied. "It is a natural spot for an invasion."

Alec studied the city's skyline in awe, taking in all the steeples, the endless array of tall buildings. He had never seen anything like it.

"And the towers?" he asked, looking up at a series of tall, square towers crowned with parapets, sticking up over the city and facing the sea.

"They were built to watch the sea," Marco answered. "Against invasion. Though, with the weak King's surrender, little good it did us."

Alec wondered.

"And if he hadn't surrendered?" Alec asked. "Could Ur fend off an attack by sea?"

Alec shrugged.

"I am no commander," he said. "But I know we have ways. We could certainly fend off pirates and raiders. A fleet is another story. But in its thousand-year history, Ur has never fallen—and that tells you something."

Distant bells tolled in the air as they continued walking, mingling with the sound of seagulls overhead, circling, squawking. As they pushed through the mobs, Alec found his stomach growling as he smelled all manner of food in the air. His eyes widened as they passed rows of merchant booths, all lined with goods. He saw exotic objects and delicacies he had never laid eyes upon before, and he marveled at this cosmopolitan city life. Everything was faster here, everyone in such a rush, the people bustling so quickly that he could barely take it all in before they passed him by. It made him realize what a small town he had come from.

Alec stared at a vendor selling the largest red fruits he had ever seen, and he reached into his pocket to buy one—when he felt his shoulder bumped hard from the side.

He spun to see a large man, older, towering over him, with a black scruffy beard, scowling down. He had a foreign face which Alec could not recognize, and he cursed in a language Alec did not understand. The man then shoved him, sending Alec, to his surprise, flying backwards into a stall, crashing down to the street.

"There's no need for that," Marco said, stepping forward and putting out a hand to stop the man.

But Alec, normally passive, felt a new sense of rage. It was an unfamiliar feeling, a rage smoldering inside him ever since the death of his family, a rage which needed an outlet. He could not control himself. He jumped to his feet and lunged forward, and, with a strength he didn't know he had, punched the man in the face, knocking him back, sending him crashing over another stall.

Alec stood there, amazed that he had knocked down the much bigger man, while Marco stood beside him, wide-eyed, too.

A commotion erupted in the marketplace as the man's oafish friends began to run over, while a group of Pandesian soldiers came running over from the other side of the square. Marco looked panicked, and Alec knew they were in a precarious position.

"This way!" Marco urged, grabbing Alec and yanking him roughly.

As the oaf gained his feet and the Pandesians closed in, Alec and Marco ran through the streets, Alec following his friend as he navigated this city he knew so well, taking shortcuts, weaving in and out between stalls and making sharp turns down alleyways. Alec could barely keep up with all the sharp zigzags. Yet when he turned and looked over his shoulder, he saw the large group closing in and knew they had a fight on their hands they could not win.

"Here!" Marco yelled.

Alec watched Marco jump off the edge of the canal, and without thinking he followed him, expecting to land in water.

He was surprised, though, not to hear a splash, and to instead find himself landing on a small stone ledge down at the bottom, one he had not detected from above. Marco, breathing hard, knocked four times on an anonymous wood door, built into the stone, beneath the street—and a second later the door opened and Alec and Marco were pulled into the blackness, the door slamming behind them. Before it did, Alec saw men running toward the edge of the canal, questioning, unable to see below as the door closed.

Alec found himself underground, in a dark, subterranean canal, and he ran, baffled, splashing in water up to his ankles. They twisted and turned, and soon there came sunlight again.

Alec saw they were in a large stone room, beneath the city streets, sunlight filtering in from grates high above, and he looked over in amazement to see himself surrounded by several boys their age, all with faces covered in dirt and smiling back good-naturedly. They all stopped, breathing hard, and Marco smiled and greeted his friends.

"Marco," they said, embracing him.

"Jun, Saro, Bagi," Marco replied.

They each stepped forward and he embraced each one, grinning, these men clearly like brothers to him. They were each about their age, as tall as Marco, broad-shouldered, with tough faces and the looks of boys who had managed to survive their whole lives on the streets. They were boys who, clearly, had had to make a way for themselves.

Marco pulled Alec forward.

"This," he announced, "is Alec. He is one of us now."

One of us. Alec liked the sound of that. It felt good to belong somewhere.

They each clasped forearms with him, and one of them, the tallest, Bagi, shook his head and grinned.

"So you are the one who started all that excitement?" he asked with a smile.

Alec smiled sheepishly back.

"The guy pushed me," Alec said.

The others all laughed.

"Good enough a reason as any to risk our lives on this day," Saro replied, sincere.

"You're in a city now, country boy," Jun said sternly, unsmiling, unlike the others. "You could have got us all killed. That was stupid. Here, people don't care—they'll shove you—and a whole lot worse. Keep your head down and watch where you're going. If someone bumps you, turn away or you may find a dagger in your back. You got lucky this time. This is Ur. You never know

42

who's crossing the street, and people here will cut you for any reason—and some, for no reason at all."

His newfound friends suddenly turned and headed off, deeper into the cavernous tunnels, and Alec hurried to catch up as Marco joined them. They all seemed to know this place by heart, even in the dim light, twisting and turning with ease through the underground chambers, water dripping and echoing all around them. They all had clearly grown up here. It made Alec feel inadequate, having grown up in Soli, seeing this place which was so worldly, these boys who were so street smart. They had all clearly suffered trials and hardships which Alec could never imagine. They were a rough lot, having clearly been in more than a few altercations, and above all, they appeared to be survivors.

After turning down a series of alleys, the boys ascended a steep metal ladder, and soon Alec found himself back above ground, on the streets, in a different part of Ur, emerging into another bustling crowd. Alec spun and looked around, seeing a big town square with a copper fountain in its center, not recognizing it, barely able to keep track of all the neighborhoods of this sprawling city.

The boys stopped before a low, squat, anonymous building made of stone, similar to all the others, with its low, slanted red-tiled roof. Bagi knocked twice and a moment later the anonymous rusted door opened. They all quickly filed inside, then it slammed closed behind them.

Alec found himself in a dim room, lit only by the sunlight streaming in through windows high above, and he turned as he recognized the sound of hammers striking anvils, and surveyed the room with interest. He heard the hiss of a forge, saw the familiar clouds of steam, and he immediately felt at home. He did not have to look around to know he was in a forge, and that it was filled with smiths working on weapons. His heart lifted with excitement.

A tall, thin man with a short beard, perhaps in his forties, face blackened from soot, wiped his hands on his apron and approached. He nodded at Marco's friends with a look of respect, and they nodded back.

"Fervil," Marco said.

Fervil turned and saw Marco, and his face lit up. He stepped forward and embraced him.

"I thought you'd gone to The Flames," he said.

43

Marco grinned back.

"Not anymore," he replied.

"You boys ready to work?" he added. Then he looked over at Alec. "And who do we have here?"

"My friend," Marco replied. "Alec. A fine smith, and eager to join our cause."

"Is he now?" Fervil asked skeptically.

He surveyed Alec with harsh eyes, looking him up and down as if he were useless.

"I doubt that," he replied, "from the looks of him. Looks awful young to me. But we can put him to work collecting our scraps. Take this," he said, reaching over and handing Alec a bucket full of metal scrap. "I'll let you know if I need more from you."

Alec reddened, indignant. He did not know why this man had taken such a dislike to him—perhaps he was threatened. He could sense the forge grow quiet, could sense the other boys watching. In many ways, this man reminded him of his father, and that only increased Alec's anger.

Still, he fumed inside, no longer willing, since the death of his family, to tolerate anything he had before.

As the others turned to walk away, Alec dropped the bucket of metal and it clanged loudly on the stone floor. The others all turned around, stunned, and the forge grew quiet, as the other boys stopped to watch the confrontation.

"Get the hell out of my shop!" Fervil snarled.

Alec ignored him; instead, he stepped past him, to the closest table, picked up a long sword, held it out straight, and examined it.

"This your handiwork?" Alec asked.

"And who are you to be asking questions of me?" Fervil demanded.

"Is it?" Marco pressed, sticking up for his friend.

"It is," Fervil answered defensively.

Alec nodded.

"It's junk," he concluded.

There came a gasp in the room.

Fervil stood to his full height and scowled back, livid.

"You boys can leave now," he snarled. "All of you. I have enough smiths in here."

Alec stood his ground.

"And none worth a damn," he countered.

Fervil turned red and stepped forward threateningly, and Marco put a hand between them.

"We'll leave," Marco said.

Alec suddenly lowered the sword's tip to the ground, raised his foot high, and with one clean kick, shattered it in two.

Shards flew everywhere, stunning the room.

"Should a good sword do that?" Alec asked with a wry smile.

Fervil shouted and charged Alec—and as he neared, Alec held out the jagged end of the broken blade, and Fervil stopped in his tracks.

The other boys, seeing the confrontation, drew swords and rushed forward to defend Fervil, while Marco and his friends drew theirs around Alec. All the boys stood there, facing off with each other in a tense standoff.

"What are you doing?" Marco asked Alec. "We all share the same cause. This is madness."

"And that is why I cannot let them fight with junk," Alec replied.

Alec threw down the broken sword, reached over, and slowly drew a long sword from his belt.

"Here is my handiwork," Alec said loudly. "I crafted it myself in my father's forge. A finer work you will never find."

Alec suddenly turned the sword, grabbed the blade, and held it out, hilt first, to Fervil.

In the tense silence, Fervil looked down, clearly not expecting this. He snatched the hilt, leaving Alec defenseless, and for a moment he seemed to contemplate stabbing Alec with it.

Yet Alec stood there proudly, unafraid.

Slowly, Fervil's face softened, clearly realizing Alec had left himself defenseless, and looking at him with more respect. He looked down and examined the sword. He weighed it in his hand and held it up to the light, and finally, after a long time, he looked back at Alec, impressed.

"Your work?" he asked, disbelief in his voice.

Alec nodded.

"And I can forge many more," he replied.

He stepped forward and looked at Fervil, intensity in his eyes.

"I want to kill Pandesians," Alec replied. "And I want to do it with real weapons."

A long, thick silence lingered over the room, until finally Fervil slowly shook his head and smiled.

He lowered the sword and held out an arm, and Alec clasped it. Slowly, all the boys lowered their weapons.

"I suppose," Fervil said, his grin broadening, "we can find a spot for you."

CHAPTER EIGHT

Aidan trekked down the lonely forest road, as far from anywhere as he'd ever been, feeling utterly alone in the world. If it were not for his Wood Dog beside him he would be forlorn, hopeless; but White gave him strength, even as grievously wounded as he was, as Aidan ran his hand along his short, white fur. They both limped, each wounded from their encounters with that savage cart driver, every step they took painful as the sky grew dark. With each limping step Aidan took, he vowed that if he ever laid eyes on that man again, he'd kill him with his own hands.

White whined beside him, and Aidan reached over and stroked his head, the dog nearly as tall as him, more wild beast than dog. Aidan was grateful not only for his companionship but for the fact that he had saved his life. He had rescued White because something inside him would not let him turn away—and yet he had received the reward of his life in return. He would do it all over again, even if he knew it would mean his being dumped out here, in the midst of nowhere, on a certain course with starvation and death. It was still worth it.

White whined again, and Aidan shared his hunger pains.

"I know, White," Aidan said. "I'm hungry, too."

Aidan looked down at White's wounds, still seeping blood, and shook his head, feeling awful and helpless.

"I would do anything to help you," Aidan said. "I wish I knew how."

Aidan leaned over and kissed him on the head, his fur soft, and White leaned his head back into Aidan's. It was the embrace of two people on a death walk together. The sounds of wild creatures rose up in a symphony in the darkening forest, and Aidan felt his little legs burning, felt they couldn't go on much further, that they would die out here. They were still days from anywhere, and with night falling, they were vulnerable. White, as powerful as he was, was in no shape to fight off anything, and Aidan, weaponless, wounded, was no better. No carts had come by for hours, and none would, he suspected, for days.

Aidan thought of his father, out there somewhere, and felt he had let him down. If he were to die, Aidan wished he could have at least died at his father's side somewhere, fighting some great cause, or at home, in the comfort of Volis. Not here, alone in middle of nowhere. Each step seemed to drag him closer to death.

Aidan reflected on his short life thus far, pondering all the people he had known and loved, his father and brothers, and most of all, his sister, Kyra. He wondered about her, wondered where she was right now, if she had crossed Escalon, if she had survived the journey to Ur. He wondered if she ever thought of him, if she would be proud of him now, trying as he was to follow in her footsteps, trying to cross Escalon, too, in his own way, to help their father and the cause. He wondered if he would ever have lived to become a great warrior, and felt deeply saddened that he would never see her again.

Aidan felt himself sinking with each step he took, and there wasn't anything much he could do now except give in to his wounds and exhaustion. Going slower and slower, he looked over at White and saw him dragging his legs, too. Soon they would have to lie down and rest right here on this road, come what may. It was a frightful proposition.

Aidan thought he heard something, faint at first. He stopped and listened intently as White stopped, too, looking questioningly up at him. Aidan hoped, prayed. Had he been hearing things?

Then it came again. He was sure this time. A squeak of wheels. Of wood. Of iron. It was a cart.

Aidan spun around, his heart skipping a beat as he squinted into the fading light. At first he saw nothing. But then slowly, surely, he saw something come into view. A cart. Several carts.

Aidan's heart pounded in his throat, barely able to contain his excitement as he felt the rumble, heard the horses, and watched the caravan head his way. But then his excitement tempered as he wondered if they could be hostile. After all, who else would be traveling this long stretch of barren road, so far from anywhere? He could not fight and White, snarling half-heartedly, did not have much fight left in him, either. They were at the mercy of whoever was approaching. It was a scary thought.

The sound grew deafening as the carts neared, and Aidan stood boldly in the center of the road, realizing he could not hide. He had to take his chances. Aidan thought he heard music as they neared, and it deepened his curiosity. They gained speed, and for a moment he wondered if they would run him over.

Then, suddenly, the entire caravan slowed and stopped before him, as he blocked the road. They stared down at him, the dust settling all around them, a large group, perhaps fifty people, and Aidan blinked up in surprise to see they were not soldiers. They did not appear to be hostile, either, he realized with a sigh of relief. He noticed the wagons filled with all sorts of people, men and women of all different ages. One appeared to be filled with musicians, holding various musical instruments; another was filled with men who appeared to be jugglers or comedians, their faces painted in bright colors and wearing brightly colored tights and tunics; another cart seemed to be filled with actors, men holding scrolls, clearly rehearsing scripts, dressed in dramatic costumes; while another was filled with women—barely clothed, their faces painted with too much makeup.

Aidan blushed and looked away, knowing he was too young to gape at such things.

"You, boy!" a voice called out. It was a man with a very long beard, bright red, down to his waist, a peculiar-looking man, with a friendly smile.

"Is this your road?" he asked in jest.

Laughter erupted from all the carts, and Aidan blushed.

"Who are you?" Aidan asked, baffled.

"I think the better question," he called back, "is who are you?" They looked down in fear at White as he snarled. "And what on earth are you doing with a Wood Dog? Don't you know they'll kill you?" they asked, fear in their voices.

"Not this one," Aidan replied. "Are you all...entertainers?" he asked, still curious, wondering what they were all doing out here.

"A kind word for it!" someone called from a cart, to raucous laughter.

"We are actors and players and jugglers and gamblers and musicians and clowns!" another man yelled.

"And liars and scoundrels and whores!" called out a woman, and they all laughed again.

Someone strummed on a harp, as the laughter increased, and Aidan blushed. A memory came rushing back of when he had once met such people, when he was younger and living in Andros. He recalled watching all the entertainers stream into the capital, entertaining the King; he remembered their brightly colored faces; their juggling knives; a man eating fur; a woman singing songs; and a bard reciting poems from memory that seemed to last for hours. He remembered being puzzled as to why anyone would choose such a life path, and not that of a warrior.

His eyes lit up as he suddenly realized.

"Andros!" Aidan called out. "You're going to Andros!"

A man jumped off one of the carts and came toward him. He was a large man, perhaps in his forties, with a big belly, an unkempt brown beard, shaggy hair to match, and a warm and friendly smile. He walked over to Aidan and put a fatherly arm around his shoulder.

"You're too young to be out here," the man said. "I'd say you're lost—but from the wounds on you and that dog of yours, I'm guessing it's something more. Looks like you got yourself into some trouble and found yourself in too deep—and I'd guess," he concluded, examining White warily, "that it had something to do with your helping this beast."

Aidan remained quiet, not knowing how much to say, while White came over and licked the man's hand, to Aidan's surprise.

"Motley's what I call myself," the man added, reaching out a hand.

Aidan looked back warily, not shaking his hand but nodding back.

"Aidan is my name," he replied.

"You two can stay out here and starve to death," Motley continued, "but that's not a very fun way to die. Me personally, I'd want to at least have a good meal first, then die some other way."

The group broke into laughter, while Motley continued holding out his hand, looking at Aidan with kindness and compassion.

"I expect you two, wounded as you are, need a hand," he added.

Aidan stood there proudly, not wanting to show weakness, as his father had taught him.

"We were doing just fine as we were," Aidan said.

Motley led the group in a fresh round of laughter.

"Of course you were," he replied.

Aidan looked suspiciously at the man's hand.

50

"I am going to Andros," Aidan said.

Motley smiled.

"As are we," he replied. "And as luck would have it, the city is big enough to hold more than just us."

Aidan hesitated.

"You'd be doing us a favor," Motley added. "We can use the extra weight."

"And the extra mouth to feed!" called out a fool from another crowd, to laughter.

Aidan looked back warily, too proud to accept, but finding a way to save face.

"Well…." Aidan said. "If I'd be doing you a favor…"

Aidan took Motley's hand, and found himself pulled into his cart. He was stronger than Aidan expected, given that, from the way he dressed, he seemed to be a court fool; his hand, beefy and warm, was twice the size of Aidan's.

Motley then reached over, hoisted White, and placed him gently in the back of the cart, beside Aidan. White curled up beside Aidan in the hay, head in his lap, eyes half-closed in exhaustion and pain. Aidan understood the feeling too well.

Motley jumped in and the driver cracked the whip, and the caravan took off, all of them cheering as music played again. It was a jolly song, men and women plucking harps, playing flutes and cymbals, and several of the people, to Aidan's surprise, danced in the moving carts.

Aidan had never seen such a happy group of people in his life. His whole life had been spent in the gloom and silence of a fort filled with warriors, and he wasn't sure what to make of all this. How could anyone be so happy? His father had always taught him that life was a serious thing. Was this all not trivial?

As they proceeded down the bumpy road, White whined out in pain, while Aidan stroked his head. Motley came over and, to Aidan's surprise, knelt by the dog's side and applied a compress to his wounds, covered in a green salve. Slowly, White quieted, and Aidan felt grateful for his help.

"Who are you?" Aidan asked.

"Well, I've worn many names," Motley replied. "The best was 'actor.' Then there was 'rogue', 'fool,' 'jester'…the list goes on. Call me as you will."

"You are no warrior, then," Aidan realized, disappointed.

Motley leaned back and roared with laughter, tears streaming down his cheeks; Aidan could not understand what was so funny.

"Warrior," Motley repeated, shaking his head in wonder. "Now that is one thing I've never been called. Nor is it something I have ever wished to be called."

Aidan furrowed his brow, not comprehending.

"I come from a line of warriors," Aidan said proudly, sticking his chest out as he sat, despite his pain. "My father is a great warrior."

"I'm very sorry for you then," Motley said, still laughing.

Aidan was confused.

"Sorry? Why?"

"That is a sentence," Motley replied.

"A sentence?" Aidan echoed. "There is nothing greater in life than to be a warrior. It is all I have ever dreamed of."

"Is it?" Motley asked, amused. "Then I feel doubly sorry for you. I think feasting and laughing and sleeping with beautiful women is about as great a thing as there is—far better than parading around the countryside and hoping to stick a sword in another man's belly."

Aidan reddened, frustrated; he had never heard a man speak of battle in such a sense, and he took offense. He had never met anyone remotely like this man.

"Where is the honor in your life?" Aidan asked, puzzled.

"Honor?" Motley asked, seemingly genuinely surprised. "That is not a word I have heard for years—and it's too a big word for such a young boy." Motley sighed. "I do not think honor exists—at least, I have never seen it. I thought of being honorable once—it got me nowhere. Besides, I've seen too many honorable men fall prey to devious women," he concluded, and others in their cart laughed.

Aidan looked around, saw all these people dancing and singing and drinking the day away, and he had mixed feelings about riding with this crowd. They were men who were kind but who did not strive to lead the warrior's life, who were not devoted to valor. He knew he should be grateful for the ride, and he was, but he did not know how to feel about riding with them. They were certainly not the sort of men his father would associate with.

"I shall ride with you," Aidan finally concluded. "We shall be traveling companions. But I cannot consider myself your brother-in-arms."

Motley's eyes opened wide, shocked, silent for a good ten seconds, as if he didn't know how to respond.

Then, finally, he burst into laughter that lasted way too long, echoed by all those around him. Aidan did not understand this man, and he did not think he ever would.

"I think I shall enjoy your company, boy," Motley finally said, wiping away a tear. "Yes, I think I shall enjoy it very much."

CHAPTER NINE

Duncan, flanked by his men, marched through the capital of Andros, behind him the footsteps of thousands of his soldiers, victorious, triumphant, their armor clanging as they paraded through this liberated city. Everywhere they went, they were met by the triumphant cheers of citizens, men and women, old and young, all dressed in the fancy garments of the capital, all rushing forward on the cobblestone streets and throwing flowers and delicacies his way. Everyone proudly waved the banners of Escalon. Duncan felt triumphant to see the colors of his homeland waving again, to see all these people, just the day before so oppressed, now so jubilant, so free. It was an image he would never forget, an image that made all of it worth it.

As the early morning sun broke over the capital, Duncan felt as if he were marching into a dream. Here was a place he had been sure he would never step foot in again, not while he was alive, and certainly not under these conditions. Andros, the capital. The crown jewel of Escalon, seat of kings for thousands of years, now in his control. The Pandesian garrisons had fallen. His men controlled the gates; they controlled the roads; they controlled the streets. It was more than he could have ever hoped for.

But days ago, he marveled, he was still in Volis, all of Escalon still under the iron thumb of Pandesia. Now, all of northwestern Escalon stood free and its very capital, its heart and soul, was free from Pandesian rule. Of course, Duncan realized, they had achieved this victory solely through speed and surprise. It was a brilliant victory, but also a potentially transient one; once word reached the Pandesian Empire, they would come for him—and not with a few garrisons, but with the might of the world. The world would fill with the stampede of elephants, the sky would fill with arrows, the sea would be covered in ships. But that was no reason to turn his back on doing what was just, on doing what was demanded of a warrior. For now, at least, they had held their own; for now, at least, they were free.

Duncan heard a crash and he turned to see an immense marble statue of His Glorious Ra, supreme ruler of Pandesia, toppled, yanked down with ropes by scores of citizens. It smashed into a thousand pieces as it hit the ground, and men cheered, stomping on its shards. More citizens rushed forward and yanked at the huge blue and yellow banners of Pandesia, tearing them from walls, buildings, steeples.

Duncan could not help but smile, taking in the adulation, the sense of pride these people had at gaining their freedom back, a feeling he understood all too well. He looked over at Kavos and Bramthos, Anvin and Arthfael and Seavig and all their men, and he saw them beaming too, exultant, reveling on this day that would be written into the history books. It was a memory they would all take with them for the rest of their lives.

They all marched through the capital, passing squares and courtyards, turning down streets that Duncan knew so well from all the years he had spent here. They rounded a bend, and Duncan looked up and his heart quickened to see the capitol building of Andros, its golden dome shining in the sun, its huge arched golden doors as imposing as ever, its white marble façade shining, engraved, as he remembered it, with the ancient writings of Escalon philosophers. It was one of the few buildings Pandesia had not touched, and Duncan felt a sense of pride at seeing it.

Yet he also felt a pit in his stomach; he knew that waiting for him inside would be the nobles, the politicians, the serving council of Escalon, the men of politics, of schemes, men he did not understand. They were not soldiers, not warlords, but men of wealth and power and influence which had been inherited from their ancestors. They were men who did not deserve to wield power, and yet men who, somehow, still held an iron grip on Escalon.

Worst of all, Tarnis himself would certainly be with them.

Duncan braced himself and took a deep breath as he ascended the hundred marble steps, his men beside him as the great doors were opened for him by the King's Guard. He took a deep breath, knowing he should feel exultant, yet knowing he was entering a den of snakes, a place where honor gave way to compromise and treachery. He would prefer a battle against all of Pandesia rather than an hour spent meeting with these men, men of shifting compromise, men who stood for nothing, who were so lost in lies that they did not even understand themselves.

The King's Guard, wearing the bright red armor Duncan had not seen in years, with their pointed helmets and ceremonial halberds, opened the doors wide and looked back at Duncan with respect. These, at least, were true warriors. They were an ancient force, loyal only to the serving King of Escalon. They were the only force of soldiers left standing here, ready to serve whatever king ruled, a vestige of what once was. Duncan recalled his vow to Kavos, thought of being King, and he felt a pit in his stomach. It was the last thing he wanted.

Duncan led his men through the doors and into the sacred corridors of the capitol building, in awe, as he always was, at its vast soaring ceilings, etched with the symbols of Escalon's clans, its white and blue marble floors, engraved with a huge dragon, a lion in its mouth. Being in here brought it all back. No matter how many times he entered, he was always humbled by this place.

His men's marching echoed in the vast halls, and as Duncan went, heading for the Council Chamber, he felt, as he always had, that this place was like a tomb, a gilded tomb where politicians and nobles could congratulate themselves on hatching plans that kept them in power. He had tried to spend as little time here as possible when he had resided in the capital, and now he wished to spend even less.

"Remember your vow."

Duncan turned to see Kavos staring back, intensity shining in his dark eyes, beneath his dark beard, Bramthos beside him. It was the face of a true warrior, a warrior to whom he owed a great debt.

Duncan's stomach clenched at his words. It was a vow he had made that haunted him. A vow to assume the kingship. To oust his old friend. Politics was the last thing he craved; he yearned only for freedom and an open battlefield.

Yet he had made a vow, and he knew he would have to honor that vow. As he approached the iron doors, he knew that what came next would not be pleasant, yet it would have to be done. After all, who in that room of politicians would want to hand him power, acknowledge him as King, even if he had been the one who had won it for them?

They passed through an open arch and another contingent of King's Guards stepped aside, revealing twin doors of bronze. The Council Doors, ancient things that had lasted for too many kings. They opened them wide and stepped aside, and Duncan found himself entering the Council Chamber.

Shaped in a circle a hundred feet across, the Council Chamber had in its center a circular table of black marble, and around this there sat and stood a huge crowd of nobles, in chaos. Duncan could immediately feel the tension in the air, the sound of agitated men arguing, pacing the floor, this room more packed than he'd ever seen it. Usually inside there sat an orderly group of a dozen nobles, sitting about, presided over by the old King. Now the room sat packed with a hundred men, all dressed in their fancy garb. Duncan would expect the mood to be jubilant here, after his victory—but not with these men. They were professional malcontents.

In their center stood Tarnis, and as Duncan and his men entered, they all stopped bickering and fell silent. All heads turned, stunned looks on their faces, looks of surprise and awe and respect—and especially of fear, fear of the change that was about to happen.

Duncan marched into the center with his commanders, while he had the rest of his dozens of men take up positions around the periphery of the room, standing guard silently all around the outskirts. It was the show of force that Duncan wanted. If these men resisted him, plotted to keep themselves in power, Duncan wanted to remind them who had freed the capital, who had defeated Pandesia. He saw the nobles glance nervously at his soldiers, then back to him, as he approached. Professional politicians to the end, they showed no reaction.

Tarnis, the most professional of them all, turned to Duncan and broke into a quick, forced smile. He reached out his arms and began to approach.

"Duncan!" he called out warmly, as if to embrace a long lost brother.

Tarnis, in his sixties, with well-tanned skin, fine lines, and soft silky gray hair that fell to his chin, had always had a pampered, manicured look to him; of course he would, as he had lived a life of pomp and luxury his entire life. His face also bore a look of wisdom—yet Duncan knew that look was just a facade. He was a fine actor, the finest of them all, and he knew how to project wisdom. That, indeed, was what had enabled him to rise to power. From all their years together, Duncan knew he was a master of appearing to feel one way—and acting another.

Tarnis stepped forward and embraced Duncan, and Duncan coldly embraced him back, still unsure how to feel about him. He still felt stung, supremely disappointed by this man whom he had once respected as a father. After all, this was the man who had surrendered the land. It was insulting for Duncan to see him here, in this hall of power, after Duncan's victory, in which he no longer deserved to be. And by the way all the nobles still looked to him, Duncan could sense that Tarnis assumed he still was king. It was, remarkably, as if nothing had changed.

"I thought to never lay eyes upon you again," Tarnis added. "Especially not under circumstances like these."

Duncan stared back, unable to get himself to muster a smile. He had always been honest with his emotions, and he could not pretend to feel warmth for the man.

"How could you have done this?" shouted out an angry voice.

Duncan turned and looked across the table to see Bant, the warlord of Baris, southern neighbor to the capital, staring back angrily at him. Bant was known to be a difficult man, a cantankerous man, as were all the people of Baris, living as they did down in the canyon, a hard, drab people. His people were not to be trusted.

"Do what exactly?" Duncan called back, indignant. "Liberated you?"

"*Liberated* us!?" he sneered. "You started a war we cannot win!"

"Now we lie at the mercy of Pandesia!" called out a voice.

Duncan turned to see a noble standing, staring back angrily at him.

"All of us will now be slaughtered, all because of your impetuous actions!" he called.

"And all this without our authority!" shouted out another noble, a man Duncan did not recognize, wearing the colors of the northwest.

"You will surrender at once!" called Bant. "You will approach the Pandesian lords, you will lay down your arms, and you will beg their forgiveness on behalf of us all."

Duncan fumed at these cowards' words.

"You all disgust me," Duncan replied, enunciating each word. "I am ashamed that I fought for your freedom."

A heavy silence filled the room, none daring to respond.

"If you do not surrender at once," Bant finally called out, "then we shall do it for you. We shall not die for your recklessness."

Kavos stepped forward and drew his sword, the sound reverberating in the room, heightening the tension, Bramthos standing close beside him.

"No one is surrendering," he said, his voice cold and hard. "Come close, and the only thing you will surrender to is the tip of my sword."

The tension in the room reached a fever pitch, both sides in a tense standoff, until finally Tarnis, the old King, stepped forward and laid his hand gently on Kavos's blade. He smiled, the smile of a professional politician.

"There is no need for division here," he said, his voice soft, reassuring. "We are all men of Escalon, all men who would fight and die for the same cause. We all desire freedom. Freedom for ourselves, for our families, for our cities."

Slowly, Kavos lowered his sword, yet he still stared coldly across the table at Bant.

Tarnis sighed.

"Duncan," Tarnis said, "you have always been a faithful soldier and a true friend. I understand your desire for freedom; we all share it ourselves. But sometimes brute force is not the way. After all, consider your actions. You have liberated the northeast, and even managed to win the capital, for now at least. For that I commend you. We *all* commend you," he said, turning to the room with a wave of his hand, as if speaking for all of them. He turned back to Duncan and rested his eyes upon his. "And yet you have also now left us vulnerable to attack. An attack we cannot possibly fend off. Not you, not even with all your men, and not all of Escalon."

"Freedom has a price," Duncan replied. "Yes, some men shall die. But we *will* be free. We shall kill all remaining Pandesians before they have a chance to regroup, and within a fortnight, all of Escalon will be ours."

"And even if?" Tarnis countered. "Even if you manage to rid our land of them before they rally? Reason with me. Will they not just invade through the open Southern Gate?"

Duncan nodded to Anvin, who nodded back.

"My men prepare even now to ride for the south and secure the gate."

The politicians grumbled with surprise, and he could see the surprise in Tarnis's eyes, too.

"And even if they secure it? Will Pandesia not storm the Southern Gate with a million men? And even if they lose those million men, can they not replace them with a million more?"

"With the gate in our hands, no force can take it," Duncan replied.

"I do not agree with you," Tarnis replied. "This is why I surrendered Escalon."

"The Southern Gate has never been destroyed," Duncan countered.

"And never has Escalon faced an army the size of Pandesia. It has never been tested," Tarnis said.

"Precisely," Duncan replied. "You don't know that we'll lose. And yet you surrendered us anyway."

"And you my friend," Tarnis replied, "don't know that we can win. Who I the more reckless of us two?"

"And what of Ur?" called out a noble. "Shall you secure its beaches with your skeleton force when the Sorrow turns black with Pandesian fleets?"

"Not my force alone," Duncan replied. "But all our men, together. Are we not all one Escalon?"

The men grumbled amongst each other, and most shook their heads and looked away in fear.

"We cannot defeat Pandesia," one lord called out. "No matter how well we fight."

"Escalon stood free for thousands of years," Duncan replied. "Are we less worthy than our ancestors?"

"No," called out another. "But Pandesia is stronger. It was not then what it is now."

As the room became filled with arguing, finally, Tarnis raised a hand, and silence fell. Duncan was surprised to see the old King still had such a command over his men.

"We cannot win," he said softly, conclusively. "And a life of servitude, a life of paying homage, is better than no life at all."

Duncan shook his head.

"A life of servitude," he replied, "is no life at all."

Tarnis sighed, at a stalemate, and the room fell silent. All looked to him, Tarnis still projecting an air of authority.

"You allow your warrior's honor and courage to guide you," Tarnis finally said. "It is commendable—but not practical. You are a warrior; you are no King, with a land to worry over. You would fight to the death, as if your livelihood; we, on the other hand, fight for survival. Escalon is indefensible against an army of that size."

"You underestimate us," Duncan replied. "We have other weapons."

In the back of his mind, he had to admit, he thought of Kyra, of her dragon.

"I have heard of your dragon," Tarnis replied, staring back at him as if reading his mind; he had always had that uncanny ability. "And of your daughter. Is this of whom you speak?"

Duncan remained silent.

"I'll have you know," Tarnis continued, "that the dragon you depend on has turned its wrath upon our people. Reports have flooded in of villages scorched to the north."

Duncan's heart fell at his words, shocked. In the back of his mind he had been hoping the dragon might come to their aid, and the news floored him.

Tarnis reached out and placed a hand on Duncan's shoulder.

"You see, old friend," Tarnis continued softly, his voice filled with compassion, "we are left with just our shields and our swords. We cannot possibly fend off Pandesia, however much your honor would like it. Our best hope, our only hope, is to reason with them. To compromise. To surrender and lay down our arms. To protect and save what we have."

He sighed.

"This is why we cannot join you," he continued. "And this is why you must surrender. Ask for mercy. They are an understanding nation. They will understand. I will use my influence to help them understand, and let you live."

Duncan grimaced back, stung by his words, losing any remaining respect he'd had for this man he once loved. He reached up and pushed Tarnis's hand off his shoulder.

"You mistake me," Duncan replied, his voice hard, official. "It was not a request." He turned and looked out at all the men in the room. "It is a command. We *are* liberating Escalon, with or without

61

you. We shall fight at dawn, as one nation, and you shall join us. If you do not, you will each be imprisoned or killed. If you hinder us in any way, you will be imprisoned or killed. I did not start this war, but I will end it."

A long, heavy silence followed, until finally Bant stepped forward.

"You have but a few thousand men at your command," he said, his voice equally defiant, determined. "I have twice as many in Baris, and we can summon many more. Attempt violence against us, and your situation will go from bad to desperate."

Duncan stared back, unwavering.

"As you say," Duncan replied. "Your men are in Baris—mine are here. You will not leave this room with your head on your shoulders if you intend to rally your men against us. The choice is yours."

The silence thickened as Bant looked about the room, seeing all of Duncan's men, uncertainty crossing his face.

"Consider, then, the King's guard," Tarnis stepped forward. "Thousands of fine soldiers stand strong here in the capital, all at my command. They answer only to the King. They will not join you. And if you threaten our men, they will stand in your way."

"True," Duncan replied. "They answer only to the King. And you are no longer that King."

For the first time, Tarnis's carefully composed face fell, as the room let out an astonished gasp.

"I am sorry, Tarnis," Duncan continued, "but you forfeited your kingship the day you surrendered Escalon. You are just an old man now; you have no authority here."

"Then who has authority as King, then?" Tarnis replied, mockingly. "You?"

"Yes," Duncan replied flatly.

An agitated grumbling filled the room, as Tarnis scoffed.

"And who named you King?" Bant called out.

"You have no right to the kingship!" a noble yelled.

They all grumbled, and Duncan faced them all bravely.

"I freed Escalon," Duncan replied. "I freed the capital. I started the revolt which all of you were afraid to. I have risked my life, and you have risked nothing. Is it you, then, who should hold power?"

The room fell quiet as he looked each one in the face.

"I seek no power," Duncan continued. "I seek only the freedom and unity of Escalon. And if I must be the vehicle, then so be it."

Tarnis shook his head in disapproval.

"No matter what you say," Tarnis replied, "the King's Guard will not answer to you. Not while I am King."

"He is right," Kavos interjected. "The Guard will not recognize two kings—no one will. Which is why you must kill him."

An outraged gasp spread across the room, and Duncan felt his stomach in knots as he faced Kavos.

"You vowed," Kavos reminded. "Now is your time to honor that vow."

Duncan contemplated Kavos's words. He had not wanted it to come to this, however little respect he had for Tarnis. He saw Tarnis's horrified look, and his feeling of anguish deepened. For the first time, Tanis stared back with a look of real fear. A long, tense silence ensued as all eyes turned to Duncan.

Duncan looked for a long time at the old King, debating, remembering all the years he had served him. He knew Kavos was right. He knew Tarnis should be killed.

Yet, finally, he shook his head.

"I shall not kill you," he said, his voice heavy, he already hating ruling. "But I cannot leave you free to roam the capital either. You shall be detained, and kept under watch."

Kavos turned to him, outraged.

"You vowed to kill him!" Kavos insisted.

Duncan shook his head.

"I vowed to assume power, and that I shall do," Duncan replied.

"You cannot have one without the other," Kavos countered.

Duncan stood firm.

"I shall not be cruel, or merciless. He is no threat to any of us."

Duncan turned to his men.

"Take him under guard," he commanded.

Several of his men rushed forward and detained Tarnis while the nobles watched, looks of panic and outrage across their faces as he was dragged out of the chamber.

A tense silence fell, and Duncan set his sights on Bant.

"I do not wish to kill you or your men. Join us. Let us fight as one—not fight each other."

Another long silence fell, a silence which did not seem to ever end. Finally, Duncan knew he had to do something to break that silence. Slowly, he crossed the room, circling the table, his men following, other men giving way, their armor clanging in the room, until finally he stopped before Bant. He disliked the man as much as anyone, and yet he knew he was king now, and he needed to do what a king would do. He had to make peace with his enemy, to unify his countrymen. If Bant followed, he knew, the others would, as would the King's Guard.

"You can kill me," Bant said, facing Duncan, "and you can kill my men. But you won't take Escalon without us."

"True," Duncan replied. "Which is why you must join us. You leave me with no choice but to kill you if you stand in our way. There is no turning back for us, and I want you by our side."

Duncan took a chance: he reached out in the silence, extending a hand. He looked Bant in the eye, waiting.

An impossibly long silence followed, until finally, Bant reached out and clasped arms with him, nodding back with a look of respect.

In that clasp, Duncan knew, the fate of Escalon had been sealed. He felt a rush of relief.

He smiled and turned to the room, and a small cheer followed.

"Tonight," he called out to the men, "we feast. And at dawn, we ride to victory!"

CHAPTER TEN

Vesuvius flailed as he plummeted toward the cave's rock floor, landing with a thud, feeling as if all his bones were breaking on impact. He lay there, limp, helpless to do anything but watch the devastation all around him. He saw the beast towering above him, stepping forward, making the ground shake, swiping his great hands and killing a dozen trolls at once. Trolls flew every which way across the tunnel, smashing into walls, and when he tired of swiping them, the giant lifted his great foot and flattened those who ran, crushing them into the ground.

The giant turned and Vesuvius's heart leapt as he saw it set its sights on him. It roared, showing sharpened teeth, then raised a foot and came down right for Vesuvius's head. Vesuvius knew that in but a moment he would be crushed to death.

Vesuvius somehow managed to muster whatever strength he had left and roll out of the way, as the giant's foot sank into the earth beside him, creating a crater dozens of feet deep. The giant, enraged, raised its other foot, and Vesuvius knew he had to think quick or else die here in this tunnel along with all of his other trolls.

Vesuvius searched his surroundings frantically and noticed something gleaming in the sunlight. He saw one of the long pikes lying there, abandoned by one of his trolls who lay beside it, dead, and he knew it was his only chance. He scrambled to his feet and ran, ducking under the giant's other foot as it came down and missed. He scurried across the cave and grabbed the pike, spun around, and charged. He raised it high with both hands and aimed for the giant's Achilles' heel, the narrowest point of the beast's body.

Vesuvius turned the pike and swung it sideways, aiming for the narrowest point, and prayed the beast did not raise its foot before he could complete the blow.

Vesuvius was surprised to feel the pike actually enter the creature's flesh; he drove it all the way through from one side of the beast's heel to the other, and he was surprised to see it emerge from the other side as blood gushed everywhere. It was a perfect strike.

The tunnel shook as the beast roared in pain, raised his foot, and stomped, creating another crater, sending Vesuvius stumbling as it barely missed. It then dropped to one knee, clearly in agony, unable to stand. It turned its head and screeched, looking everywhere for Vesuvius, off balance, reeling from the blow.

"THE PIKES!" Vesuvius shouted to his trolls.

His remaining trolls rushed forward and grabbed pikes as he led the charge. As the beast knelt there, its head lowered, Vesuvius jammed another pike into the back of the giant's neck. Beside him his trolls did the same, stabbing the beast in the neck and chin and face and shoulders.

The giant roared in agony and frustration; it reached up, grabbed the pikes, and yanked them out, snapping them in half as he gushed blood. It swiped back, killing several of Vesuvius's men, and Vesuvius narrowly missed being killed.

Knowing he needed a decisive blow, he grabbed another pike, rushed forward and this time swung upwards, beneath its chin, into its throat.

The giant flailed, reaching for the pike, but clearly weaker, gushing blood, unable to pull it out. It stumbled in agony, blind with fury, flailing its fists and smashing rock in every direction. Huge boulders and chunks of rock fell from the walls and crushed several of Vesuvius's trolls. A boulder fell on Vesuvius's foot, and Vesuvius shrieked as it felt as if it had broken his foot.

But the giant, hurt badly, this time fell to both knees, lowering his head to the ground. Vesuvius rushed forward, the rest of his trolls too scared to approach, and knew this was his final chance. In one last, mad dash, he grabbed an abandoned pike, raised it high overhead, let out a great shriek, and brought it down on the back of the beast's exposed neck. He brought it down with everything he had, driving it down with both hands, and as he did he felt it lodging deep into the beast's brain.

The beast slumped silently; then its eyes began to close as its great body went limp. It fell to the side, crushing several more trolls as it did, then lay there, unmoving.

Dead.

Vesuvius stood there, gasping, and surveyed the damage. There before him lay the dead giant, hundreds of dead trolls, piles of rubble, dust swirling in the air. He could hardly believe it. It was over.

Vesuvius heard a commotion and he looked out, past the settling clouds of dust, and in the distance, he saw hundreds more of his trolls arrive. Here came his nation of trolls, ready to follow him, ready to invade. Knowing they needed his leadership, he forced himself to his feet, despite his pain, wiped the blood from his mouth, and turned and looked up. There, at the top of the tunnel, was the sunlight, shining down amidst the dust and rubble. All was silent. The dragon was gone.

Escalon awaited him.

"NATION OF MARDA!" he shrieked to his army. "ATTACK!"

In the tunnel there echoed the shouts of thousands, all raising their halberds high, rushing forward, a nation ready to invade, to instill their bloodlust and violence on anyone and anything that stood in their path. All ready to rip Escalon to shreds.

*

Vesuvius sprinted through the open countryside of Escalon, his army behind him, beneath him the ground of Escalon, frozen snow and ice crunching beneath his feet, and it felt surreal. Here he was, breathing Escalon's air, feeling its wind, actually south of The Flames, in the land he had always dreamed of. It was a feeling he never thought he'd have. All those humans of Escalon, protected by The Flames, who thought they were so superior to the nation of Marda, had thought they were safe, untouchable. They had underestimated him. *Everyone* had underestimated him.

Vesuvius ran and ran, the snow melted in places in the charred countryside left by the dragon, the ground still smoking from its breath, until he crested a hill and saw a valley below. At its bottom sat a simple village, smoke rising from chimneys, farmers going about their work, women, children, cattle sharing the streets. They had no idea, Vesuvius realized with a smile, of the hell about to descend upon them.

Vesuvius grinned from ear to ear. He would rape all these women, he decided, torture all the men, take some slaves back with him, and murder whatever was left. On second thought, perhaps he would just murder them all.

"TROLLS OF MARDA!" he shouted. "I PRESENT TO YOU YOUR FIRST PRIZE!"

His trolls cheered as they raised their halberds and charged behind him, all racing down the slope, Vesuvius's legs unable to carry him fast enough.

The wind in his hair, the ground softening beneath his feet, Vesuvius had never felt so overjoyed. In but moments he reached the village, and he raised his halberd high as he saw the first face, the first human of Escalon to turn and stare and look him in the face. Here was the first human to see trolls, for the first time in history, in her native country, and her look of terror was priceless. It was a woman, perhaps in her thirties, staring back at him with such horror and fear and disbelief that it made everything he'd ever done in life worth it.

Vesuvius raised his halberd, swung it around, and just as she began to scream, he chopped her head off.

A shame, he thought—she would have made a fine plaything. But he had a ritual of always killing the first person in battle, and that, not even for her, he could not break.

As her body collapsed, all around him his trolls rushed forward and set torches to the village, stabbed spears into men's hearts, hacked down women and children, anything and everything they could get their hands on. Shouts of terror filled the air as the humans fled, none able to go fast enough.

Vesuvius joined them, and he soon felt himself covered in blood, his arms and shoulders tired from all the killing. He laughed aloud, praising the heavens for this day. If he could freeze this moment in time, he would.

For he knew that soon, very, very soon, all of Escalon would be his.

CHAPTER ELEVEN

The baby dragon emerged from his egg in a bout of rage, landing with his feet on the ground of Escalon, still breathing fire as the pack of wolves turned and fled. He arched his neck, his red scales still slimy, squinted, and breathed until his fire ceased.

He took his first wobbly steps, one foot after the next, learning how to walk, stretching, feeling his wings, beginning to get an understanding of himself. He could feel the fire coursing in his belly, through his veins, wanting to emerge. He could feel his strength slowly rising up within him. He leaned back and let loose the fire again.

The wolves ran, but not fast enough, and the dragon watched in satisfaction as the pack shrieked, in flames, flailing on the ground. He stepped forward, still wobbly, and breathed down on them again and again, unsatisfied.

The pack was soon burnt to a crisp, and the baby dragon turned and looked out at the forest. There, on its periphery, were several more wolves. They stood there, unsure.

The dragon wanted more. He ran forward, hobbling, slipping, falling to the ground face-first, then getting up again. He tried to flap his wings, but they were not strong enough, and after lifting into the air for a few feet, he fell back to the ground. He slipped and fell again, and yet he still charged for them.

He breathed fire as they all turned and fled, and suddenly, his flames ran out. Standing there, dry, parched, unable to fly or run, the baby dragon realized he had met the limit of his power. He tried again and again, and yet no flames came. How long would his flames take to regenerate? He wondered. How long would he be defenseless?

The dragon looked around with a new sense of appreciation for his surroundings. He was vulnerable; he felt it. He looked up and searched the sky for his father, but he was nowhere to be found. He felt the power in his veins that he would one day have—but right now, he did not have it yet.

No sooner had he had the thought when he heard a branch crack behind him. He turned and braced himself as he saw several soldiers approaching, wearing blue and yellow armor, face visors down, long shields held out before them, looking back warily.

"What have we here?" asked one.

Another soldier raised his visor, studied the baby dragon, then searched the skies for its father. Seeing nothing, he looked back to the dragon.

"Looks like someone forgot its baby," he said cruelly.

A soldier stepped forward and examined the broken shell, puncturing it with his long spear. Slimy liquid emerged from it.

"Barely out of its shell," he observed. "Weak, then. The better for us."

The soldiers, emboldened, cruelty in their faces, approached.

The dragon stood its ground proudly, arched its back, and tried to breathe fire.

But this time, to his dismay, only a trickle came out.

The soldiers laughed as the dragon felt his first jolt of fear. Before he could react, a soldier stepped forward and smashed him on the side of his head with his shield.

The dragon stumbled as he felt a wave of pain rush through his body. He knew that one day he would be able to kill all these men with a single breath; yet that did him no good today.

Still, the dragon, born a fighter, was determined not to give up, no matter how outnumbered, how bleak his situation. As a soldier approached, the baby dragon waited, then, at the last second, he reached around with his sharp claws and sliced the soldier's face. Blood gushed as he left a nasty wound, forcing the soldier, shrieking, to drop his shield and stumble back.

Yet another soldier charged from behind and jabbed the dragon in his back with his spear; the dragon shrieked as it punctured his still-soft scales.

"Don't kill it!" commanded a voice.

A soldier, bigger than the others, with different markings, clearly their commander, stepped forward.

"We need it alive!" he continued. "This will be the greatest prize we have ever captured."

Another soldier came forward with his shield, wound up, and smashed it across the jaw.

The dragon felt another jolt of pain as it swayed; yet somehow it mustered the strength to spin back around and claw the man across the stomach.

Another soldier smashed it from behind.

And another.

A dozen more soldiers pounced on it, smashing it from all sides, its ears filled with the clanging of metal. One blow at a time, his strength weakened, his world went dark.

Yet still he fought, lashing out, struggling to break free, screeching his young screech, managing to claw a few more soldiers in the face.

Yet it wasn't enough. Soon, despite all his efforts, he found himself on his side, in the grass, losing consciousness. He looked up, searched the skies, and hoped, wished, for but one thing.

Father, he called in his mind. *Why have you abandoned me?*

CHAPTER TWELVE

Kyra stood before Alva, her second uncle, and stared in disbelief. Despite herself, she felt supremely disappointed. Kolva had been everything she had ever hoped for in an uncle, had given her a sense of pride, of lineage; she had looked forward to spending time with him, to train with him, and she was proud to call him her mentor.

But this boy before her, Alva, hardly four feet tall, looking ancient, puny, sitting in a tree, appeared to be no mentor, no warrior, no sorcerer, wizard, or monk, no all-powerful being whom, she had imagined, would teach her everything she would need to know to become the greatest warrior of all time. Instead, there sat a mere boy, younger even than her little brother, Aidan, smiling down at her mysteriously, his face covered, prematurely aged. She felt as if she were being mocked. Had she crossed Escalon for this? To train not in the famed Tower of Ur, but rather here, in the woods, with a boy?

Kyra felt like crying. She also hated that this strange boy was her uncle, that she shared a bloodline with him. She had to admit, she felt ashamed. It made her wonder about herself.

She didn't know what to say or do; she wanted to flee this place, to go back to the tower, to pound on the doors until a warrior let her in. Someone she could respect, someone who had the power to teach her, to help her master her powers. She felt as if she were wasting her time.

"You are ready to leave," Alva observed, his voice like a child's, still smiling. "You are tense. Your hand rests firmly on your staff, and you think of the bow on your back, the wolf and Andor at your side. You think of returning to the tower. Perhaps even of returning to your father."

Kyra reddened as he read her mind perfectly. She felt violated; she had never experienced anything like it before. A long silence fell over them.

"I mean no offense," she finally said. "But I have crossed Escalon to train. You are half my age and half my size."

She expected him to take offense, but instead, to her surprise, he still smiled.

"And yet," he said, sitting on the branches, cross-legged, looking down at her, "I have lived centuries longer than you have."

She frowned, confused.

"Centuries?" she asked. "I don't understand. You look young. And you look nothing like me."

Kolva stood at the edge of the clearing, patiently awaiting Alva's command, and Kyra looked from Kolva to Alva, her two uncles, saw the stark difference in appearance between them, and wondered how they could both share her bloodline.

"We don't choose our relatives," Alva replied. "Sometimes family can disappoint us. We search for pride in our ancestors, pride in our relatives. But this pride is meaningless. The pride you seek must come from within."

Kyra shook her head, feeling overwhelmed. She wanted to discount this boy, and yet, as she stood there, she had to admit she sensed a tremendous energy coming off of him, a power she could not quite grasp.

"I must return to my father and help him," she said.

"Maybe you *are* helping him," Alva replied. "Right now. By standing here."

Kyra was perplexed; she had no patience for riddles.

"I haven't time for this," she said. "I must train."

"You are training right now," he replied.

She raised her eyebrows.

"Training?" she asked, wondering if he were mocking her. "I'm standing in the woods, far from battle, talking to a boy sitting in a tree. Is this training? Can you teach me to wield a staff, to fire arrows, to become a great warrior?"

He smiled, unflappable.

"Is that all you wish to learn?" he asked. "I can teach you far more than that."

She stared back, wondering.

"Those things of which you speak are trivial," he continued. "They have little to do with true power. Any warrior can wield a weapon. What I teach is far more than that. What I teach is the source behind the weaponry; the hand that wields the sword; the spirit that guides the hand."

She stared back, not understanding what he meant. She did not know what to say or feel.

"I thought..." she began, then trailed off. "I thought...you would lead me to my mother. That, if you were my uncle, you would reveal who she is. Who *I* am."

He closed his eyes and shook his head, his smile beginning to fade.

"Too many questions," he replied. "Questions that cloud you. You are full of demands—from myself and from the universe. Sometimes the universe is not ready to yield answers. Your mother understood that."

Kyra tensed at the mention of her mother.

"You knew her then?" Kyra pressed.

He nodded.

"Very well, indeed," he replied. "We both did."

Kyra looked to Kolva, who nodded back.

"And what was she like?" she asked, so eager to know.

Alva opened his eyes and looked down at her, a twinkle in his eyes.

"Just like you."

Kyra felt a flood of excitement at the thought, eager to know more.

"Tell me more."

He closed his eyes and shook his head.

"Release all questions and demands, or you will be unable to train. Let go of everything you have, everything you are."

Kyra stared back, unsure.

"I had expected to arrive at a place with a great training ground," she replied. "With great warriors to train with."

He shook his head.

"Still fixed on illusions," he replied. "I offer you much more. I offer you this," he said and spread his arms wide.

She looked around and saw nothing but trees.

"What is *this*?" she pressed.

"You do not see the trees before you," he replied sadly.

Kyra could contain her impatience no longer. She felt sure she was being tricked, that she was being tested, that this was all somehow part of her test.

"I do not wish to offend you," she repeated, "but my time is short. I cannot let my father die out there while I stand here, wasting time."

Kyra turned, hurried across the clearing, and mounted Andor. She directed him toward the woods and prepared to kick and ride off, unsure where she would go—anywhere but here.

Yet as she prepared to ride off, she looked at the woods before her, and was shocked. Instead of trees she saw rolling hills, shining in the sun. She saw gold and silver castles, a fantastical landscape of waterfalls and rivers and lakes. She saw a place unlike anything she had ever seen.

Behind it, she saw a massive army, all black, forming on the horizon.

Then the landscape changed, and the woods reappeared.

She spun back around, her heart pounding, unsure what had just happened. Alva raised a hand, and as he did, Andor, to her shock, suddenly sat.

Kyra studied Alva in awe, and finally began to realize just how powerful he was. She realized, finally, that she had met her true teacher.

"What was that vision I saw?" she asked. Then, hesitant, "Who are you?" she asked, her voice barely above a whisper.

He smiled wide.

"Soon, my niece," he replied, "you shall find out."

CHAPTER THIRTEEN

Dierdre sat proudly on her horse, leading the group of liberated girls through the familiar streets of Ur, and feeling a sense of pride at her homecoming. It felt good to be back in familiar terrain, back in her father's stronghold, and it felt good, most of all, to be able to help these girls, to spare them the anguish that she had met herself.

Yet Dierdre felt a wave of mixed emotions as she rode these packed, familiar streets, each corner filled with a childhood memory, but also with a sense of sadness. It was here, after all, that the Pandesians had taken her away; it was here that her father and his men had done nothing to stop it, had allowed her to be given away like chattel in some cattle trade. All because some lord in some far off empire had declared that Escalon women were the property of men. It was here, in her own city, that she had been betrayed, where her father, whom she had idolized most of all, had let her down.

Dierdre rode on, determined, anticipating the confrontation to come with her father, looking forward to it and dreading it at the same time. A part of her loved her home city, with its glistening canals, its cobblestones, steeples, domes and spires, its ancient temples, its air filled with the sound of foreign traders and the sight of foreign banners. Yet a part of her wanted to run from it all, to start fresh somewhere else. She passed through the arch of the ancient temple, and a part of her wanted to lead these girls elsewhere, anywhere else in Escalon.

Dierdre knew she couldn't run from her fears. She had to confront her past, confront those who had betrayed her, teach them what it meant to sell away a life. These men, her father most of all, had to be held accountable for their actions. All through her life Dierdre had always been one to avoid confrontation, yet now she knew that to run away from it would be cowardly. If she did not face them, make them own what they did, it would endanger other daughters, and other girls would suffer the same fate she had.

As Dierdre turned into the crowded marketplace, people stopped and stared, looking up in wonder at the caravan of girls riding so proudly down the center of the streets. Ur was a city that had seen it all, given its exotic visitors from all corners of the world, yet this sight stunned people. After all, they were a group of young, beautiful girls, exhausted from their long journey perhaps, but riding proudly through the streets like a band of warriors. Dierdre felt intensely protective of each one of them and was determined to find each a home—or give them a spot fighting beside her, whatever they chose.

As Dierdre rode proudly down the center of the street, she knew the dangers of being so conspicuous; she knew the Pandesian presence was everywhere, and she knew that word would spread soon of her arrival, if it hadn't already. They would come looking for her, to her father's fort. But she refused to hide in her hometown. She reached down and tightened her grip on the hilt of her sword; if they came for her, she was ready.

As she rode, Dierdre thought of her friend, Kyra, alone, on her way to the Tower of Ur, and she wondered if she had made it. She vowed to herself that, as soon as she got these girls situated, as soon as she had the weapons and support she needed, she would find her somehow, join forces with her. She felt that Kyra was like a sister to her, the sister she never had, the two of them having suffered so much together at the hands of the Pandesians.

Dierdre turned a corner and felt a rush of excitement as she saw her father's stronghold, the ancient stone fort, low, crowned with parapets, on top of which stood many of her father's men. They were unarmed, of course, given the Pandesian presence in the city and the law against Escalon men bearing weapons. Yet still they were allowed at least to inhabit the fort, her father having at least some semblance of the strength he once had here as a warlord. It was just a façade, though, she knew. With the Pandesians occupying them, they were hardly the free and proud warriors they had once been. And that was about to change—if she had any say in it.

Dierdre surveyed the fort's familiar walls, its thick, ancient oak doors, studded with iron, saw her father's men standing guard outside, dressed in the chain mail of Escalon warriors, and she felt at home. As she neared with her girls, they all stopped and looked over at her in shock. She stared back, cold and hard, realizing she was no longer the young, innocent girl who had left here. She was a woman now—a woman who had seen too much, who had been to hell and back. She was no longer willing to bow to the rights of men.

"Dierdre?" a soldier called out in surprise, rushing forward. "Why have you returned? Did your father not marry you off?"

"*Marry*," she spat back with disgust, anger rising in her voice. "A convenient word."

The soldier studied the girls with her, clearly amazed.

"And who are these girls?" he asked.

Dierdre dismounted, gestured to the girls, and they dismounted, too, as more of her father's men gathered around in amazement.

"These are the liberated *women* of Escalon," Dierdre replied. "They are under my protection."

"Protection?" the guard asked with a smirk.

Dierdre's face darkened.

"I shall see my father at once. Open those doors," she commanded.

The men looked at each other in wonder, more, she could see, due to the newfound authority in her voice than anything else.

"Is he expecting you?" a soldier asked.

Dierdre glared back with steely eyes.

"I am not asking you to open the doors," she replied. "I am telling you."

The men hesitated, looking to each other, then finally one nodded and the others stepped back and opened the doors wide. They creaked as they slowly gave way.

"Let your father deal with you, then," one of the guards said sternly, dismissing her as she walked past.

Dierdre paid him no mind. She walked proudly, leading the girls through the doors.

The ancient, musty smell of the place hit her as she walked in, that smell she recalled so well, the smell of a true fort. It was dim in here, as she remembered, lit only by sporadic tapered windows that let in narrow shafts of light.

They walked through the stone corridors, empty, and she looked up and saw the marks on the wall, the empty spots where her father's trophies used to hang, his finest weapons, shields, suits of armor, banners from clans he had defeated in battle. Yet these, too, were gone now, vestiges of what once was, another insult from Pandesia.

Dierdre continued down a long corridor until she spotted the familiar set of arched doors that led to the Great Hall. Muffled sounds arose from the other side and a soldier stood guard before it—but when he saw the look of determination on her face, he did not hesitate—he stepped aside and opened the doors for her. As he did, a wave of sound and noise hit her like a wall.

Kyra steeled herself as she entered, the girls behind her.

Dozens of her father's men lounged about the hall, furnished only with a long, square wooden table, open in the center, men passing in and out. A large fire burned on either side, dogs resting before it, fighting over scraps. Men were drinking, eating, clearly discussing matters of war. It was a group of warriors without a war, without a cause, idle, weaponless, stripped to the shell of what they once were.

At the head sat her father, seated before the huge square table which served as a place to feast, to meet, or alternately as a council table for matters of importance, matters of war. Matters they had not discussed in too many years.

As Dierdre and her girls entered, the men soon noticed, and a silence fell over the room. She had never thought to see such an amazed look on their faces, as one at a time they turned and watched her enter. They looked as if they were staring at a ghost.

Dierdre marched right up to the center of the table, to her father. He stopped talking to the warrior beside him and looked over at her, his jaw dropping in astonishment. He stood, rising to his full height.

"Dierdre," he said weakly, shock in his voice. "What are you doing here?"

She noticed his face flush with concern, and she was reassured to see that, at least, he seemed to care. She had been forged by suffering, was no longer the same person, and her father clearly realized, even if these men with him could not. His face filled with concern and guilt as he hurried from his seat and stepped forward to embrace her.

Yet as he reached for her, she held out a palm and stopped him.

He looked at her questioningly, his face filled with pain.

"You do not deserve a daughter's embrace," she said coldly, her voice deep, filled with an authority which surprised even her. "Not a daughter you gave away."

His face darkened with guilt, yet it also became set, as it sometimes did, with stubbornness.

"I had no choice," he countered, defensive. "I was obliged by law."

"Whose law?" she asked.

He furrowed his brow, clearly not appreciating being questioned. He was not used to her standing up to him like this.

"The law thrust upon all of us, all of Escalon," he replied.

"The law you *allowed* to be thrust upon you," she countered, unwilling to back down.

His face flushed red with anger and shame.

"Dierdre, my daughter," he said, his voice broken. "Why have you returned? How did you leave? How did you cross Escalon alone? What has happened to you? I don't know the voice of this woman who is speaking to me."

She stared back, feeling a mix of sorrow and defiance, recalling how much she had once loved this man and how badly he had betrayed her.

"That is right, Father. You don't know me anymore. I am not the same girl who left you. Not since you gave me away like a piece of property. Not after what I have suffered. I am a woman now. Tell me, Father, would you have given away one of your sons as easily as I? Or would you have fought to the death if they had come to take them?"

He stared at her, and she stared back. As she did, she felt, for the first time, rooted in place, no longer feeling a need to be quiet, to back down, as she always had. For the first time, she realized she had equal strength, equal fierceness, to her father. She no longer needed to recoil from his steely brown eyes, eyes which she herself had.

And then, slowly, the most amazing thing happened. For the first time since she had known him, her father's look of defiance morphed to one of guilt, of sorrow, as his eyes welled with tears.

"I am sorry," he said, his voice broken. "For whatever has happened to you. I never meant for anything bad to come of it."

She felt like crying, but she would not give in; instead, she turned and faced all the other warriors in the room as she spoke.

"Do you know the daily beatings I suffered? How they tortured me? How they locked me in a cell? How they passed me from one lord to the next? I was left for dead. And how I wish I had died. If it had not been for a dear friend, I would be dead right now. She saved me. A girl, a *woman*, who had more strength and courage than all of you men. No one else came for me—not one of you. Every day I woke and I was sure you would come—I was sure that there was not one of you who wouldn't risk his life to save a girl from torture."

She sighed.

"And yet, not one of you came. You, brave warriors, who pretend to be the bearers of chivalry."

She looked at all of the faces, and one at a time, she could see them all look away or look down, all shamed, all with nothing they could say.

Her father's face fell, pained, as he stepped forward.

"Who hurt you?" he demanded. "I did not give you over to be tortured; I gave you to be nobly wed to a Pandesian lord."

Dierdre threw a glance of hatred back at him.

"*Nobly wed?*" she seethed. "Is that what you call it? A fancy term to justify your spinelessness."

His face reddened with shame, he unable to respond, and as she surveyed all the other men in the room, they hung their heads low, none able to say a word.

"Pandesia has done what they have done not just to me," she called out, her voice stronger, "but to all of you. You should know this. You should know that when you hand off your daughters, you hand them off not to be wed, but to be beaten, tortured. They torture them even now, as we speak, in all corners of Escalon, in the name of their great law. And you all sit here and allow it to happen. Tell me: when did you all stop becoming men? When did you stop standing up for what was right?"

She looked at all their faces and could see them begin to transform with indignation.

"You all, great warriors, men whom I respected more than any in the world, have become weak, cowardly men. Tell me, when did you forget your oaths? Was it the day you laid down your weapons? How long do you think it will be until Pandesia comes not just for your women, but for you, too? Is that when it will mean something to you? When the sword is at your throat?"

81

She stared them all down, and not one of these men was able to say a word in response. The room hung thick with a heavy silence, as she could see their minds turning.

"You all disgust me," she said, indignation coursing through her veins. "It is not Pandesia I blame, but *you*—you who allowed this to happen. You don't deserve the right to be called warriors. Not even men."

She stood there, waiting for her father's response. But for the first time in his life he stood there, speechless.

Finally, when he spoke, they were the words of a broken man, a man who looked much aged since she had strode into the room, a man who looked filled with regret.

"You are right," he said, his voice subdued, broken. She was surprised; never in her life had he admitted he was wrong. "We don't deserve to be called warriors. And I didn't realize that until this day."

He reached out and placed a hand on her shoulder, and this time she allowed it.

"Forgive me," he said, his eyes welling with tears. "I never knew how wrong I was. It is the greatest shame of my life, and I will spend the rest of my life making it up to you, if you allow me to."

Dierdre felt her own eyes well at his words, all of her pent-up emotion rising to the surface, remembering how much she had once loved him, trusted him. But she fought it back, unwilling to show these men any emotion, still unsure if she would be able to truly forgive.

Her father turned to all his men.

"On this day," he boomed, "my daughter has taught us all a lesson we have forgotten. She has reminded us what it means to be a warrior. Of the warriors we once were. And of what we have become. She is the bravest and best of us all."

The men grunted in affirmative response, banging the table with their cups.

Her father stood to his full height, welling with pride once again, a gleam returning to his eyes that she had not seen in years.

"On this day," he called out, "we shall take up arms once again, even at the risk of our lives, as our women have so bravely done!"

The men cheered, their faces brightening.

"We shall learn what it means to become warriors once again. The enemy lies before us. We may die confronting him—but we shall die, once again, as men!"

The men cheered loudly, rising to their feet.

"Bring me that scroll." He gestured to a squire.

The boy rushed across the room and removed from the wall a scroll with Pandesian writing, several feet long. Her father held it out for all to see.

"The Pandesians declare that their laws must be hung in our meeting halls. Removal is upon pain of death," he reminded.

He held the scroll out before them and then slowly tore it in half, the sound filling the air.

The men let out a great cheer, and Dierdre felt her heart warming as her father threw the scraps to the floor.

"We shall fight Pandesia," he said, turning to Dierdre, "and you shall point the way."

Her father reached for her, and this time she embraced him back, as the men cheered.

Life, she felt, maybe, just maybe, could begin again.

CHAPTER FOURTEEN

Aidan held on as the wagon jolted him on the bumpy roads. White was finally asleep, resting his head in his lap, Motley across from him, and he took in the country scene in wonder. The caravan of wagons, with its jugglers, acrobats, actors, musicians, and all manner of entertainers, was full of life, everyone telling jokes, laughing, playing instruments, singing songs and jostling with each other—some even managed to dance. Aidan had never seen a group of people so carefree, so unlike the grim warriors he had grown up with in his father's fort. Where he was from, men stayed silent unless they had something to say. He barely knew what to make of these people.

Seeing all of this was like a veil being pulled back on the lighter side of life, a side that had never been revealed to him. He had no idea that life could be this carefree, that one could be *allowed* to be this carefree, that it was okay to be this happy and foolish. It was something he was sure his father, a serious man with little time to waste, would frown upon. Aidan had a hard time grasping it himself.

They had been riding for days through the countryside, twisting and turning their way through deep and dark woods, their destination never in sight. As they went, Aidan marveled at the foreign landscape, snow giving way to grass, twisted black trees giving way to perfectly straight glowing green trees that lined the road. The air was different this far south in Escalon, too, balmy, heavy with moisture; even the sky seemed to take on a different tint. Aidan felt a mixture of excitement and apprehension the further they went, eager to see his father, yet realizing he was further from Volis than he had ever been. What if, after this huge journey, his father was not there?

Aidan felt a twitching in his lap and he looked down at White's paw as Motley came over, knelt beside him, and checked his dressing. This time, White didn't whine as Motley wrapped it up again. Instead, he licked Motley's hand.

Aidan reached over and gave White some water in a bowl and a small treat—a piece of dried meat that Motley had given him.

White snatched it hungrily, then licked Aidan's face, and Aidan could already see his dog's spirits returning. He knew he had a friend for life.

There came another burst of laughter and a shout from the wagon beside them, as a group finished a song and drank from sacks of wine. Aidan frowned, not understanding.

"Why are you all so happy?" he asked.

Motley looked back at him, puzzled.

"And why wouldn't we be?" he countered.

"Life is a serious business," Aidan said, echoing something his father had drilled into him many times.

"Is it?" Motley countered, a smile forming at the corner of his mouth. "It doesn't seem so serious to me."

"That is because you are not a warrior," Aidan said.

"Is being a warrior all one can do in life?" Motley asked.

"Of course," Aidan countered. "What else is there?"

"What else?" Motley asked, surprised. "There's a whole world out there outside of killing people."

Aidan frowned.

"Killing people is not all that we warriors do."

"*We*?" Motley smiled. "Are you a warrior then?"

Aidan puffed out his chest proudly and used his most mature voice.

"I most certainly am."

Motley laughed, and Aidan reddened.

"I have no doubt that you will be, young Aidan."

"Warriors do not just kill people," Aidan persisted. "We protect. We defend. We live for honor and pride."

Motley raised his sack and drank.

"And I live for drink, women, and joy! Cheers to that!"

Aidan stared back, frustrated that he was unable to get through to him.

"How can you be so joyful?" he asked. "There is a war to fight."

Motley shrugged, unimpressed.

"There is always a war to fight. This war, or that war. A war that you warriors begin. Not *my* war."

Aidan frowned.

"You lack honor," Aidan said. "And pride."

Motley laughed.

"And I have lived very joyously without either!" he countered.

Several musicians rode up beside them, laughing and singing. Aidan wracked his brain, trying to figure how to make him understand.

"Honor is all there is," Aidan finally said, recalling a saying from the ancient warriors he had read.

Motley shook his head.

"I require a lot more than that," Motley replied. "Honor has never gotten me a thing. Besides, there's honor in other things besides fighting."

"Like what?" Aidan asked.

Motley leaned back and looked up at the sky as he seemed to think.

"Well," he began, "there is honor in making someone laugh. There is honor in entertaining someone, in telling a story, in taking them away from their woes and troubles and fears, even if just for an afternoon. Transporting someone away to another world holds greater honor than all of your swords combined."

Motley took another swig.

"There's honor in being humble, in not being so puffed up with pride like most of your warriors," he added. "There's even honor in laughter. Your problem," he concluded, "is that you've been around warriors too long, growing up in that fort. Your vision is single-minded."

Aidan had never considered any of this before. For him, he wanted nothing more in life than to be around his father's warriors, to hear stories of battle and honor recounted again and again by his father's hearth. For him, honor meant nothing else. He had never heard words spoken such as this, and he marveled at this man and his words and his brightly colored clothes, at all of his friends, all these people who seemed so foolish to him, who seemed to trivialize life.

And yet, as Aidan pondered the man's words, he wondered if perhaps there could also be other side of life, another type of man out there, different ways to live. After all, he had to admit there was some truth to the man's words: Aidan himself had never experienced any greater feeling than being carried away by a story, getting lost in the fantasy of ancient worlds and battles. They were what inspired him, what sustained him. And if this man could recount such stories, then maybe, perhaps, there was honor in him after all.

"Is that what you do?" Aidan asked, curious, looking the man up and down. "You tell people stories? Are you a bard, then?"

"I don't just tell stories," Motley replied. "I create worlds. I ignite the imagination. I inspire. I invite people into a world of fantasy, a world they could not enter on their own. What I do is no less important than what your father does."

"No less important?" Aidan demanded skeptically. "How can you say such a thing?"

"Without me," Motley replied, "who would tell the tales? After the warriors have won their battles, who would recount them to the masses? And if no one recounts them, they will not live on. All your father and his men had done will not even be a memory."

As Aidan pondered his words, Motley took another long swig on his sack and sighed.

"Besides," he continued, "your father's wars are mostly mundane. For every dramatic battle worth mentioning there may be a year of trivialities. My stories, though, are never mundane. My stories extract the life from your father's mostly dull journeys. My stories are not dry histories, are not encyclopedias; they are what matters most in them, what is worth remembering."

Aidan frowned.

"My father defends kingdoms," he said. "He has many people under his protection. You tell stories."

"And I defend kingdoms of my own," Motley replied, "and I, too, have many people under my protection. It is a different kingdom—one of the mind—and a different sort protection—one of the heart and of the soul—but it is of equal worth. The kingdom of the mind, after all, comes first. It is what enables men to dream, to imagine, to plan, and eventually to conquer the kingdoms of the world. The inspiration they draw, the lessons they learn, the strategies they deduct, are all from my stories. After all, what is life without story, fantasy, the legends we tell each other? Ask yourself, young Aidan: where does story end and life end begin? Can you ever truly extricate the two?"

Aidan furrowed his brow.

"I don't understand," he said.

Motley leaned back, took a long swig of his sack, and studied him.

"You're a wise boy," he replied. "You *do* understand. I can speak to you as an adult, and I know you listen. You just need to think on it. To let go of all your preconceptions. And I know you have a lot in there."

Aidan looked out as the cart rolled and bumped, watching the landscape change again and again as a heavy mist rolled in and out. He wondered. Was there any truth to what this man said? Were there other virtuous paths in life aside from being a warrior?

A long, comfortable silence descended over them, interrupted by nothing but the sound of the carts jostling on the rough country road and the occasional laughter and music of the others.

"When we die," Motley finally said, breaking the silence Aidan thought would never end, his voice more tired, heavy with drink, his face partially obscured by the mist, "we have nothing left in this world. Not our siblings, not our parents, not all the whores we've slept with, and not even the drink in our bellies. All we have left is memory. And our memories often trick us. They become half-truths, distorted truths, part real and part how we wished them to be. Our memories morph over time, like it or not, to fantasy. *Fantasy* is all we have left. Fantasy will always trump memory. When you look back on life, when you try to grasp whatever it is that you have left, you will not cherish the fading memories, but the fantasies that became so real they are now a part of you. And those fantasies are driven by story."

Motley leaned forward, impassioned, a sudden intensity in his stare.

"You see, young Aidan, too often our lives are too mundane. Or too complicated. Or too unjust. Or too mysterious. Or too unresolved. Our lives can be messy stuff, with no resolution, sometimes even stopped in the middle. But our stories, our fantasy—well, those are different things altogether. They can be everything our lives cannot. They can be perfect. *They* are what sustain us."

He breathed deep.

"*More* than that," he continued, "we are not only sustained by our stories. If we live with them long enough, we *become* our stories. Do you understand? The legends we read, the fantasies we choose—they sink into us. They became a part of our fabric. They come to define us. They become as much a part of us as our real memories—even more significant, because our memories are thrust upon us, while our fantasies we *choose*. Whenever you hear a great fantasy, such as the ones I tell, it will change you. *Forever.*"

Motley finally sat back, sighing, taking another swig on his sack.

"So you see, boy," he concluded, "I don't just tell stories. I change people's lives. As much, if not more, than your father. Your father's swords are temporary; my fantasies shall live long after."

Motley folded his hands on his chest, closed his eyes, and just like that, to Aidan's surprise, he was snoring.

Aidan marveled at this man, so unlike anyone he'd ever met, wondering where he had come from. He looked around and he had to admit that he was in awe of all these people, so happy, so carefree. Aidan had never seen such joy in his father's fort. Were the people of Volis missing something these people were not?

The cart rode on for hours, jolting its way, Aidan holding White beside him, trying to shelter him from the bumps, his wounds still tender. Aidan looked out and watched the passing terrain, trees turning from green to purple to yellow to green again, and just as he wondered if these woods would ever end, suddenly, they gave way to a great open plain before them.

Aidan sat up, feeling a rush of excitement as the vista changed dramatically. The sky opened up as the forest gave way, and the sun shone through in the open plains. He sensed they were close now. The ride was smoother, their horses moved faster, and as Aidan stood in the cart, eager to take it all in, he was stunned at what he saw.

There, on the horizon, emerging from the mist, sat Andros, the capital. It took his breath away. It was the most remarkable place he had seen in his life, stretching across the horizon, as if it filled the world. He looked as hard as he could, but he could not see where it ended. Before it was an enormous temple, soaring in the clouds, and through its center, an open arch, was its massive entry gate, mobs of people hurrying in and out. Aidan studied the parapets, expecting to see the royal yellow and blue banners of Pandesia, the battlements lined with Pandesian soldiers—and yet, as he surveyed the city walls, he was delightfully shocked to see none. Instead, his heart raced to see, the banners of Escalon hung proudly. He blinked, wondering if his eyes were misleading him.

They were not. The capital, he realized with a thrill, was back in his people's hands. And that could only mean one thing: his father had taken it. He had won.

And that meant something even more important, Aidan realized with a thrill: his father was here, inside.

"Look!" Aidan called out excitedly, kicking Motley's leg as he stood, staring out at the approaching capital, not believing how anyone could sleep through such a moment. The horses gained speed and Motley finally opened his eyes, startled. He looked around, then sat up and glanced at the approaching capital—but then he just as quickly sat back down, to Aidan's astonishment. He folded his hands on his chest and closed his eyes again.

"Seen it a million times," he said, yawning.

Aidan looked from Motley back to the capital in disbelief, his heart soaring with excitement, wondering how anyone could be so indifferent to life, so indifferent to one of the greatest views in Escalon. A series of horns sounded from the carriages, startling Aidan as the musicians blew beside him.

"What are they doing?" he asked Motley.

"Announcing our arrival," Motley replied curtly, eyes still closed.

The horns sounded a series of short blasts, in an unusual rhythm, unlike anything Aidan had heard before.

"But why?" Aidan asked.

"It's good for business," Motley replied. "It lets them know we're coming. After all, this is the capital, and we're not the only game in town—we'll have a lot of competition."

The horns sounded repeatedly as the horses increased their speed, and soon they reached the massive wooden drawbridge. They passed over it, horses clomping, and Aidan felt a thrill as they merged with the throngs. He looked down and recognized a few of his father's men guarding the drawbridge, at attention, and he laughed aloud at the sight, delighted that his father had really won, that he was really here. Riding over this bridge brought back vague memories of when he was young, living here with his father, when the weak King was still in command. It seemed like a lifetime ago.

Yet Aidan also felt overwhelmed as he studied the size and scope of the city, realizing it would be no easy feat to find his father behind its walls. The capital seemed to be as large as a country itself.

There came the sound of cheering and laughing in the streets, as the throngs gathered around their carriage. Aidan kicked Motley again, still sleeping.

"You don't understand!" Aidan called out. "The capital! It's free! It's ours!"

Motley opened his eyes wide and this time he jumped to his feet, seeming surprised. He saw the Escalon banners, saw the festive crowds and, for the first time since Aidan had met him, he looked truly stunned.

"I had not expected this," he said to himself, taking it all in with wonder.

"We are free!" Aidan called out, elated.

Motley shrugged.

"Free or not, hardly matters," he replied. "The crowds are festive. That will be good for business."

"Is that all you care about?" Aidan snapped. "Pandesia has been defeated by my father! That is what matters."

Motley shrugged.

"Money matters," he replied. "So I shall thank your father for that. Perhaps I shall tell a tale about him."

Motley saw the festive crowds rushing the cart, silver coins in hand, and he beamed.

"You see, young Aidan?" he said. "Warriors do not receive half the adulation that we do."

Aidan, burning with a desire to find his father, could not waste another minute. He leapt over the side of the cart, White joining him, landed hard on the dusty ground, and ran through the gates.

"Aidan!" Motley called out.

But Aidan did not look back. He was already pushing his way through the crowd, into the capital, getting lost in the masses as he was determined, no matter what it took, to be reunited with his father once again.

CHAPTER FIFTEEN

Merk sat on the stone floor in the Tower of Ur before the roaring fireplace, a dozen other warriors beside him, sitting in a loose circle, and as they all stared silently into its flames, he contemplated his life here. It had been a long day on duty, watching, and few of these men had much to say. They chewed on their sticks of dried meat, and Merk chewed, too, realizing how hungry he was from his journey, grateful to be able to stretch his aching legs at last, after so many hours of sitting at that window and watching the countryside.

Merk glanced around at the other men, men who, like him, seemed to have no other place to go in the world, men with hardened faces. They were, like he, lost souls, broken people; yet each, he knew, must have something special in order to have made it through these doors. What had driven them all here?

The distant crashing of the ocean waves filtered in through the windows, while a gust of wind tore through, as it did every so often. That, and the crackling of the fire, provided the only noise while they all sat somberly, each lost in his own world. Merk felt this place was like a monastery, each of these warriors like monks, each resigned to his own personal vow of silence.

Yet Merk wanted to do more than just watch—he wanted to protect. He wondered when his duties would change. Surely, he hoped, he would not be confined to this tower forever? Doomed to sit by a window and watch?

Merk glanced about the room and his eyes paused on Kyle, the mysterious boy with the long, golden hair, who sat apart from the others. There was clearly something different about him. With his surreal, glowing gray eyes, he did not appear to be of their race. But why would a true Watcher be stationed with them?

Merk turned and looked at his new commander, Vicor, who sat at the head of the circle, staring into the flames, and took a long swig on a sack of wine as it was passed around. The sack soon ended up in Merk's hands and he took a long swig. He was surprised to find the wine spicy and warm, rushing to his head. It felt good.

"Tonight," Vicor finally said, breaking the heavy silence, "we patrol."

He scanned the circle of men and his eyes stopped on Merk.

"We shall leave the tower and patrol on foot."

Merk felt a rush of excitement at the thought.

"What will we be looking for?" Merk asked.

Vicor gave him an impatient look.

"Anything hoping to kill you," he answered flatly. "We patrol at night, after our days of watching. We take shifts in rotation."

"Why not patrol during the day?" Merk asked.

As Vicor stared back at Merk, it was clear he did not like being asked questions.

"Because our enemies prefer to attack us at night."

It suddenly occurred to Merk that all those nights he had sat outside, petitioning to get in, these men must have seen him. And yet, they had let him sit there.

"Why did you not approach me, then?" he asked Vicor.

Vicor shrugged.

"New petitioners come to our doors all the time," he replied. "It is not our place to decide on their fate. We let the others in the tower decide. Those camped at our doors hold no threat."

"Then what does?" Merk asked.

"Trolls," he answered without hesitation. "They invade in small groups from Marda, when they slip past The Flames. Lone attacks."

Merk was surprised to hear this.

"I thought The Flames kept them out."

Vicor shook his head.

"Enough of them slip through."

"And they make it all the way here?" Merk asked

"Enough do."

After a long silence, Vicor continued.

"From all corners of Escalon, from all corners of the world, they all want the same thing: The Sword of Flames. It is our job to guard it."

"Is it here, then?" Merk asked even though he knew he shouldn't, dying to know.

Vicor looked away. Then, after a long pause, he replied: "That is something you will never know. Nor I. It is our job to watch, only. Whether it sits here or in the Tower of Kos matters little, anyway. Our job is just as sacred, either way. This tower holds many secrets, and many treasures—some even more valuable than the Sword."

Merk's curiosity was piqued.

"What could possibly be more valuable than the Sword?" he asked.

But Vicor looked to the others, and they all looked away and fell silent. Merk realized he was an outsider; he still needed to earn their trust.

"This tower is not what it seems," Vicor finally replied. "There are many floors you will never get to see, many secret passageways that lead to places you cannot imagine. Going somewhere in this tower without permission is on pain of death."

He gave Merk a serious look, and Merk made a mental note not to explore.

"So we watch all day and patrol all night," Merk said. "Do we ever sleep?"

Vicor smiled halfheartedly.

"In shifts," he replied. "You get two hours before dawn."

"Two hours?" Merk repeated, surprised.

Vicor suddenly stood, and all the men stood with him. He looked at Merk and as he did he threw down a sword, a beautiful sword inscribed with the ancient markings of the tower. It landed on the stone, clanging at Merk's feet.

"You'll join us tonight," he said to Merk.

Merk reached down and picked up the sword, holding it up, running his finger along the blade, in awe of its craftsmanship.

"You want to be a Watcher," Vicor concluded. "Let's see if you can earn it."

Merk followed the group as they walked single file out the door and hurried down the stone spiral staircase, flight after flight. He fell in behind Kyle.

"You carry no weapon," Merk observed, as they descended flight after flight.

Kyle glanced back.

"It would slow me down," he replied.

Merk was puzzled, but had little time to process it as they reached the main floor and he saw the others continue down another flight, past the floor with the golden doors. They were soon underground, descending deeper and deeper, Merk baffled as to where they could be going—when suddenly they stopped on a floor, went through a small, arched door, and entered a long tunnel, lit by torches. It twisted and turned, Merk feeling claustrophobic as he was right behind the others, and it finally ended in a small flight of stone stairs. They ascended again, and a small stone door was opened.

Merk was shocked to find himself emerging to the outside, exiting the tower from a secret passageway carved into the stone. He felt the moist, cool ocean air on his face in the night, and it felt odd to be back outside again. The stone doors mysteriously closed behind them and Merk stopped and looked up at the tower. He was in awe at its height.

Merk heard the crashing of the ocean, louder here, and he looked around in the black of night, lit only by their torches, and saw the men begin to spread out. They all headed away from the tower, toward the woods.

"What is our assignment?" Merk asked Kyle, coming up beside him. "What are we looking for?"

Kyle was silent for a long while, moving quickly, never taking his eyes off the woods, until finally he replied.

"An enemy takes many forms," he answered mysteriously, still looking straight ahead.

Merk walked with the others, and they fell into a groove, hiking into the night. It felt like a silent meditation.

For hours they patrolled, and he did not see or hear anything, only the sound of leaves crunching, of him and the others walking in the woods. He found himself wondering about the nature of this place, the nature of his service here. Was he really serving Escalon? It didn't feel like it. He could not even be sure the Sword of Flames was in this tower. He felt as if his special skills were not really being put to use. Was this what it meant to be a Watcher?

Hours more passed, and Merk, deep in the woods, suddenly heard a noise before him. It sounded somewhat like a crow, yet with a sound that was more shrill. It cawed again and again, and as Merk listened, he sensed it was something more sinister. A harbinger of something to come.

The others, following Vicor, had just turned back around and were now all heading back to the tower. A part of Merk wanted to go with them—yet another part, the part that demanded duty, felt he could not go back until he had explored.

"Wait!" Merk called out to the others.

All the men stopped, and Vicor came up beside Merk as he studied the woods.

"It's your first watch," said Vicor, after a long silence. "There's nothing there."

"Nice try," mocked another of the men, patting him on the back as he snickered and turned away.

They all turned back for the tower, but Merk stood his ground, alone, refusing to go. He had always trusted his senses, and that was what made him the most feared assassin in Escalon. Now they were telling him that something was out there.

Merk watched the woodline for several minutes, waiting. Yet nothing happened. The sound did not come again.

He debated turning back himself, when suddenly, he, standing there alone, heard the snap of a twig. The hairs rose on the back of his neck as he knew for sure this was no crow. There came a howling noise, and suddenly there came a rustling. Something was charging through the woods, right for him.

A moment later there appeared the face of a hideous creature, and Merk could see, with dread, that it was no man, no beast—but the face of a disfigured, overgrown troll. He knew instantly that he had on his hands the fight of his life.

The troll charged him, nearly twice his size, and Merk blinked as he saw dozens more appear behind it. He raised his sword, ready to christen it, knowing he didn't stand a chance. But that didn't stop him. He charged, throwing caution to the wind, letting honor take its place, ready to do what he had been born to do—even in the black of night.

CHAPTER SIXTEEN

Duncan sat at the head of the long banquet table in the great Hall of Feasting, and he looked out at the massive crowd of soldiers gathered before him with unease. He knew he should be happy by what he saw—after all, there, before him, was what he had craved to see: all his warriors here in Andros, feasting, reveling in their victory. There were Kavos's men and Seavig's men, all of them together, taking the very seats the Pandesians had had, feasting on the finest delicacies, drinking the best wine, and celebrating, as they deserved to, for taking the capital against all odds. Duncan reflected on how they had managed to take their victory from Volis to Esephus, to the Lake of Ire and on to the peaks of Kavos—and now, finally, to the capital itself. It was surreal. They had sparked a movement in Escalon, and had spread freedom throughout half the land. It had been a spontaneous uprising, sparked by Kyra, something none of them could have ever planned. Seeing the statues toppled, as he had today, capped the victory of a lifetime.

Duncan knew he should feel victorious, relaxed. And yet he did not. For before him sat, amidst his men, an uneasy alliance of others, Bant's men on the other side of the table, joined by the nobles and King's Guard, men who were, he suspected, still loyal to Tarnis. It was a fragile alliance of combating clans and interests, all, despite being of Escalon, with different agendas and viewpoints, a table of men who coveted the kingship, and who had opposing ideas for ousting Pandesia. Duncan could feel the tension in the air, barely masked, each side keeping to itself. And as the wine flowed, he sensed that tension rising.

Duncan looked out and he wanted so badly to think that this was a unified group of his countrymen, fighting for one cause. After all, they all wanted freedom. Yet he could also sense that for each of them, the cause before them was different, and the path to achieve it even more so. The more Duncan observed them, the more he began to realize that before him was not one people, but a group of competing interests who inhabited the same isle. He began to see that Escalon had never truly been one people, but in name only. It was really a disparate collection of strongholds sharing a border, each with strong-headed warriors and warlords, each concerned

97

only with his own region. The King's job, Duncan was realizing uncomfortably, was to be the glue that held them all together, this alliance which felt as if it were hanging by a thread. It gave Duncan a fresh respect for the old King. Despite his faults, somehow Tarnis had, at least, held them all together. Unity, he realized, could be harder to achieve than victory.

Duncan also felt a sense of dread as he looked over and spotted Enis, Tarnis' son, easily distinguishable in his aristocratic dress, his shifty eyes, and with the long, vertical scar along his ear. He glared coldly at Duncan until Duncan finally stared back, and he looked away. With his hollow eyes and hungry stare, Duncan trusted him the least. Duncan thought back to their troublesome encounter, shortly after he had imprisoned his father. Enis had insisted that he would be the best king to take his father's place, and had practically begged Duncan to put him in power, promising all sorts of alliances in return. Duncan, sickened by this disloyal son, had sent him out of his presence. He hated having him here at this table, and he would not if Enis were not close with Bant, the King's Guard and all the nobles. Just one more sickening side effect of politics.

The feast went on for hours, the room filled with music, women, drink, a feast designed to cement their brotherhood. Duncan wished he could take Escalon on his own, but he knew he needed Bant and his men, needed the King's Guard. Liberating a few towns was one thing—taking an entire land, securing its borders and ruling it were all quite another. Duncan needed them, especially as Pandesia was most surely preparing for a counterattack.

While the others ate and drank, Duncan barely touched his food. He hated being King already. He hated politics, hated ruling, hated having to detain Tarnis, who had once, whatever his faults, been like a father to him. Yet he had been left with little choice. It was death or detainment, and Duncan was glad at least that he had chosen the latter. That choice, he knew, had also strained his alliance with Kavos, who was still fuming that he had left him alive, and his alliance with Bant and the nobles, who were simmering, too. From all sides, Duncan felt his alliance fracturing.

Duncan looked over at Arthfael, taking solace at the sight of him, as always, and beside him, he noticed Anvin's empty seat, his most trusted commander. As he thought of the mission he had sent

Anvin on, he felt a fresh pit in his stomach. Anvin was riding right now, he knew, throughout the night, for Thebus, to secure the Southern Gate before it was too late. Duncan wondered if he would make it in time, before Pandesia invaded like a tidal wave from the south. Duncan wanted nothing more than to join his friend, but he knew he was needed here, to cobble together this alliance before the next attack.

The men before him drank and reveled, all celebrating as if they would not be up at dawn, riding into more battle. Duncan had seen it before with his soldiers—it was their way of steeling themselves for a possible death, of numbing themselves to the fear of battle. He would not deny them their pleasure. Even his own sons, he could see, red-faced, had had one drink too many. Despite their reddened cheeks, despite their drunken arrogance, Duncan knew now was not the time to rein them in.

Seeing them, though, made his heart hurt, as he thought of his missing daughter. Where was Kyra now? he wondered. Had she made it? He wished, above all, that she could be here with him— she, and her dragon. How he needed them now.

"The men of Baris are by far the most superior warriors of Escalon!" exclaimed a harsh, drunken voice.

A shout rose through the crowd.

Duncan gritted his teeth as he looked over to see a drunken Bant slam the table with his mug, punctuate his boasting to his men, speaking loud enough to goad Duncan's men across the table. Bant's men cheered in the affirmative, while Duncan's men darkened. It was almost as if Bant were looking for a way to provoke Duncan and his men, to break the alliance. Perhaps, Duncan figured, Bant was just trying to save face from giving in today, and to push back a bit.

Duncan would not take the bait. As the man holding this alliance together, he knew he had to choose his battles and to exercise restraint, the same restraint he had always loathed as a warrior. As much as he despised the blowhard men of Baris, for the sake of Escalon, he knew he had to take a deep breath and find a way to hold his alliance together.

"Baris has also the finest stronghold in all of Escalon! I challenge you to find one better!" Bant continued, to the drunken cheers of his men.

"You mean that rat-hole deep in a canyon you call a city?" called out a voice from the other side of the table.

A hush came as all eyes followed the voice. Duncan looked over and his heart fell to see what he had suspected the second he'd heard the voice: his son, Braxton, beside his brother Brandon, staring back at Bant. *No*, Duncan silently willed his braggart sons. *Not now.*

"And as for the best warriors," Brandon chimed in, "ten of your men could not face one of us."

Duncan's men cheered this time, as Bant reddened. He scowled back, staring Duncan's boys down.

"We have more victories, boy, than you will ever count," Bant seethed, placing both palms on the table.

Brandon scoffed. "Victories!" he mocked. "Is that what you call your cattle skirmishes!?"

"The only victories you can claim," Braxton added, "are kissing the old King's ass!"

The room roared and hooted.

Bant, humiliated, stood, murder in his eyes. He laid fists on the table as he faced off with them.

Duncan, infuriated, knew he had to stop this before it got out of control.

"Boys!" Duncan hissed, needing to silence them. They were young and stupid and had taken Bant's bait perfectly.

He expected them to look over at him, but his two boys, flush with wine, seemed not to hear him. Brash and young and impetuous, they stood there and faced Bant.

"Tell me," Braxton added, "how did it feel today to kiss our father's ass?"

Bant turned purple. He spit on the table, while all his men stood beside him, indignant, as if preparing to fight. Bant turned and faced Duncan.

"My men are no longer with you!" he snapped. "You can attack Pandesia alone and die alone—our alliance is over!"

His men cheered as Bant drew his sword, his men with him.

Duncan's men stood, too, on their side of the table, drawing swords, Kavos, Bramthos, Seavig and Arthfael at their front, all appearance of civility gone. They all faced off, about to leap at each other, and Duncan knew he had to take action fast.

Duncan pushed back his chair, stood at the head of the table, slammed a fist on the table, and shouted:

"ENOUGH!"

All the men turned and faced him, sensing the authority in his voice.

"There is only one path to victory!" Duncan called out, his voice booming, the voice of a great commander. "The enemy lies at our gates, an enemy that will take all that we have, all that we are, to conquer. And shall we sit here, like children, fighting amongst ourselves?"

He slowly stared down the men on both sides, red-faced, as they all still held their swords, facing off. They did not set down their weapons, but at least, for now, they stood still.

"I shall not tolerate such an insult from your offspring!?" Bant called out.

Duncan looked at his boys, dreading dealing with this. He knew his boys were right, and he hated asking them to apologize, especially to this blowhard. But too much was at stake, and good leaders did what they had to.

"You shall apologize to Bant!" he commanded. "Both of you!"

His sons frowned back, still drunk.

"We shall not apologize for speaking the truth!" Brandon called out.

"This man has been provoking us all night!" Braxton called. "Should he not apologize?"

"If he is the great warrior he claims to be," Brandon added, "let us see if he can back up his claims!"

Duncan felt his stomach turning in knots as he felt all his plans crumbling before him.

"You little turds!" Bant glowered at them. "I've been killing men before you were weaned, and if your father wasn't standing here I'd drive this sword through your hearts right now."

"Try it!" Seavig suddenly called out, standing beside Brandon. "And my sword will find a spot in yours!"

"And mine through yours!" countered one of Bant's men.

Both sides of the table began to yell at one another, until finally Bant jumped up on the table and spit.

"Our pact is finished!" Bant called out.

All eyes turned to him and fell silent.

101

"We shall retreat to Baris!" he shouted. "And when Pandesia kills you all, we shall be the first to celebrate!"

Bant suddenly jumped down, turned, and stormed out of the hall, and as he did, his men joined him, half the hall emptying out with him.

As he watched them go, Duncan watched his alliance go with them, and he knew that there was little he could do to keep his kingdom from falling apart.

CHAPTER SEVENTEEN

Kyra swung her staff in every direction, slashing at branches all around her in the wood, while Alva sat at the far end of the clearing, very still in the grass, his back perfectly straight, watching. Beside him sat Leo and Andor, both, amazingly still, as if peaceful in his presence. Breathing hard, covered in sweat as the morning sun broke through the trees, Kyra spun and slashed as she had for hours, striking at branches, at imaginary foes, as Alva had instructed her to do, breaking branches, sending leaves flying, the crack of her staff ringing throughout the wood. She ran from one tree to the next, feeling judged in Alva's watchful eyes.

Kyra still didn't know what to make of him. He seemed part human, part something else, and while he was boyish, he also had an ancient, timeless quality. She sensed he had lived for thousands of years. She could not understand how he was her uncle, and she was impatient to know more about her mother. What secrets, she wondered, was Alva holding back? When would he tell her?

Finally, Kyra reached out and slashed a branch, breaking it in half, feeling a sense of victory as the large limb fell to the ground. She then turned and threw her staff, aiming for a leaf across the clearing, and was satisfied to see it was a perfect throw.

Kyra, breathing hard, turned and looked at Alva, feeling a sense of victory, and expecting his approval. Yet she was surprised to see him still staring calmly ahead, expressionless. He remained silent, to her dismay, as if withholding his approval.

"I have hit every target and completed every test!" she called out, indignant.

He slowly shook his head.

"You have yet to complete a single test," he replied.

Kyra stared back, disappointed, confused.

"Not a limb is left standing!" she cried.

He closed his eyes.

"You hit every one," he finally replied, "and yet you hit none at all. Your mind still impedes you."

Alva suddenly jumped to his feet, with a speed that threw her off guard. She was shocked he could move that fast. Slowly, he approached and stopped about twenty feet away.

"When you meet your enemy," he continued, "your *true* enemy, your mind must be empty. Now, it is full. Take me, for example."

He raised a hand, and to Kyra's amazement, her staff, lying on the ground, lifted into the air and flew across the clearing, landing in his palm. She stared back in wonder, as it dawned on her that he had far greater powers than she realized.

"Attack me," he said, matter-of-factly.

He stood there, across the clearing, relaxed, waiting. He barely moved his hand, and her staff flew through the air toward her. She held out a palm and it landed inside. She looked down at it, speechless.

Kyra stood there, hesitant, not wanting to attack him.

"I will not strike a boy," she finally called out. "A defenseless one, no less."

He smiled.

"I am your uncle. And I have more defenses than you shall ever know. Now come!"

Kyra felt she had no choice but to obey, so she rushed forward half-heartedly, raised her staff, and aimed delicately for his shoulder.

But when her staff came down he was no longer there. She turned every which way and found him, to her shock, standing behind her.

"But…how?" she asked, flabbergasted. "You disappeared, then reappeared again."

"I am waiting," Alva replied. "Strike me."

Kyra raised her staff in frustration, then this time swung down with more speed.

Again, she missed, Alva dodging it easily, as if she were swinging in slow motion.

Kyra lunged and slashed, more determined, each time missing him, Alva easily evading her. She drove him across the clearing, her staff whooshing through the air, missing every time. She swung with all she had, her fastest speed, and yet still she could not touch him. She could not believe it; she had never encountered anyone like him.

Finally, as he evaded a particularly fast strike, Kyra stood there, defeated, gasping for air, and realized she wasn't going to

104

catch him. He was a better fighter than she. She could not understand it. In a bout of frustration, she charged, raised her staff high, and brought it down with all she had, sure she would strike him.

But she found herself stumbling forward, striking air, and, humiliated, landing in the grass on her knees.

Alva stood beside her, smiling down.

"You're too fast," she gasped, defeated, on her hands and knees.

He shook his head.

"No," he replied. "It is your mind that is too fast. You use your mind, and not what lies inside you. You fear the powers within you."

"Yes," she admitted, realizing he was right.

Kyra stood and faced him, ashamed. She had never missed a target with her staff in her life, and she had missed him again and again. It was humbling. She was not the warrior she thought she was.

"There are parts of you that you have never explored," he replied. "You cling to the warrior's way. And that limits you."

"Teach me," Kyra said, eager, her heart pounding, realizing he was alluding to something that had always been just beyond her grasp. "Teach me how to get the power you speak of."

"You know it yourself," he replied. "You have felt it before."

She remembered: Theos. Her fight against Pandesia. Those moments in battle that had been a blur, when she had not even been aware of what she had been doing.

"I have," she said, realizing. "When I summoned Theos, he came. When I fought in Volis…I felt… bigger than myself." She paused. "But I could not summon it again. I…lost that power."

He was silent for a long time, then finally he spoke.

"Why doesn't your dragon come now?" he asked.

She sensed that he knew the answer, and she desperately wanted to know. But she was at a loss. It was the very same question that had been burning through her mind all these days, ever since she had departed Argos.

"I…don't know," she replied.

She looked at him, hoping for an answer.

"Tell me," she pleaded.

But Alva merely stared back, expressionless in the long silence that followed.

"Try to summon him now," he said.

Kyra closed her eyes and with all her might, she tried once again to summon Theos.

Theos, she thought. *I need you. Come to me. Wherever you are, come to me. I beg you.*

After a long silence, Kyra opened her eyes, and was dismayed to feel nothing. There came no dragon on the horizon, no sound of screeching, no flapping of wings. Nothing but silence.

Kyra stood there, teary-eyed, feeling powerless. She realized the limitations of her power, and she wanted desperately to learn why.

"If you could summon your dragon," Alva finally said, "if you could control him, you could end the war that rages inside you, and within Escalon. You could save your father right now. But you cannot. Why?"

She shook her head, unable to reply.

"That is why you are here. That is what you are here to learn. Not this," he said, grabbing her staff and throwing it down to the ground. He stepped forward and touched her forehead, between her eyes. "But this. The true source of your power. You will never grasp it until you throw down your weapons and start fresh."

As she pondered his words, she suddenly heard a snarl that raised the hair on the back of her neck. Alva stepped aside, and as she looked past him, into the woods, she saw, approaching, a Salic. She froze. It was a terrifying creature that she had only read about, with a black hide, red eyes, three red horns, and was the size of a rhinoceros. It drooled, revealing its sharpened fangs as it crept toward her.

Alva stood there, his back to it and somehow not caring. And for some reason, the beast fixed its gaze only on her.

"This forest brings forth what we fear the most," Alva said calmly, not even turning to look. "What we fear to face. What do you fear to face? *Who are you, Kyra*?" Alva demanded, his voice suddenly booming, deep, filled with authority.

At the same moment the Salic pounced. It charged for her, and she raised her staff and slashed.

But with a single claw swipe it swatted it away.

Kyra stood there, defenseless, as it leapt into the air, its claws out for her chest, and she knew that, in moments, it would tear her apart.

CHAPTER EIGHTEEN

Merk braced himself as he faced the group of trolls charging for him, snarling, curled fangs protruding from their cheeks, all raising their halberds as they emerged from the wood. He had trusted his instincts, had combed these woods while his fellow Watchers had turned back, and he had proved himself right. Yet it had also left him out here alone, vulnerable, far from the others. He realized with dread that he would have no choice but to take on the entire pack by himself.

Merk steeled himself as the first troll attacked, allowing his killer instincts to take over; he felt a sense of calm wash over him, entered that place he always returned to, where he could separate himself from the violence about to happen, could quiet his fear even in the face of mortal danger. He'd faced multiple attackers many times before, and even though they had not been trolls, he felt an odd sense of comfort in the situation. Fighting, after all, was what he had been born to do, as much as he tried to turn his back on it.

As the first troll swung the hatchet down for his head, a blow strong enough to cut a tree in half, Merk waited for the last moment then stepped aside, feeling the whoosh of the blade beside him. He smashed the troll in the solar plexus with the hilt of his sword and as it keeled over, he spun around and chopped off its head. It rolled onto his feet, the blood hot and sticky on his boots.

Another troll charged, halberd high, and Merk spun and swung his sword sideways, chopping off its head before it could reach him. Its halberd fell to the ground as the headless troll collapsed at his feet.

Another troll came, and another, and Merk twisted his sword, raised it high overhead with both hands, and thrust it straight down into the chest of the next one, driving it in so deep he was unable to extract it. The creature shrieked as it dropped to its knees, and as the other troll brought down his halberd, Merk, weaponless, dropped to his knees, ducking as the blade grazed his hair. He then reached down, grabbed the halberd off the ground, swung sideways, and chopped the troll's legs out from under him. The troll shrieked as it fell to the ground, and Merk, not hesitating, swung around and chopped its back.

Another troll charged and swung his halberd for Merk's face, and Merk, still on the ground, raised his halberd high overhead, turned it sideways, and blocked with the shaft as it came down. His arm shook from the blow, the steel shaft clanging and sparking as the blade struck it, the force of it knocking Merk onto his back. The troll landed on top of him and leaned in, its grotesque face snarling inches away, and Merk, struggling with all he had, leaned back and kicked it between its legs, dropping it. It nearly landed on top of Merk, but he rolled out of the way at the last second, then jammed the blade of his dagger into its throat.

The move, though, left Merk's back exposed, and he sensed more trolls behind him. He glanced back and saw a fast and powerful troll racing for him, lowering the hatchet for his exposed back, and knew he could not react in time. He braced himself, already anticipating the pain of the blade cutting through his flesh. He knew he would die—yet he took some solace in the fact that he had taken many of these creatures with him, and had helped protect the realm.

As he braced himself, there came a sound of something whizzing by his head, and Merk spotted out of the corner of his eye a golden spear fly by, barely missing his ear. He heard a grunt and a cry as the troll behind him suddenly fell to his knees. It landed beside him on the ground, motionless, a spear impaled in its head.

Merk, stunned that his life had been saved, looked over and was amazed to see the last person he had ever expected to see out here: Kyle. He must have circled back for him, more aware than the others, and just in time to save his life. Merk was shocked at his prowess, at the speed and accuracy of his throw—and that he would care enough to save his life.

"DUCK!" Kyle yelled.

Merk ducked low and as he did, a halberd flew over his head, wielded by another troll whom Merk had not seen. Kyle raced across the clearing with a speed unlike any Merk had ever seen, a blur, a flash of light, as he reached the troll standing over Merk and kicked it in the chest.

It was no mere kick: it sent the troll soaring through the air, fifty feet across the clearing, where it smashed into a tree with such force that it cracked the tree in half. The troll slid down, limp, dead.

Merk sat there, stunned, as he watched the boy in action. Kyle sprinted through the clearing, like a blur of light in the darkness, smashed one troll with his hands, elbowed another, kicked another. He crossed the clearing and snapped one's neck, crossed back and punched another under the chin, sending it up into a tree. They were like molasses around him, and within moments, the trolls' bodies piled up, dozens of them lying in the clearing, motionless.

Merk stood and stared in the silence, speechless. All was eerily still, just the two of them alone in this clearing with dozens of dead trolls. Merk breathed hard, amazed, most of all, at how Kyle stood there, looking so relaxed, as if he had exerted no effort at all. Who was he? Merk wondered. Where had he come from? What race was he? He realized he had vastly underestimated him.

A commotion ensued as Merk's fellow soldiers finally circled back and caught up, rushing into the clearing, and they all stopped and stared in amazement as they saw Merk and Kyle and the piles of dead trolls. Merk saw them looking at him with awe, as if they had clearly not expected something like this from Kyle. A look of respect crossed their faces as they realized what he had done, that he had faced them alone, and that his instincts had been right.

Kyle stepped through the carnage, reached down, and extracted his long golden spear from the chest of a troll, wiping the blood as he inspected the body. The others seemed impressed by him, too, yet not surprised.

"These are no mere trolls," Kyle said, stepping forward and shoving one over with his boot. "Look at their dress, their weapons."

Merk examined them, but could not understand.

"They are unsinged," Kyle explained. "Somehow, they did not pass through The Flames."

Merk looked back at the others, who all stared back, fear and intensity in their eyes, and slowly, the realization began to dawn on him, too.

"Marda," he said, his voice grave in the black of night, "has broken through."

CHAPTER NINETEEN

Anvin galloped through the stone gates of Theb.
dozen warriors behind him, all kicking up a cloud of dust in .
barren desert, struggling to breathe. It was so hot down here in the
south, arid, desolate, nothing to breathe in but dust off the desert
and waves of heat. Anvin had never been this far south, and he felt
as if he were in a foreign country; he was amazed he was still in
Escalon. It was hard to believe that, when he had set out from Volis,
there had still been snow on the ground. The plains of Thebus, cut
off by the mountains, had their own, desert climate, and had always
been a separate region within Escalon.

It had been a long and hard journey, past Everfall, past the
Devil's Gulch, across the endless, dusty desert of Thebus, one that
would break many other men. Anvin had not stopped since Duncan
had dispatched him from Andros, leading this small, elite group of
Duncan's best men on this perilous mission. He knew the
importance of this mission, knew what was at stake, and knew he
could not let Duncan know, not with the fate of Escalon riding on it.

Joining Anvin were the elite of Duncan's men, all willing to
face death unblinking, exactly what Anvin needed for a mission that
would more likely end in their deaths than not. After all, taking and
holding the Southern Gate, the portal to all of Escalon, the only
thing standing between them and Pandesia, would be no small
undertaking. The strip of land, the chokehold at the gate, was
narrow enough for a few thousand men to hold back one million—
but the gate would have to be secured, closed in time, and held long
enough for Duncan to arrive with reinforcements. And for that, he
would have to reach Fort Thebus first, and rally the local soldiers.

As they finally rode through the high stone arch heralding the
fort, this place which lay but a mere day's ride from the Southern
Gate, Anvin knew that Fort Thebus, as the southernmost stronghold
of Escalon, was the key. Anvin glanced about and saw the harsh
and bland buildings, the sand color blending in with the desert, a
place of sand and wind and rock, built of squat, low buildings. It
was a place with no beauty to it, as if it all had been sucked dry by
the arid sand and sky. It was no place for people, a remote outpost
that the warriors of Thebus had somehow managed to live in. Anvin

ook his head, marveling at what strong stuff they must be made of to live such a bleak life, so cut off from Escalon. They were the last defense of the south, a place that had always remained loyal to Escalon. And, sadly, it had been betrayed more than any other place, when the weak King had opened the gates and surrendered Escalon.

As Anvin charged through the fort with his men, passing through dusty streets, a place its residents did not even bother to embellish, he saw the faces looking back at him, warriors lined up loosely, with their sandy hair and beards, blond from too much sun. They all watched him skeptically. They were men who squinted into the sun, with too many lines around their eyes, who had seen it all here. They watched, silent, like the plains around them, all their hands resting on the hilts of their swords, as if equally ready to embrace or kill their fellow countrymen.

Anvin continued riding to the main entry of the garrison, surprised to see there were no doors here, no gates. He rode through an open-air arch, the weather so warm here that there was never a need to close doors, a place so barren there was no need to defend it. After all, anyone approaching Thebus would be spotted a hundred miles away.

He rode into the inner courtyard of the fort, and as he did, he spotted more warriors standing about, waiting. Their leader, Durge, stood in their center, surrounded by dozens of his men, clearly having spotted them far off and anticipating their arrival.

Anvin finally came to a stop, breathing hard, every muscle in his body hurting from the long ride with no break. He dismounted, all his men with him, and he faced Durge.

Durge stood there, staring back, expressionless, with his sandy hair and wide jaw and broad shoulders, an inscrutable man, perhaps in his forties. Hand on his sword, as if ready to kill or embrace him, he stood there like a rock, a man who had seen it all, who trusted no one, and who did not care. A hard man for a hard place.

Anvin stepped forward in the silence, wondering if Durge remembered him.

"It has been many years since we fought side by side," Anvin began.

Durge stared back silently, as the wind howled through this dusty place.

"The battle of Briarwood," Durge finally replied, his voice slow and hoarse, scratchy, like the sand around him.

Anvin nodded, relieved.

"We killed many men," Anvin replied.

"Not enough," Durge added, meaning it.

Anvin studied him in the silence.

"It is curious that you have no door, no gate," Anvin replied. "What do you do when an enemy approaches?"

For the first time, Durge smiled.

"We need no door," he replied, "because we crave enemies. We would enjoy being attacked—it is, after all, what we live for. Why should we cower behind gates?"

Anvin smiled back, having no doubt that this warrior's words were true.

"I bring urgent business from the capital," Anvin continued.

Durge shrugged.

"Nothing is urgent here," Durge replied. "And the capital's business is not my business," he concluded, his voice cold and hard.

Anvin knew he was facing an uphill battle, and that he had to phrase his next words carefully. Durge was clearly a proud man, and one not to be controlled.

"I know you are free," Anvin replied. "And that you answer to no man. It is no command I bring, but a request—one that comes from our new King."

Durge looked interested for the first time.

"What new King?" he asked.

"Tarnis is imprisoned," Anvin said proudly. "Duncan stands as King."

Durge seemed truly caught off guard. He leaned back and stroked his long blond beard, thinking.

"Duncan," he reflected. "A warrior I respect. A serious man. I never thought he would desire to be King."

"He does not," Anvin said. "He desires only freedom for Escalon."

Thebus pondered.

"And what does Duncan request of us?" Durge asked, his tone a bit more accommodating.

"He wishes nothing of you," Anvin replied. "He wishes to give you something."

Durge's eyes narrowed.

"And what is that?"

"Freedom," Anvin replied. "The thing that no man can give you. The thing that you must take for yourself."

Thebus watched him for a long time, as if pondering.

"And how is this new King going to give us our freedom?" he asked. "We stand but a day's ride from the gate. Beyond that gate lie millions of Pandesians. We are flanked by the Sea of Sorrow on one side and the Sea of Tears on the other, and in those waters sit a million more men. What freedom does he speak of?"

Anvin took a deep breath, preparing.

"Duncan does not cower and hide, as Tarnis did," Anvin replied. "He strikes his enemies harshly and quickly. We have freed Volis and Argos and Esephus and Kos—and now, Andros. Powerful cities. Half of Escalon is free—and the other half will soon be, too. But we need your help to secure the Southern Gate. If not, we will be invaded anew by the hordes of Pandesia, and all of Duncan's efforts will be for naught."

Thebus squinted, stroking his beard, then turned and walked to the edge of the courtyard, to an open arch, and looked out at the dusty plains. He stood stroking his beard for a long time in silence.

Anvin came up beside him, waiting, knowing he had to give him time.

"The Southern Gate, is it?" he said, still looking out.

Anvin waited patiently, as Durge stared, clearly mulling it all over in his mind. Anvin followed his gaze and in the distance, faintly on the horizon, he could see the golden arches of the Southern Gate, gleaming in the sun.

"A mighty thing it is," Durge remarked, studying the horizon. "Built by our forefathers, a construction we could never manage today. The tallest and thickest structure in Escalon. Built to withstand invasion, war. It has lasted for centuries, and for centuries it has kept out Pandesia."

He turned to Anvin and frowned.

"Until Tarnis came along," he continued. "He undid all that in a single stroke. He opened the gates without a fight, made a deal. Worst of all, he told no one. One day we awoke and found ourselves surrounded, prisoners, without even a chance to fight. He betrayed us all. He never gave us a chance to defend the gate, our sacred duty, and that is something we men of Thebus shall never give."

Durge sighed.

"Now here you come, with a new King, and new promises," Durge continued. "Our men were compromised once before by politics, and I vowed—never again."

"You were not alone in the betrayal," Anvin replied. "Tarnis betrayed us, too. And Duncan is no Tarnis."

Durge stroked his beard.

"A new King, yes," he reflected. "But politics are always the same. Power is always the same. How long until your precious new King is corrupted, like all the others?"

Anvin frowned.

"Duncan is a warrior. He has always been a warrior, and he always shall be."

"Perhaps he shall," Durge replied. "And yet, perhaps those closest to him shall not."

"You shall never know until you take the chance, shall you?" Anvin pressed.

He sighed, stroking his beard, pondering. A long, heavy silence fell over them, until finally Durge turned to him.

"We can take back the gate," he finally said. "That is easy enough to do. Yet holding it is another matter. When the hordes of Pandesia invade, they will come with a greater force than ever. And if Duncan and his men are not at our backs, then this time, we shall all be slaughtered. All of my men—and you along with them."

Anvin stepped forward and mustered all the seriousness he could.

"You have my sacred vow," Anvin said. "Duncan will not betray us. He rides for us even now. When we take the gates, when Pandesia approaches, Duncan and his men will show up to help us. He has given his sacred vow, and he shall never betray us. If he does, I shall gladly be the first to die."

Durge studied him, seeming to be impressed by his seriousness.

"We need your help," Anvin pressed, sensing this was the moment. "Are you with us? Are you for freedom? Or shall you squat here in this empty fort you call a home and pretend to be free?"

Anvin knew he was taking a chance in provoking Durge, and yet he sensed he had to. Durge's eyes darkened with violence as his jaw locked, and Anvin could see the anger coursing through him.

But then, just as quickly, he smiled.

"The gate, then," he replied, and smiled wide. "Today is as good a day to die as any."

CHAPTER TWENTY

Alec sat inside the steamy forge, before the anvil, surrounded by boys and men on all sides, the room too hot, filled with clouds of steam and the sound of hammering steel. Alec, too, hammered away, pounding a molten-hot sword again and again as it turned white, sparks flying, sweat stinging his eyes and Alec no longer caring. Beside him sat Marco and his new friends, all part of the resistance, all getting ready to take up arms against Pandesia.

As Alec pounded away, with each blow of his hammer he thought of vengeance. He thought of the Pandesians that this weapon would kill, thought of his brother and father and mother. His village. His people. Alec knew all of these new weapons he was forging would be a drop in the bucket against the vast Pandesian army; yet he also knew that every sword he made, every axe, every shield, would mean at least one more Pandesian dead, one more chance to defend Ur. And that gave him a great sense of satisfaction.

Alec finished his sword, raised it high, inspected it, then dipped it into the vat of water; another cloud of steam immediately filled the room, accompanied by a loud hiss. He inspected the final product, switching hands with it, until he finally laid it down in the pile of new swords, satisfied.

Alec took a break, wiping sweat from the back of his head and surveying the room. This forge was more airy than his father's, with large open arched windows which let in fresh air and bright sunlight, light from the canals making this pace far less oppressive. He looked out and could see all the passing ships, their masts and sails floating by the window, flying banners from all corners of the world. Such an international city, Ur exuded a sense of peace and calm, of commerce, and belied the oppression his people lived under, the occupation of Pandesia—and the great war which Alec knew was coming. His land, he knew, was crying for vengeance.

Alec paced the forge, walking up and down the rows of boys and men, surveying everyone's work. All of these boys were still amateurs, and he had to adjust each one's work as he went.

"Your strike is uneven," he said to one boy, shifting his elbow. "That sword will be jagged."

He stopped beside another.

"The hilt is bent," he said, straightening his wrist. "You hammer at the wrong angle."

One boy at a time, one weapon at a time, he went, fixing, adjusting. All the boys looked to him, deferring to him—even Fervil, the master smith deferred to him, finally realizing the fine quality of Alec's work. He stopped as he came across an older man hammering a shield, and snatched it from his hands, impatient, as the man stared back.

"This shield will stop the blow of no sword," Alec rebuked. "Its metal is too thin—and the strap is too tight."

Alec, who used to be so calm and good-natured, found himself getting frustrated, snapping when he should not. He wondered at his recent anger and impatience, wanting to stop it but unable. He felt he was not the same person he was since the death of his family, and he hated who he was becoming.

Alec stopped and took a deep breath, forcing himself to calm, to release his anger. He did not want to let it out on anyone else. He went to a window and looked out, watching the ships go by, and he wiped an unexpected tear from the corner of his eye, quickly so the others would not see, surprised by its appearance.

Alec flinched as he felt a palm on his shoulder, and he looked over to see Fervil the smith beside him.

"Go easy on them," he said. "They are not like you or I. They are not smiths. They are all here to help the cause."

Alec closed his eyes and took a deep breath, knowing he was right.

"I am sorry," he said. "I just feel so frustrated. We don't have enough men. We don't have enough weapons. And there is not enough time. All of this, everything we're doing," he said, scanning the room, "it's not enough. What shall we do when the whole of the Pandesian fleet arrives? When the great ships enter these canals?" he said, as he watched another large Pandesian vessel sail past.

"We are doing the best we can do," Fervil replied.

Alec shook his head.

"It's not enough," he replied. "Swords and shields won't stop ships. We can't take on entire fleets with this."

118

"What would you have us do, then?" Fervil snapped back, frustrated himself. "Build a fleet of ships? Close up the sea? These swords are all we have, and they will have to do."

Alec quieted, something Fervil said striking him. An idea was dawning. As he looked outside and studied the canals, an idea overcame him. He felt a rush of excitement as it dawned on him.

"You're wrong," he said, breathless with excitement. "We have quite a bit more."

Alec suddenly ran to the tables, examining all the steel, all the half-forged weapons lying on the tables, partly finished axes and maces. Unsatisfied, he scoured the room until he found what he was looking for: there it was, lying in a dark corner on the stone floor.

"What are you doing?" Fervil asked, following him.

Alec picked up one end of a huge, thick chain, originally designed for an anchor.

"Help me!" he cried out to the others.

Marco and the other boys stopped what they were doing, ran over, and helped him lift the chain, each struggling under its weight. It was like lifting a massive snake.

As all the boys grabbed it, they helped Alec drag it over and lay it down with a clang on the wooden table. He unraveled it as the others brushed aside swords and shields to make way, sending them clamoring to the floor. He then stretched out the chain with the others on the twenty-foot-long rectangular table, the chain amazingly heavy, weighing at least a hundred pounds. He unraveled it until it covered the whole length of the table.

Alec stepped back and surveyed it, smiling.

"This will do," he said.

"Do for what?" Fervil asked, puzzled.

Alec turned to him, impassioned.

"How wide is the canal?" Alec demanded.

Fervil shrugged. "Thirty feet?"

"Then we shall make this forty," Alec replied. "We will need more chain."

"But why?" Fervil pressed. "What is this madness?"

Alec turned and scanned the room, ignoring him, concentrating. He stopped when he found what he was looking for: a group of long spikes, meant for spears.

"I need all of those," Alec said to Marco and the others, who rushed to get them. "And we shall forge more."

"I need those spikes for spears!" Fervil called out. "We cannot spare them! What are you doing? What is the meaning of all this!?"

Alec grabbed the spikes and spread them out on the table, alongside the chain, then stepped back and surveyed his creation, while the others did, too. There, spread out on the table, was a twenty-foot chain, spikes placed every few feet, and as Alec looked at it, his heart warmed with his idea. It could really work.

The others must have realized, too, because slowly the room fell quiet as they studied it.

"You mean to trap the harbor," the smith said softly, finally realizing.

Alec turned to him, smiling.

"I do," he replied.

Alec leaned over and touched a spike, feeling it, admiring how sharp it was.

"We shall trap the floor of the canal," he replied, "and then we shall wait. When the Pandesians arrive, we shall raise it. Instead of a man, we shall take out a ship; instead of a few soldiers, we will kill a few hundred. And the broken ship shall clog the canals, block their entire fleet, make landing impossible."

They all studied it in silence, clearly in awe.

"Risky," Fervil finally replied, walking up and down, inspecting his potential handiwork. "The work this would require, and the chances of success—"

Suddenly, the door to the room slammed open, and all the men turned and looked. Alec blinked, and as he saw who was entering, he wondered if he were seeing things.

In walked the most beautiful girl he'd ever seen, tall, about his age, with long hair, beautiful brown eyes, a proud face lined with character. Even more shocking, she had a dozen girls in tow. She led them proudly, no fear in her eyes, an air of defiance about her, as if she had a chip on her shoulder.

"Dierdre," Fervil said, surprise in his voice, clearly recognizing her. "Did your father send you?"

She stepped into the room and stared back with a hard gaze.

"I sent myself," she replied.

Fervil stared back questioningly.

"Why?" he asked. "And who are these girls with you?"

Dierdre walked proudly into the room, as if she belonged, and Alec felt his heart beating faster; she was so beautiful, it was hard to think around her. He had never seen anyone like her in Soli.

"I've come to arm us all with weapons," she replied, confident. "And to give these girls a chance to work at the forge. This is our cause as much as yours."

A few of the boys in the room snickered, while the rest looked at each other in wonder. Fervil shook his head.

"This is no place for girls, and no girls will be wielding swords," he replied with authority. "Or forging them. You would be of best use at your father's fort, helping the other women prepare whatever is needed."

But Dierdre held her ground, darkening.

"You don't seem to understand," she replied, her voice hard and cold. "It was not a question—it was a command."

All eyes in the room stared as an awkward silence fell over the room, and as Alec stared at her, he experienced something he had never felt before. It was more than admiration—it was love. He was smitten. It was even more surprising to him, because ever since the death of his family he had felt nothing but emptiness and grief. And yet, looking at her, something shifted within him. Here she stood, so gorgeous and brave, so strong and proud, and in her he found a role model of courage in the face of adversity. He felt a reason to live again.

Alec suddenly stepped forward, unable to control himself.

"I do not think it such a foolish idea," he called out, defending her, and breaking the tense silence.

Everyone in the room looked to him, and his heart beat faster to see Dierdre look at him, too. Her eyes were mesmerizing.

"I'd be glad to assist you," he said, stepping toward her. "I can teach you how to forge weapons. Who knows? Maybe you'll do a better job than this lot."

He smiled warmly, and expected her to smile back—but she did not. He could see layers of grief in her eyes, and as she merely stared back at him silently, he sensed she was lost behind walls of sadness. He wondered what had happened to her.

Dierdre nodded to the girls, and as they stepped forward Alec gestured to the boys to make room for them at the table. Alec motioned for Dierdre to sit, too, but she did not. Instead, as all the boys and men in the room went back to work, returning to their weapons, or surveying Alec's chain, she walked up and down the tables, observing the weapons. She stopped before a sword, one of Alec's favorites, a long thin sword with a silver handle, lighter and thinner than the rest, and sharper, and held it up. Alec could tell by the way she examined it that she was someone who grew up around weaponry.

"A fine choice," he said.

"Will this pierce a man?" she asked.

"Yes," he replied, wondering at the source of her anger.

"Even through armor?" she pressed.

He nodded.

"That and more," he replied, sensing the depth of her rage. "Who is it you hope to kill?"

She turned and they locked eyes, and hers were icy cold and deadly serious.

"Any Pandesians I find," she replied, her voice intense.

For the first time in as long as he could remember, Alec smiled wide, feeling his heart warm again.

"I think you and I," he replied, "shall have a lot in common."

CHAPTER TWENTY ONE

Aidan walked the streets of the capital in wonder, jostled by the crowds and not caring, looking up in awe at the tallest buildings he'd seen in his life. He had seen all the great forts of his father's stronghold, yet he didn't know buildings could be as tall as this. Everything here was new, different, the shapes of these buildings, the angles of their doorways, their windows, the immense statues and fountains before them, and he could not get enough. He spun in every direction, taking it all in. He did not remember any of this from when he'd lived here as a child, all of it but a vague memory, and as he went, turning down cobblestone alleyways, walking in and out of squares, past temples, White at his side, keeping up with him, sniffing at all the vendors' food, he felt as if he could walk for weeks and still not cover half of this immense city.

Everywhere someone was selling something, yelling for his attention, all trying to get Aidan to stop, to look, to listen, to touch; music filled the air, roving musicians everywhere, competing with the shouting of merchants and barking of dogs. Everyone was in a hurry. Everywhere, jubilation hung in the air, the joy of a liberated people. Aidan took a great sense of pride in knowing it was all thanks to his father.

Aidan searched for any sign of his father or his soldiers as he walked, on a mission to find him, but saw none. As he emerged from an alleyway, he found himself in a huge, circular intersection, spanning a hundred yards, at its center a towering fountain. Around it milled thousands of people, some sitting by its edge but most hurrying every which way. The circle was bordered by tall, ancient buildings, built of a fading marble, as if they'd sat there forever. Between the buildings Aidan spied alleyways, dozens of them, turning in every direction.

Aidan felt a sudden sense of panic as he realized he was lost. These alleys could lead anywhere. Every square just led to another square. He had no idea how to navigate this city, much less find his father. He scanned the courtyard, looking for any signs of his father's men, but saw none.

There arose a whining and Aidan looked down to see White rubbing up against him. Recovered from his wounds, White was clearly out of his element here—and clearly starving. Aidan felt hungry, too, and he reached into his sack and fingered the few gold coins he had left. He figured it was time to put them to use.

He suddenly felt a strong hand on his wrist, and he looked up to see a large, unshaven man with a big belly staring down at him, with a misshapen jaw and eyes that exuded hate.

"What's a boy like you doing with all that gold?" he demanded.

He did not wait for a response as he tightened his grip on Aidan's wrist, squeezing so hard that Aidan thought he might break it.

"Want to hand it over here, and escape with your life?"

Aidan welled with panic as the man reached for the sack; he looked around and saw no one there to help him. He spotted a small, gleaming dagger in the man's other hand, pointed at his throat, and he didn't know what to do. He realized he could not part with this gold. It was all he had.

There came a horrific snarl as White suddenly leapt forward and clamped his teeth down on the man's wrist that was holding Aidan. White was so fast and strong, his teeth so sharp, that the man shrieked as, in a flash, his hand was severed.

He turned and fled, grabbing his stump, shrieking, and he disappeared into the crowd as quickly as he had appeared.

Aidan looked over at White, still snarling, as if still angry, and then, to Aidan's amazement, he
bounded off, chasing after the man through the crowds, not done with him yet.

"White!" Aidan yelled.

But White wouldn't listen. Aidan chased him down, out of breath, until finally he caught up with him, several blocks away, leaping on the man's back and sinking his fangs into the back of his neck. The man fell still on the ground, until his shrieking stopped. Dead.

White's vicious look softened as he turned and spotted Aidan. Aidan looked at him with a whole new respect as he knelt down and stroked his head.

"Thank you," Aidan said, as White leaned over and licked him.

Aidan noticed a few passersby look over at the dead body, but none stopped. In a city like this, Aidan supposed, a dead body was nothing worth stopping for. Still, he didn't want to take any chances of getting into trouble.

"Let's go."

Aidan guided White away, and the two of them merged quickly back into the crowds. White bounded ahead, and as Aidan hurried to catch up, he wondered where he was going.

"White!" Aidan called out.

Aidan turned a corner, wondering what trouble his newfound friend could be getting into next, when he spotted White at the far side of a square, sticking his nose in a rack full of meat. Aidan smiled; he had been following his noise. The vendor did not look happy.

Aidan hurried over and held out a gold coin to the woman. He had to admit he was enticed by the smell, too, his stomach growling.

The vendor took the coin and examined it skeptically in the light, looking down at Aidan.

"What will you have?" she finally asked, curt.

"The whole rack," Aidan said, realizing how hungry White must be.

She reached over and handed him a long stick holding chunks of roasted meat, dripping with sauce. Aidan handed one to White first, and White snatched it from his hands, chewing the meat off the stick, pulling off one chunk after the next. The vendor handed him stick after stick until finally the entire rack sat empty. Aidan could not believe how much White could eat. He saved the last stick for himself, and he savored every bite of the steak, as the sauce dripped down his chin.

"Something to wash it down?" the woman asked.

She handed him a bowl of water and he set it down for White; then she handed him a small sack of liquid.

Aidan squirted it down his throat, expecting water, and he coughed as he realized there was something else in it. He felt it rush to his head, and he realized: it was wine.

"What's in here?" he asked, shocked.

The woman smiled down, missing a tooth.

"Something a bit stronger," she replied. "Time for you to become a man. Welcome to the capital."

The wine rushed to his head, and Aidan did not like the feeling. He felt disoriented.

"Have you seen the men of Volis?" he asked her, eager to know.

"You mean all those new soldiers?" she asked. "The ones that freed the capital?"

He nodded.

"What would you have with them?" she asked.

"They are my father's men," he said proudly.

She looked at him for a long time, as if suspecting he were lying.

"Check the Southern Square," she said. "Soldiers usually station there."

She pointed down an alleyway, and Aidan continued on, following her directions.

Aidan headed down a series of endlessly long alleyways, emerged into another square, then turned down a side street, White always at his side. He emerged from a series of tall, narrow buildings, and the city opened up again.

As Aidan entered this new square he looked up, dwarfed by buildings hundreds of feet high. One building, with tapered golden doors, looked like a temple, while another had soaring columns and resembled a library. Several of the buildings had golden domes, shining in the sun, and everything here looked as if it had stood for centuries.

Aidan roamed through the new square, looking for any sign pointing to the Southern Square of the city.

"Do you know the way to the Southern Square?" Aidan asked a passerby, a man who looked slightly less rushed than the others. But the man merely shook his head and rushed off.

Aidan turned in every direction, seeing an endless array of alleys and squares, and he felt lost and overwhelmed.

Suddenly, there came a voice.

"Help me, please!"

He looked over and saw a girl about his age, sitting on the street, legs crossed, a forlorn and helpless look on her face. Covered in dirt, she looked as if she hadn't eaten in months, wasting away, flies on top of her that she didn't even bother swatting away.

"I need something to eat," she added, her voice hoarse. "Anything."

Aidan's heart broke for her. He examined his sack, looked in at all of his coins, and hesitated for a moment, knowing it was all he had left in the world. Then, feeling a rush of compassion for her and knowing it was the right thing to do, he stepped forward and placed the entire sack in her palm.

She looked up at him, and slowly her eyes filled with shock. Then she welled with tears, as she stood to her feet.

"What is your name?" she asked.

"Aidan."

"I am Cassandra," she replied. "And I shall never forget this."

She reached forward and hugged him, then she turned and disappeared into an alley.

Aidan stood there, penniless, but feeling good that he had done the right thing. While he feared for his future, penniless now, he didn't regret it.

Music suddenly drifted up from the far side of the square, and Aidan turned and was shocked to see a huge platform rolling through and atop it, jugglers, musicians, and, he was thrilled to see, some of the actors he had ridden into town with. At center stage was Motley.

"Ladies and gentlemen of Andros!" he boomed, as the crowd gathered close. "I present to you a tale of no parallel!"

Aidan desperately wanted to find his father, but as he looked out at the falling night he knew his search would be futile in the dark. And as he felt the exhaustion in his legs from a long day of searching, he knew he needed a break. So instead, he allowed himself to merge with the crowd, toward the stage, and settle in for the entertainment. After all, his new friends, he knew, would know this city, and if anyone could help point him to Southern Square, to his father, it would be them.

CHAPTER TWENTY TWO

Merk stood atop the Tower of Ur, watching the breaking dawn spread over the world, staring out at limitless sky and ocean, and he felt as if he were being reborn with the world. The view was breathtaking. From up here, he could see it all: the crashing of the Sorrow in every direction, the barren, windswept peninsula of Ur, the treetops of the great wood. Beyond them, he could see across all of Escalon. The sky broke and shifted in color, the sun's rays slowly flooding the land, while gales of wind ripped through off the ocean, strong enough to nearly knock him off the side of the tower. He gripped the low stone wall, steadying himself, and looked down over the edge. His heart raced as he saw the ground, hundreds of feet below.

Merk realized how lucky he was to be alive, to wake on this day, and he felt like a new man. His life had been spared last night, thanks to Kyle, and it profoundly affected him. He had never come that close to dying, and he had never had someone save his life before. It was an almost religious experience, and he felt something shift within him. He was beginning to feel something more profound stirring inside.

The sound of hammering filled the air all, and as Merk finished his break and went back to his own hammering, nailing the iron pegs deep into the stone like all the others atop the tower, he turned and looked for Kyle. He spotted him on the far side of the roof, hammering away with the others, testing and retesting a rope as he threw it over the side. Merk did not recognize all of the dozens of Watchers up here with the men, warriors emerging from somewhere in the tower, from all different floors, men with hardened faces he did not recognize. It seemed all the men in the tower had been mobilized since last night's confrontation, and now they all prepared for war.

Merk finished hammering in his peg, then threw his rope over the edge and tested it. It uncoiled all the way until it hit the bottom, then he coiled it up again, slowly pulling it up, his palms burning.

Satisfied, Merk prepared to hammer in the next rope, and as he did so, he made his way over to Kyle, wanting to thank him.

"I still don't see the point of this," Merk remarked to Kyle as he hammered in yet another peg.

Kyle did not look at him, staying focused on his work, his hammering.

"These ropes will help us fend off attack," he explained. "They give us another option of defense and offense. They can also prove, more importantly, to be another escape route."

"Escape?" Merk asked, surprised. "Do we not fight to the death here?"

"Not for us," Kyle explained. "But for the Sword."

Merk thought about that.

"Then it lives here?" he asked, curious.

Kyle glanced at him, then looked away.

"Whether it does or not, we must cover all contingencies," he replied, "from above and below."

Merk wondered.

"Are there tunnels beneath the tower, then?"

Kyle continued to hammer, not meeting his eye.

"Our tower is mysterious," he finally replied, "even to those who have served here for centuries. Not all is revealed to everyone, at every time. Each of us has pockets of knowledge about this place, different roles to play. Some know the rooftop, others, the tunnels. Some guard the Sword, if it is here, and others the windows."

Merk studied Kyle as he hammered alongside him, and he wondered. Had this boy lived for centuries?

A silence fell over them as the Watchers kept to themselves, immersed in their work, many giving Merk a newfound look of respect. A few, though, he could sense, seemed jealous, or perhaps embarrassed that Merk had pressed on and spotted the trolls when they turned back.

"I didn't have a chance to properly thank you," Merk finally said to Kyle.

"For what?" he replied, still not looking, still immersed in his hammering.

"For saving me last night."

"I didn't save you. I did my duty."

"But you saved me in the process," Merk insisted.

Kyle shrugged.

"That was not my intent," he answered flatly.

Merk felt hurt by that.

"Are you saying you would not have cared if I had died?" Merk pressed. For some reason, it mattered to him. No one had ever cared enough to save his life before, and he wanted to know if that was what had really happened.

Kyle fell silent for a long time as he inspected his rope, pulling it tight, twisting it.

"I have seen many men come, and many go," Kyle finally said. "I have seen many die. That is the nature of man, is it not?"

Merk tried to understand.

"And what is the nature of your race?" Merk asked. "Do they not die?"

Kyle shrugged.

"You have mortality," he replied. "We have our vulnerabilities."

"Like what?" Merk asked.

Kyle fell back into silence as he continued hammering, and as he went back to work himself, Merk felt stung by him. He had hoped to make a friend in him, but Kyle seemed oddly aloof. It irked Merk all the more because all his life he had kept to himself, never reaching out to anyone before to befriend them. A gale of wind blew through, and the tower suddenly felt more cold and lonely than before.

"Figure you're special, do you?" came a harsh voice.

Merk turned to see one of the Watchers, Pult, a rugged man, unshaven, with a big square jaw and dark eyes staring back at him, a face filled with hostility.

"Because you spotted the trolls last night?" the man added. "And we didn't?"

Merk was not looking for a fight, especially from his newfound friends, but he knew that bullies were everywhere, and that he could not risk showing weakness on a first encounter. Weakness emboldened bullies, and he could sense this man was territorial, that he hated him for no reason. He had been around hate long enough to spot it when he saw it.

"You said it," Merk replied, not backing down, not wanting to appease this man. "Not me."

The man reddened, clearly not expecting such a response.

"Let me tell you, stranger," the man said, stepping close. "I've seen many drifters like you come into this tower. And I've seen just as many go. I've seen too many disappear in ways that are mysterious." He smiled and stepped closer, but a few feet away. "There are too many ways to get hurt in this place."

Merk smirked and, deciding to show no fear, turned his back on the man. He bent over the tower wall and tested his rope.

"And I've seen blowhards all my life," Merk replied, his back to him. "They like to talk. They bore me. *I* like to take action. If you have something to say, draw a dagger. Otherwise, you're just talk."

Merk suddenly felt a kick in his back, and a moment later, he felt himself sliding over the side of the tower. He was stunned—he had not expected this man to attack him here, in daylight, before all the others.

Seconds later Merk was over the edge of the tower, sliding, falling, and he reached out and grabbed the rope with both hands, swinging a few feet from the top. He slammed into the stone as he swung, winded, and his heart pounded as a gale of wind blew him from side to side. He looked down, saw the drop hundreds of feet below, and knew it would kill him.

Merk reached to pull himself up on the rope, when suddenly a hand came down—a young, smooth hand—and pulled him up in one quick motion, with surprising strength.

Merk landed back on the rooftop, on his hands and knees on the stone, gasping. Irate, he looked everywhere for the bully, but he was nowhere in sight. The rest of the crowd kept their eyes on their work, either not wanting to get involved, or not caring if Merk survived.

Only Kyle stood over him, and stared down at him.

"Saving you's getting to be a full-time job," he remarked, shaking his head, then went back to his work.

Merk, still stunned, was grateful as he slowly regained his feet.

"Why?" Merk asked, approaching him. "If you don't care, why bother saving me?"

Kyle grinned, still looking down at his hammer.

"I like not being the only outsider here," he finally replied. Then Kyle turned to him: "And I have to admit, things are a bit more interesting with you around."

CHAPTER TWENTY THREE

Anvin galloped south through the hot and barren plains of Thebus, the air stifling with every step, racing into the sun, Durge at his side and their dozens of men behind them as they headed for the Southern Gate. They rode on, the thundering of their horses' hooves filling the air. Anvin's heart raced; the next few hours would determine his destiny, and the destiny of Escalon. He had never ridden all the way to the gate, and as they went the land narrowed to a strip of desert, bordered on either side by the two seas. On either side of him the water sparkled, the glare blinding, heat coming off the ground in waves and not a breeze to be found. This strip of land was all that separated the two seas, the mainland of Escalon from Pandesia, and Anvin knew that whoever held it controlled the gateway to Escalon.

Durge rode up beside him, and Anvin looked over to see a maniacal smile on his face, as if he were getting ready for bloodshed. Durge looked as if he had been born for a day like this.

"Do you think it was wise, bringing only two dozen of your men?" Anvin called out, recalling the hundreds of men Thebus had left behind in his fort.

Thebus, covered in dust, looked straight ahead, studying the horizon with a deadly intent.

"Taking the Southern Gate is not hard," he called back defensively. "Holding it is. The Pandesians know this—that is why they leave but a few dozen men to guard it. They don't expect an attack from the north—after all, who would be foolish enough?"

Anvin studied the gate as they approached, wondering.

"What matters is holding it," Durge continued, "and for that we need not a few hundred men, but a few thousand. We need your Duncan's men, and all those reinforcements you vow will be coming."

Anvin understood.

"They will come," he reassured. "Duncan never breaks a vow."

As they closed in on the gate, a half mile away, Anvin wondered about something.

"Tell me," Anvin called out. "When Tarnis surrendered the Southern Gate and opened it for our enemies—why did you obey?"

Durge's face reddened with anger as he continued to ride, locking his jaw, clearly bringing back bad memories.

"When your King commands," he replied, "you obey. That is what loyal soldiers do."

"And now?" Anvin asked.

They rode on in silence, until finally, Durge spoke.

"I shall not make the same mistake twice," he replied. "If I am asked again to choose between my King and my honor—I will serve my honor first."

They rode on, horses thundering across the plains, entering the long, narrow stretch of land that spanned the channel and leaving in their wake a cloud of dust. Anvin's heartbeat quickened as they approached what could only be the Southern Gate. It gleamed from here, filling the skyline, a massive golden arch hundreds of feet high, the largest gate he had ever seen. It had huge iron spikes on its portcullis, which sat raised, keeping the gate open, allowing access to Escalon from all of Pandesia. Anvin would change that—or die trying. Whoever held that gate, Anvin knew, could keep the world at bay, could protect Escalon from any invasion. It was a natural bottleneck, and thousands of men of Escalon, properly positioned, could beat back millions.

Atop the gate, to Anvin's disgrace, he saw the Pandesian banner, the insidious yellow and blue, flapping in the wind smugly, and at its base, he spotted a dozen Pandesian soldiers, standing lackadaisically on guard, their backs to them, facing south. Of course, they did not even bother to face Escalon. They never could possibly expect an attack.

"The worst job for a Pandesian!" Durge called out to Anvin. "To be stationed at the gate. They bask in the sun all day long, and they can expect no action."

"Not until today," Anvin corrected.

Durge drew his sword.

"Not until today," he echoed.

Anvin lowered his head and kicked his horse and they all galloped, racing across the peninsula, a band of warriors charging together for their destiny. Anvin charged beside Thebus, leading his men as they raced down the barren stretch of land, the sun beating down, sweat stinging his eyes as he blinked into the sun. The light was blinding, bouncing off everything, the water now surrounding them on both sides, and but a few hundred yards ahead lay the Southern Gate, gleaming, reflecting more light than the two seas.

Anvin felt his heart slamming as they approached, knowing these next moments would determine everything, would be the sum of all he had ever fought for as a warrior. If they took the gate, they would, for the first time in years, shut off Escalon from the outside world, from invasion, would seal it off for its final step toward freedom. But if they failed—all of Pandesia would bear down on them with the weight of an ocean, and they would all be killed.

Anvin thought of Duncan, counting on him, and he gripped his sword, knowing he could not let his old friend down.

"Aim for the hornblowers first!" Durge cried.

Anvin looked at him, puzzled.

"See the ships?" Thebus cried, pointing to the sea.

Anvin looked and on the horizon saw hundreds of black ships, sailing the yellow and blue banners of Pandesia.

"That's why there are so few men at the gate," he added. "They need only sound the horns, and all the ships shall come to their rescue. They must not sound those horns!"

Anvin followed his finger and saw standing up high, on platforms raised on the gate, about twenty feet off the ground, a soldier on either side, each holding a horn several feet long. They faced south, their backs still to them.

"I'll take the one on the right," Anvin said, gripping his spear. He galloped faster, praying he could get close enough before his target turned around.

"And the other is mine," Durge replied.

"And you, the crank turner," Durge commanded one of his men, pointing with his sword.

Anvin followed his gaze and saw a soldier standing by a huge crank, hands at the ready, his back to them, too.

"If that gate is closed before we can reach it," Durge added, "we are finished."

They bore down, horses thundering, fifty yards away, then forty, then thirty, Anvin's throat so dry he could barely breathe. He studied the hornblower on the right, counting the steps until he was close enough to throw his spear. He knew it would have to be a perfect throw, or else risk losing it all.

He was just a few more yards from throwing when one of the Pandesian soldiers suddenly turned, hearing them. His eyes opened wide in panic. He reached out and shoved the soldiers beside him, and as one they all turned and looked.

"NOW!" Durge shouted.

Anvin knew he needed a few more yards to ensure an accurate throw—yet he had no choice. He took a deep breath, steadied his shoulder as best as he could, and raised the heavy spear, praying—and then let it fly.

Anvin held his breath as he watched his spear fly; his palms were sweaty as he released, and he had no idea if his throw was true. He also watched Durge's sword, flying at the same time, turning end over end as it neared its target.

The hornblower on the left, Durge's target, turned and raised the horn to his mouth, and as he did, Durge's sword impaled him in the chest. He dropped the horn and fell off the platform, dead.

At the same time, Anvin's hornblower turned, at just the moment when the spear was set to impale his body. Anvin was appalled to see that that lucky turn had saved him, to see his spear sail by his target, merely grazing his arm and knocking him off balance.

Anvin was relieved to see that, at least, the hornblower cried and fell from the platform. And yet somehow the steep fall, which should have killed him, did not. He crawled on the ground, alive, inching his way toward his horn, which had fallen but a few feet away.

Anvin was flooded with panic, knowing there was no time. He was still ten yards away when the hornblower reached out and grabbed his horn. He raised it to his mouth with shaking hands, took a deep breath, and, with puffed cheeks, was about to blow.

Anvin allowed his blind instincts to take over. He leapt from his horse while still at a full gallop, the world rushing by him, raised his sword, and swung for the hornblower. He felt his blade slashing flesh, and he looked over to see the soldier slump to the ground, decapitated, the horn still on his lips, his cheeks still puffed—thankfully, silent.

Anvin hit the ground hard, rolled and rolled, and gained his feet, never slowing. He charged the other soldier holding the crank, knowing time was short, and as he ran, he saw the other crank turner, dead on the ground, in a pool of blood, killed by a spear in the back.

Anvin tackled the soldier to the ground just as he began to turn the crank and lower the massive portcullis. He landed on top of him and tried to choke him, but as soon as he did, he was kicked hard in the back by a Pandesian soldier—then clubbed by another. He turned to see a third Pandesian pouncing, a sword coming down for him before he could gather himself. He had left himself too vulnerable, he realized, by rushing out ahead of the pack.

As he braced himself for the blow, his men arrived, their horses galloping through, and Anvin watched with relief as one decapitated the soldier above him, sparing his life. Another killed the Pandesian beside him with a spear through his chest. Anvin spotted another Pandesian run for the crank, and saw a hatchet turn end over end as it flew through the air and lodged itself in his back.

Durge and his men overtook the gate, horses galloping, slashing and killing Pandesians on all sides, who had no time to put up a defense. They swept through like a desert storm and slaughtered them all in a blur. A few Pandesians had time enough to just grab for swords and shields, yet barely had they lifted them when they were hacked down. And with the hornblowers dead and the cranks out of their control, there was little they could do to alert the others. They were quickly surrounded and killed.

Soon, all the Pandesian soldiers lay in heaps, their blood staining the sand, while all fell silent.

"He's getting away!" someone yelled.

Anvin turned to see a lone Pandesian had escaped. The soldier mounted his horse and took off, galloping south at lightning speed toward Pandesia. Anvin knew if he got away, all would be lost.

Anvin didn't hesitate. Without thinking he mounted his horse and rode after him. He bore down him, as fast as he ever rode, air cutting into his lungs, hardly able to breathe. They rode, just the two of them out there alone, and the terrain shifted as they went farther from the gate, left the peninsula, and entered the mainland of Pandesia, the ground morphing to hard rock. Their horses' hooves clattered, and Anvin knew they were riding in Fields of Ore. A stretch of black stone, it was no terrain for riding.

Anvin's horse was slipping and sliding on the slick stone, and soon, it stumbled and fell—while the Pandesians did, too. He hit the ground hard, bruised from the hard landing, feeling pain in every corner of his body. His only solace was that the Pandesian up ahead was in the same position as he.

Anvin rolled and summoned all his effort to regain his feet. The Pandesian was slower to get up, and Anvin, forcing himself to his feet, charged for the man, about twenty yards ahead, beneath the blistering heat of the sun. The Pandesian stumbled, and he bore down on him.

Anvin was but yards away, preparing to tackle the soldier, when suddenly the soldier did something Anvin could not expect: he turned, raised a small hidden spear, and threw it at him.

At the last second Anvin's reflexes kicked in, and he dodged as it grazed his shoulder.

The soldier looked up and, fear in his eyes, turned to run, weaponless. Anvin, knowing that a slippery chase on the slick rock could end poorly for them both, instead drew his sword, planted his feet, reached back, and threw it.

He watched the blade tumble end over end until it finally found a spot in the soldier's back. He grunted and fell face-first on the rock. Dead.

Anvin walked over, breathing hard, stood over the soldier and grabbed his sword. He then turned and looked back at the shining gate in the distance. He saw all of his men, triumphant, the gate in their control. It was the most beautiful sight of his life.

All them cheered in the distance, and Anvin knew they had done it.

The gate was theirs.

CHAPTER TWENTY FOUR

Kyra stood in the forest clearing, breathing hard, overwhelmed with frustration. Her hands were raw, her quiver empty, already having fired all her arrows at her targets. She had missed them all.

Kyra felt like a failure. She could not understand how she had missed every single shot, as she had not missed a shot in years. Every time she fired, somehow the tree moved. The skinny trees were very much alive here, dodging her arrows; she could not even hit a leaf. Her arrows had whizzed by harmlessly, landing on the forest floor, while Alva had sat there and watched all morning, silent, expressionless. Failing in front of him had worsened her shame. He was never disapproving, and he never tried to correct her—in fact, he never said anything. He just observed, and his observing set her on edge. She never had any idea what he was thinking. Was this what it meant to train someone?

She stood there, reflecting, and she thought back to her encounter with the Salic. She had been certain, as it had pounced, that it was going to kill her; yet it had vanished just as its paws had touched her. Somehow, that was more unnerving to Kyra than anything. She didn't understand this place, and she didn't understand Alva. She just wanted to train somewhere with real warriors, real opponents and real teachers.

"I don't understand," she finally said, breathing hard, exasperated. "How am I missing? Why are you not correcting me?"

Alva stared back calmly, seated on the forest floor across the clearing.

"No one can correct you," he replied. "And I, least of all. You must find your own way."

She shook her head.

"How can I? I don't know why I'm missing. Those should have been easy shots. I don't understand this place."

There came a long silence, the only sound that of the wind rustling through the trees, of the distant ocean waves, crashing somewhere far off. Finally, he took a deep breath.

"This place is *you*," he said. "All that you see is a mere reflection of what lies inside you. A target too hard to reach; a fast-moving opponent."

Kyra furrowed her brow, struggling to comprehend.

"I don't understand," she replied. "I feel as if I arrived here as a warrior, and yet now, I am nothing. I no longer know a thing."

He smiled for the first time.

"Good," he replied, to her surprise. "Very good. You are beginning to learn."

She frowned.

"Beginning to learn?" she echoed. "I don't know what I'm doing. I had thought you would introduce me to new weaponry—magical halberds and spears and axes and swords and shields. I thought I would learn and do all the things that warriors do in advanced training. But it feels like it's been weeks here, and I've done none of that. I've chased moving targets; I've run up and down valleys; I've watched trees sway in the wind; I've followed a trail of ants. What kind of training is this? I don't even believe that you are my uncle."

She added emphasis to her final words, wanting to provoke some reaction from him, but Alva merely stared back calmly.

"Don't you?" he asked.

"You won't tell me anything about my mother," she added. "Or about myself. I thought I would come here and find answers. Instead, you've raised more questions. I am wasting my time," she concluded, unable to take any more. "I must leave. And I must return to my father. He is at war, and he needs me. It was a mistake to come here."

Kyra stood there, breathing hard, upset with herself and at the end of her rope.

Alva, though, sat there calmly, unfazed, expressionless. Kyra felt on the verge of breaking down and crying, and yet nothing seemed to faze him.

"The only war that rages lies within yourself," he finally replied, calm. "It is a far more interesting war, and a far more powerful one. Have you asked yourself why you cannot summon your dragon?"

Kyra blinked, wondering. It was a question she had been grappling with herself.

"I…don't know," she admitted, feeling crushed. She was starting to wonder if she had ever been able to summon him to begin with, if she had ever had any true powers, or if it had all just been a dream.

"You cannot summon him," he replied, "because you are too busy thinking, planning, training. You still think you can control the world around you—and that is your greatest failing. You cannot control anything. Not the woods around you, not the universe, and not even your skills. As soon as you realize that, as soon as you stop trying to control, you will allow the power in. You can never be one when you are in opposition—and when you try to control, you are in opposition."

Kyra closed her eyes, trying to grasp the concept of his words. She understood what he was saying intellectually, yet she could not grasp it viscerally yet.

"Take me, for example," he said, surprising her as he suddenly jumped up and walked over to her. "You hold a very fine staff, a staff that you love, a staff that could kill many warriors. And here I hold," he said, picking up a stick off the floor, "a thin stick."

He stopped about ten feet away in the clearing and held it behind his back with one hand.

"I am a small boy," he continued, "with an aging disease. A harmless boy with a small stick. You are the great warrior Kyra, more powerful than most men I have encountered, and you wield a powerful weapon. You should be able to defeat me easily, should you not?"

She looked back, confused, appalled at the idea of fighting him.

"I would never harm you," she said. "You are my teacher. Even if I don't understand what it is you are teaching me."

He shook his head.

"You *must* fight me," he replied. "Because you look with your eyes, but not with your heart. You listen with your ears, but not with your mind. You still think that what you see is real. You still have not lifted the great veil of the universe."

He sighed.

"Until you pull it back, you will never see for sure, never understand that all you see is the world of illusion."

Kyra pondered his words as he stared back calmly.

"Attack me," he finally commanded.

She shook her head, horrified.

"I will not," she replied.

"I command you," he said firmly, his voice darker, ancient, suddenly scary.

Kyra felt she could not disobey. She walked slowly toward him, a knot in her stomach, stepped forward and halfheartedly swung her staff at his shoulder.

To her surprise, Alva swung around with his stick and swatted her staff, knocking it from her hands. She looked at him in shock; an enemy had never made her drop her staff before.

"I said *attack*," he commanded.

Kyra retrieved her staff and faced him again with trembling hands, unsure what to do. She stepped forward and attacked again, a little bit harder this time.

As she swung, though, he spun around, knocked it again from her hand, and leaned back and kicked her in the chest.

To her shock, his kick knocked her halfway across the clearing, and she landed on the forest floor, winded.

She sat there and stared back at the boy in wonder. He stood there, still smiling, looking as if he had not moved at all, and for the first time, she felt fear. She realized she had vastly underestimated him, and she wondered who he was. Finally, she was beginning to understand that all was not what it seemed.

"The greatest warriors do not present their hand in battle," he said. "They deceive. They project weakness, inexperience. They disarm foes who judge by appearance. Now—attack me."

This time, Kyra, angry, still smarting from the blow, ran, grabbed her staff, and charged him with all her might, no longer holding back.

She swung, and to her surprise, she missed, hitting air as she stumbled forward. At the same time she felt a crack in her back, and she turned, red-faced, to see Alva standing behind her, stick in hand. She fumed, her back stinging from the blow.

"Good," he said, "you no longer patronize me. Now let us see what you can do."

Kyra let out a shout of frustration, raised her staff with both hands, and slashed at him. He raised his stick and blocked it easily. She swung left and right, pushing him back across the clearing with a dizzying array of blows, blows strong enough to take down a dozen warriors.

Yet each time he calmly raised his skinny stick with one hand and blocked, deflecting her blows as if he were wielding a steel shield.

As she thought she was gaining ground, driving him all the way back to the edge of the clearing, he slashed upwards, catching her staff from beneath and sending it flying up out of her hands. He then stepped forward and jabbed her in the solar plexus, and she fell to her knees, defenseless before him, her staff on the ground.

She knelt there, feeling like crying, feeling lower than she ever had in her life. She was defenseless, ashamed, and she felt as if she had no skills whatsoever. Had her skills been an illusion? Had she ever been good?

She slowly looked up at him in shame, but also in awe at his powers. Clearly, he was no mere human.

"Who are you?" she asked.

"The question is not who I am," he replied. "Who are *you*? That is what you fail to grasp."

"Who am I, then?" she asked. "You know. Tell me."

He looked at her for a long time, expressionless.

"You are more than a mere girl, Kyra," he finally replied. "Which is why you—and you alone—must answer that question."

*

Kyra hiked deeper and deeper into the forest, as she had been for hours, utterly alone, having left Leo and Andor behind, needing time to be with herself. Still reeling from her encounter with Alva, still trying to understand everything he'd said, she hiked deeper and deeper into the mysterious forest of Ur, past glowing, light green trees, swaying in the wind, their long leaves rustling, their shapes constantly changing. She replayed her encounter with Alva in her head, again and again. How had he beaten her so soundly? How could she have been so ineffective? What had he meant when he'd said the answers lay within her? What was the veil of the universe?

The training had been much harder than she imagined, not only physically, but mentally and spiritually. It would have been easier if she had had traditional targets, weapons, opponents to fight against.

But this training of the mind was stumping her, pushing her farther than she had imagined. She was afraid she could not achieve what her uncle wanted of her. Did that mean she was a failure?

She closed her eyes as she went, trying to summon that deeper part of herself, to turn on that energy she had once experienced.

But try as she did, nothing came. She was no one now. Nowhere.

So many people in her life had had faith in her. Had she not deserved it?

Alva had urged her, after their sparring, to seek out the Pool of No Reflection, deep in the forest of Ur, and had pointed the way. She was so lost in her thoughts that, as she looked up at the sound of a bird, she forgot why she had even come this way—when her eye was caught by a glistening red color. Kyra hurried toward it and found herself at the edge of a clearing. She stopped, amazed at the sight. There, hidden in the thick wood, was a small red pond, its waters shimmering. She sensed a strange power emanating off of it, even from here. It must be the pool Alva had spoken of.

Kyra stepped forward cautiously and knelt beside it. She looked down, searching for her reflection, hoping.

Yet she found none.

It was as Alva had said. This pool did not reflect the outside world; instead, it reflected only what lay inside, what one was unwilling to see within one's self. Kyra hoped for the waters to show her something, to help point the way.

But she waited for a long time, staring down, and was disappointed to see nothing. All she heard was the rustling of the leaves, high overhead.

What was it the universe demanded of her? she wondered. Why couldn't she be like everybody else?

There came a sudden snap behind her, and Kyra turned, on edge, reaching for her staff. A noise raced past her, like a weapon racing through the air, and she looked over and was astonished to see a silver spear flying in her direction.

It whizzed by her, and Kyra realized it wasn't meant for her. She turned and was shocked to see the spear puncture the breast of a Pandesian soldier—standing but a few feet away from her, sword raised high. He grunted and fell, and as his sword fell to the ground, she realized he had been about to stab her in the back. That spear had spared her from death. How stupid she had been to let down her guard.

Kyra wheeled, peering into the wood, wondering who had thrown the spear, who had saved her, and why.

Another snap followed, and she turned in the other direction and her heart caught in her throat. There, but a few feet away, was the most striking boy she had ever seen. He stood tall and proud, looking about her age, with broad shoulders, a smooth face, a chiseled jaw, and fine, golden hair longer than any man she knew, down to his waist. He stared back with flashing steel gray eyes, and as he did, she felt her breath leave her. She couldn't look away if she tried. For the first time in her life, she was mesmerized.

The boy looked away. He stepped forward, extracted his silver spear, and rolled over the Pandesian soldier with his foot.

"They are everywhere," he said, his voice as hypnotic as his face. "Searching for you. This one was a scout. That means an army follows on his heels."

She could barely process his words, her mind reeling.

"You saved my life," she said, her voice barely above a whisper.

He looked away, combing the woods, and it pained her that his eyes would not meet hers.

"I mustn't stay here," he said, examining the treeline. "You must not, either."

She stared at him, unable to look away.

"Who are you?" she asked. "Why did you save me?"

He looked down.

"I have been waiting for you," he said, his voice so soft she barely heard it. Then he looked up and met her eyes. "For my entire life. For you and for no one else. For now and forever. And it is you, most of all, who I am forbidden to see."

He looked up at her, his eyes watery, sparkling gray, and she knew, at that moment, two things: He was not human. And she was in love.

"I saved you because I love you," he continued. "I always have, and I always will. And I saved you because I can never again see you after this day."

He slowly reached out and touched her cheek, and his touch electrified her.

144

Then suddenly, just as quickly, he withdrew his hand and bolted off, disappearing into the wood.

Kyra stood there, left all alone, and looked out in wonder. Had she imagined it all?

She knew, from the way her heart was beating, from the feel of his skin still on her cheek, that she had not. She felt different from having met him. For the first time in her life, she didn't think of battle, or training. For the first time, all her worries left her.

She thought only of the boy. The magical, mystical boy who had appeared like a lightning storm and disappeared just as quickly. She knew, as certain as she knew herself, that seeing him again would mean the ruin of them both.

And that, no matter what, was exactly what she had to do.

CHAPTER TWENTY FIVE

Duncan marched quickly through Fort Andros beneath the moonlight. He walked across ancient stone floors, past endless marble walls, his armor rattling, joined by several of his men, and he tried to shake from his mind his troubling thoughts. He walked past a series of arches and columns that looked out over the inner courtyard of the capital building, and his heart lifted with pride to see his hundreds of soldiers milling about, Kavos's and Seavig's men with them, Bramthos and Arthfael beside them, all preparing, waiting for the dawn. In but a few hours, they would march from this place, attack what remained of the Pandesian garrisons, and battle would come for them all.

Duncan turned down another corridor and saw a row of torches lighting the night, dozens more of his men lined up along the walls. Duncan had ordered the extra guard, and he was glad he had: that feast had turned into a fiasco. The alliance of Escalon splintered, his men nearly coming to blows with Bant. Duncan felt he was holding all his men together by a thread, and that he could trust no one.

Duncan was deep in thought as he marched, his mind teeming with a million anxieties, unable to sleep even if he had wanted to. With Baris leaving the alliance, Duncan had not only lost half his manpower, he knew, but had also made a great enemy in him. The men of Baris were vindictive and sneaky, and now not only would he have to defeat Pandesia, but he would also have to watch his back from within his own land—all thanks to his hot-headed sons. Bant, though, would likely slink back into his canyon, take no sides, and if Pandesia won, bank on their neutrality to spare them. Neutrality would spare no one in this war, though. Duncan knew that.

Duncan shook these worries from his mind; he had bigger ones to focus on. At daybreak he would lead half his men to ride south, for the Southern Gate, to relieve Anvin and hold back the Pandesian invasion. Along the way he would liberate and clear the southern cities, and secure the south. The other half of his army, led by Kavos and Bramthos, would be dispatched north and west, to secure Ur, its ports, and the north and west of Escalon. Without Bant, though, his men would be stretched thin; he would have to rely on whatever men he picked up along the way, on the people of Escalon aiding him in spontaneous revolt. If he could just seal the Southern Gate in time, and the ports of Ur in time, then, Duncan knew, Escalon could hold.

Duncan turned down corridors, marching and marching, until he reached a narrow stone staircase. He descended, deeper and deeper, impatient, as the staircase twisted and led him to the lower levels of the capital building. Walking these halls brought back memories.

As he reached the lower level, Duncan felt a knot in his stomach as he remembered where he was going: to visit Tarnis, locked up below. Duncan had received a scroll urging a word with him. He had been skeptical, wondering Tarnis could want from him now that he was imprisoned. A part of him wanted to ignore him, yet he knew Tarnis still wielded power and influence with his many connections in the capital, and he thought it wise to at least hear him out. He also still held, he had to admit, some warmth for him for old times' sake, and his nostalgia tugged at his strings of compassion.

"You are wasting your time," came a hurried voice beside him.

Duncan turned to see Kavos marching beside him, his face hard and lined, unsmiling. He did not look happy.

"Nothing Tarnis can say will make any difference," he continued. "Words from a prisoner are meaningless, and he is but a weak old man trying to worm his way back into power."

Duncan considered that as he walked.

"Perhaps," he replied. "Yet still, I must hear him out. There comes no harm in listening, and a ruler who does not listen is a foolish ruler indeed."

They reached a massive stone arch, secured by iron bars and guarded by Duncan's men, and as Duncan paused before it, Kavos reached out and grabbed his arm, giving him a meaningful look.

"Do not trust him," he urged. "We cannot trust any of them. You did him a great service by not beheading him. Remember: loyalty is not an entitlement. And loyalty misplaced is the most dangerous thing of all."

Duncan pondered his words.

"It is just a conversation," he replied. "I shall make no rash decisions. Regardless of what this old man has to say, we ride, all of us, at dawn, and I am as anxious for battle as you."

Kavos didn't seem convinced.

"We are men of war," he continued. "Not men of talk. Don't forget that. We are not like Tarnis. We are not like any of the others here. You will be unlike any King Escalon has ever had. Finally, one of *us* will be on the throne. You will be King second—and warrior first. But don't assume, even for a second, that the others are like you."

With that, Kavos turned and marched away.

Duncan turned and nodded to his guards, who bowed their heads in respect and opened the iron gates.

Duncan entered the small stone courtyard, open-aired, the moonlight shining down, and in the far corner spotted Tarnis sitting against a wall, hands on his knees, looking dejected, but a fraction of the man that Duncan once knew. Several of Duncan's guard stood along the walls, torches burning high above them.

As Duncan entered, Tarnis looked up, and his eyes lit at the sight of him. He jumped to his feet and hurried toward him.

"I knew you'd come," he said, smiling. "You were always the only warlord I could trust."

Tarnis reached out to embrace him with a warm smile—but Duncan stood there coldly, not allowing his embrace.

"I am no warlord anymore," Duncan replied, cold and hard. "I am your King."

Tarnis stood there, and his face fell in disappointment as his arms slowly fell. He appeared humbled. It felt funny for Duncan, after serving so many years on the King's council, to be on the other side of it—but he had to make sure Tarnis understood the new power structure and was not under any illusions.

"Forgive me, my King," Tarnis replied, his voice broken. "I meant no offense. It takes time to get used a new title. After all, it was not so long ago when you called me King."

Duncan gritted his teeth, thinking of the battle awaiting him at dawn and having little patience for this man.

"Why have you summoned me?" Duncan demanded, short.

Tarnis sighed.

"What I have to say is for your ears only," Tarnis said, and glanced at Duncan's guards, lining the wall.

Duncan stared back at his friend, his impatience growing but sensing an important message, and he reluctantly turned and nodded to his soldiers.

They immediately turned and filtered out, leaving the two of them alone in the courtyard, closing the iron gate behind them with a bang.

"Quickly," Duncan said. "My time is short."

"Walk with me," Tarnis said, placing a hand on Duncan's shoulder. "Grant me at least this much."

They turned and walked, Duncan indulging him. It was a warm night here in this southern climate, the breezes temperate, the moon lighting their way as they passed beneath torches in the courtyard. Duncan recalled what a slow talker his old King could be, partly because he was a slow thinker, never quick to rush to judgment, and partly for effect.

"For many years you served at my council table," Tarnis finally said, nostalgic. "I made a lot of good decisions, decisions that benefited Escalon. I made some bad ones, too, I will be the first to admit. You are King now, and you must know what it means, what it really means, to be King. It means you will encounter the bad along with the good."

Tarnis took a deep breath as they walked.

"Surrendering Escalon," Tarnis continued, "was a bad decision. I know this now. And I am truly and deeply sorry for it. But I did what I thought, at the time, was best for us all."

They continued on in silence, Duncan wondering what this was all leading to. He could not help but wonder, too, if he would feel the same way when he was King.

"You will come to learn that when you are King," Tarnis continued, "you will make many good decisions, and many bad ones, too. You can only hope that the good outweigh the bad. In my case, I was not so lucky. So many excellent decisions, all forgotten, all wiped away by that one bad one."

They walked in silence, Duncan pondering his words.

"There is no shame in making bad decisions," Duncan finally replied. "All decisions are forgivable, as long as they come from a place of honor. Your decision to surrender our country held no honor. That was your mistake. That was a bad decision, but more importantly, it revealed a character flaw. Moments of danger, of crisis, reveal character. I have seen it many times on the battlefield. And at the end of the day, we can only be judged by our character."

Duncan expected Tarnis to argue, but to his surprise he nodded back in agreement.

"I cannot disagree," he replied. "And you shall be a wise king—wiser than I clearly thought. I displayed a flaw in my character, true. Yet I also displayed many virtues in that same bad decision. Compassion. Humility. There is honor in these, too."

Tarnis sighed as they continued on, Duncan feeling impatient, wondering what this was all leading to.

"Make no mistake," Tarnis continued, "you, too, will encounter moments of flawed character as King. Yes, even you, with all your chivalry and honor. What you don't yet understand is that to be King means nothing more than embracing compromise. Your job is to hold together the loose alliance we call Escalon. Yet we are not truly one land—we never have been. We are a series of competing strongholds. And oftentimes, too often, as King, you must bend to keep them all together. *Unity*." Tarnis shook his head. "As if it were some great goal. What is so great about unity? Why is it so important that we all be one land, one name, one banner? Why not just be competing strongholds, each ruled by its own warlord?"

Duncan contemplated his words as they walked.

"Then we could not fend off an invasion," Duncan replied.

"I was a master politician," Tarnis continued. "As was my father, and his father before him. I was good at what I did, just as you are good at what you do. I could not wield a sword, as do you—and yet, you could not stomach all the lies and machinations as I had to suffer in that council of nobles. We each have our talents, our strengths and weaknesses. It doesn't make either one of us better than the other."

They stopped, and Tarnis turned and looked at him, eyes filled with compassion.

"I elevated you above all my warlords," Tarnis said. "I made you my most important warrior. And you, in turn, kept me alive when you had no reason to—a far greater gift, to be sure. Now I wish to return the favor."

Duncan stared at him, wondering.

"How?" he asked.

"By saving your life in return," Tarnis replied.

Duncan frowned.

"My life needs no saving."

Tarnis smiled and shook his head.

"If only that were true," Tarnis replied. "At dawn, you will recklessly wage war on all of Pandesia. You know as well as I do that you cannot win. Even if you cleared our land, secured the Southern Gate, they will send the hordes of the world against us and will not stop until all we know is dead and gone."

Duncan gritted his teeth, unmoved.

"That is the difference between you and I," Duncan replied coldly. "You wage wars only when you can win. I wage wars when honor and duty compel them."

"What if I brought you victory another way?" Tarnis asked. "With honor, and without losing a life?"

Duncan stared back, suspicious.

"And how can you do that?" he asked.

Tarnis smiled.

"I have built much good faith with Pandesia," he replied. "I did not resist their invasion, I complied with their demands, and as a result, they hold me in high esteem. They listen when I speak to them. I have got a message to them—and they have responded. I have negotiated a truce for you."

Duncan raised his eyebrows, shocked.

"A truce?" he asked, indignant. "And who are you to negotiate a truce for a land you no longer rule?"

Tarnis shook his head.

"More than a truce," he insisted. "A victory. *Your* victory. A victory never before achieved. After all, the great Pandesia has never backed down in its history, has never before conceded, as they are willing to do to you. They will leave our shores. There will be no more bloodshed. Victory will be yours. At dawn, their Lord Governor has vowed to me he will appear before you and accept defeat before you and all your men."

Duncan stared back, skeptical.

"And what is their price in return?"

"A safe retreat," Tarnis replied. "Nothing more. They want to spare the remainder of their army and ensure them safe passage from our borders."

Tarnis paused, as Duncan let it sink in.

"Don't you see, Duncan?" Tarnis pressed. "I am handing you a complete victory."

Duncan felt unsure.

"It sounds too good to be true," Duncan replied.

"Does it?" Tarnis asked. "They know we have their men surrounded. They know we have momentum. They have many important Lord Governors still here. They fear for their lives, and they have petitioned Pandesia, too. They know Escalon is difficult to hold—and they have more important kingdoms to conquer. They have already taken from our land the best that they can take, and they are ready to move on."

Duncan stared at Tarnis long and hard, debating. His heart began to warm thinking of handing his people a victory, of no more bloodshed, of Escalon being free.

"If it is as you say, an unconditional victory," Duncan began slowly, thinking, "then yes, I shall allow them to retreat. I have no reason to slaughter troops who have conceded defeat. Indeed, my honor compels me to make sure they retreat unharmed."

Tarnis smiled.

"A wise decision," he said.

Duncan studied him.

"And what about you?" Duncan asked. "What compels you to care so much to broker a truce for a new King who has ousted you?"

Tarnis furrowed his brow.

"I love my country," he replied. "As do you. We just have different ways of showing it."

Duncan waited, sensing more.

"And yet," Tarnis continued, "aside from the general welfare of Escalon, there is one small thing I would ask of you for my brokering this truce."

Duncan stared, wondering, while Tarnis took a deep breath.

"It is no command, old friend," Tarnis continued, "but a request. A small favor. I know I stand in no position to make requests, but I appeal to your love and your mercy and our once-strong friendship."

"Tell me," Duncan urged, curious.

"I have a daughter Tarnis finally announced.

Duncan stared back, shocked. He knew the King had a son—an impetuous and unlikable young man—but he had never heard any word spoken of a daughter.

"A daughter?" Duncan asked.

Tarnis nodded.

"My only daughter. Illegitimate. My only surviving issue outside of my son. I could not allow her to be raised here. Her existence would have been a threat—I have always kept her location secret. You are the only one I'm telling."

Duncan stared, wondering.

"What is it you wish from me?" he asked.

"Her safety," Tarnis replied. "You are the only one I trust. She means more to me than all I have left in the world."

Duncan could see Tarnis's expression, and for the first time since he had known him, he detected true sincerity in his words.

"Where is she?" Duncan asked.

Tarnis took a deep breath and looked around, as if afraid someone might be listening.

"At the tip of the Devil's Finger," he said, his voice low. "In Knossos."

Duncan was shocked to hear it; Knossos, he knew, was an extreme, remote place, inhabited by warrior monks in the Tower of Kos, and not much more. It was nearly impossible to reach and as secluded from Escalon—and the world—as any island could get.

"I trust you with my life," Tarnis added. "Because she is what remains of my life. I do not ask you to reinstate my title—nor do I ask for freedom. I will serve you as King. I ask only that you find her. And protect her. I fear word has leaked of her existence, and that nefarious forces close in on her even now."

Duncan took a deep breath, satisfied Tarnis was genuine, and approving of his love for his daughter. It made him think of Kyra.

"Consider your daughter safe," Duncan said. "You may have made mistakes, but you are a fine man, in many ways. I am glad I did not kill you."

153

The old King laughed heartily, smiling wide, a look of relief crossing his face for the first time.

"As am I," he replied. "To victory, my friend."

Tarnis reached out his forearm, and Duncan reached out and clasped it. As he did, he thought of the truce to come, and he felt a sense of imminent victory welling up inside of him as a new dawn began to break over Escalon.

Finally, victory was his.

CHAPTER TWENTY SIX

Dierdre hurried out the forge with the others as the horns of war sounded. They echoed throughout the streets of Ur, again and again, each blast sending a chill up her spine. They were horns of warning, horns of danger, horns she had not heard since she was a child, last sounded only when Ur had been invaded by Pandesia. They were horns that could only mean one thing: a Pandesian warship had arrived.

Dierdre's heart slammed as she ran outside, followed by her girls, the boys and men from the forge dropping their weapons-in-progress and racing into the crowded streets. She was jostled as all around her the streets filled, the masses flocking for the canals, all eager to see. Dierdre pushed her way to the water's edge, shoving people aside, and beside her Alec did the same, joined by his friend Marco and the others. She could not help but wonder about him, as she had from the first moment she had seen him. There was something different about him, some sense of tragedy lurking behind his eyes. She felt he was a kindred soul, could sense that he had suffered as she had.

As closed off as Deidre was to the world, and especially to men, she had to admit there was something about this boy that she liked. She tried to suppress her feelings, knowing she was in no mood to be in love, not after what she had been through. Not to mention, now was not a time to love—but a time for vengeance. For doing to Pandesia what they had done to her.

Dierdre shook these thoughts from her mind as she finally reached the water's edge. She leaned forward, craned her neck, and caught sight of what everyone else was gaping at—and her heart fell at the sight. There, at the far end of the canal, sailing into the city, was a massive, gleaming black Pandesian warship, flying their banners, dozens of cannons at its side, being sailed by hundreds of soldiers in full armor, weapons at the ready. Dierdre looked behind them and saw no other ships following and she was thankful, at least, for that. It seemed to be a lone ship, leading the way, perhaps, for the fleet. The horn sounded again and again, and as they sailed deeper into the heart of the city, unmistakably toward them, their visors drawn, these men clearly had come for a reason. Dierdre felt a pit in her stomach as she knew instantly why they had come: for her.

While the entire city flocked to the canals, Deidre strengthened her grip on her staff, resolved not to be taken captive. She would kill them, or die trying. There would be no running for her—not anymore.

Sensing motion, she turned and watched Alec run off into the crowd, disappearing.

"Alec!" Marco called out. "Where are you going!?"

But Alec did not respond as he vanished, leaving Dierdre wondering, too. He did not seem the type to run from danger.

"They're coming for you," Fervil said, coming up beside her, concern in his face. "You know that, don't you?"

"I do," she replied.

"Go to your father," he urged. "He'll be gathered with his men. A war is about to start, and you're going to be in the middle of it. I'm sure he is looking for you."

Dierdre realized he was right, and without hesitating, she turned and ran, pushing her way through the thick crowd, rushing to find her father.

The throng thinned as she made it farther from the canals, and finally she had room to run through the streets. She turned down familiar alleyways, left and right, and as she heard footsteps behind her, she turned and was surprised to see the girls she had liberated following her.

She stopped and looked at them all, breathing hard.

"Go back," she urged. "Stay with the others. You will be safer. Take shelter in the forge."

But they shook their heads adamantly.

"Wherever you go," said one, stepping forward, "we go."

"Wherever you fight," said another, "we fight."

"We are through running, too," said another.

Dierdre, seeing they would not be deterred, felt a rush of gratitude for their loyalty. She turned and ran and the girls joined her, all navigating their way alongside the canals, as she led them toward where her father and his men would surely be amassed.

Finally, Dierdre emerged from a narrow alleyway and burst out into a wide, open square of cobblestone, framed by ancient buildings on all sides, at the canals' end. It was where the ships must stop, leading to the deepest point in the city, and as she suspected, Dierdre saw her father at its edge, surrounded by his men. There he stood, a hundred warriors behind him, facing the canal and watching it anxiously as the Pandesians approached.

Dierdre pushed her way through the crowd, the men parting ways for her and the girls, until she reached her father's side.

He turned at the sight of her, and his face fell in relief.

"Dierdre," he exclaimed. "Are you okay? My men were searching for you everywhere."

She could see the genuine concern his eyes, and it helped her forgive him.

"I am, Father."

"Have you seen them coming?" he asked urgently. "Have you heard the horns? You know they come for you."

She nodded back, stoic, resigned.

"I do."

"They will surely demand I turn you over. You know this," he said, more of a statement than a question. She could hear the anguish in his voice.

She nodded, wondering what he would do.

"And will you?" she asked.

He sighed, looking exhausted, irritated.

"Would you have me sacrifice our entire city to save one girl?" he asked.

Dierdre's heart sank. Had he not changed after all?

"I would have you be my father," she replied coldly.

"Death is coming," her father said, setting his jaw, tightening his grip on the hilt of his sword. "I don't want you staying here. Take these girls, and flee. My men will escort you. We have many safe tunnels and forts in which to hide you."

She shook her head.

"Don't you understand, Father? Have you not listened to anything I said? I do not wish to run. I do not wish to hide. I wish only for a chance at justice. A chance not to back down in the face of men."

Her father sighed, anguished; and yet she could also see the pride in his eyes. As he stared, horns sounded, again and again.

"That ship is but a messenger," he continued. "Behind it lie a million more. We cannot defend this city. Do you realize what will happen once they are victorious?"

"I do not fear death, Father," she said, meaning it. "I've already faced it. Now, all I fear is not living proudly."

He looked into her eyes long and hard, and slowly, he smiled.

"You truly are my daughter."

His words meant the world to her.

"And you, Father?" she asked. "What will you do when they come for me?"

She searched his eyes, and she could see that he was grappling with this himself.

The horns sounded again, more urgently, and she turned and saw the Pandesian warship suddenly close, looming down on them. Its cannons aimed at them, dozens of archers training bows on them, and dozens more men holding spears, it was a floating army, ready to attack.

Dierdre felt a cold dread as they approached. The ship came to a stop perhaps twenty yards away, near the end of the canal, its huge masts rising to the sky, casting shadows down upon them. Thousands of citizens of Ur flocked to the edge, looking up at it, gathered to watch the confrontation.

A heavy silence fell over the city as Dierdre stood beside her father, looking up at the ship, waiting. The ship floated there in the water, its wood creaking, as the soldiers stared down ominously, weapons at the ready. Dierdre could feel them all pointed at her and knew she could die at any moment. Yet somehow, she was unafraid.

The Pandesian commander finally stepped forward, his armor clinking, and stood at the edge of the bow, hands on his hips, the sun behind him, his hundreds of men behind him, looking down at them like a God from the sea. His armor gleamed in the sunlight, and from this angle, looking up, the warship seemed indomitable. And somewhere out there, Dierdre knew, were thousands more ships, waiting to arrive. Yet still, she was determined to make a stand.

The commander began to speak, his voice booming.

"His Glorious Ra, The Supreme Lord Emperor, ruler of all the great cities of Pandesia, God of the South and Titan of the West," the commander boomed, his voice echoing with authority, "has commanded us, the legion of the fourth of the fleet of Pandesia, to enter Ur first, and to give you one chance. Behind us, a fleet of death spreads across the Sorrow. Hand over the girl now, she who has defied Pandesia, who has murdered our Lord Governor, and we shall spare this entire city the destruction it so deserves. It is a supremely generous offer," he added, "and we shall not make it twice."

He paused.

"Defy us," he continued, "and we shall rain down ash and fire on this city until, a fortnight from now, it is but a memory."

Dierdre glanced at her father and could feel the torment and anguish within him. She saw all the citizens looking to him for a response, and she knew this would be the defining moment of his life—and of her relationship with him. She watched the emotions flash across his face, and her heart pounded. Would he do it again? she wondered. Would he cave and hand her over?

If so, she resolved, she would not go. She clenched the spear in her hand tighter, and knew that if he tried to hand her over, she would let it fly, and kill at least one before they took her.

Finally, after a long, tense silence, her father cleared his throat.

"You have thousands of arrows trained upon us," he boomed back, "and thousands more spears. Behind that, you have every manner of weaponry."

He paused.

"And my answer is no," he continued. "I shall not turn over my daughter—or *any* of our daughters. Not now, and not ever. You can take our lives. You can destroy our city. But you will never have what you truly want—our freedom."

The crowd gasped, and Dierdre felt a rush of admiration for her father and, finally, a sense of vindication. Her father had come back to her, the man she had always loved and admired and looked up to.

She watched with glee as the face of the Pandesian commander reddened.

"It is your graves!" he called out, then turned to his men.

"SAIL FORWARD!" he shouted.

The sails were hoisted, and the great ship began to move again, closing in on them.

"ARCHERS!" the commander shouted.

The archers raised their bows, and Dierdre's heart slammed, bracing herself. The ship sailed closer, and Dierdre knew they would soon reach the edge, disembark, and engage in a bloody hand-to-hand war—assuming the arrows and spears did not kill her first. She stood there, beside her father, awaiting a certain death, when suddenly, an unexpected noise shattered the silence.

Dierdre looked down to the water, wondering what was happening. It sounded like a rattling of chains at the bottom of the canal, and as she peered down below into the canals, she was shocked to find Alec and several boys on one side of the canal, down below, hidden out of sight, and Marco and his friends on the other.

"NOW!" Alec yelled out.

Alec and the boys beside him gave a great tug, while Marco and the other boys tugged on the far side of the canal, and Dierdre watched in amazement as a huge iron chain emerged from the water, spikes spread out alongside it. A tremendous noise of cracking wood followed, and Dierdre watched in awe as the hull of the massive warship floated right into the spikes.

Alec and the others quickly wrapped the iron chain around iron footings in the harbor, again and again, then let go, right before the chain went taut. The Pandesian ship continued to sail into it, still gaining speed, unable to maneuver, its men dumfounded, still not understanding what was happening.

The ship lurched and rocked violently and its men stumbled forward. The cracking grew louder and the boat listed sharply as water rushed into its hull, and it began sinking, bow first, into the canal.

The air suddenly filled with the shouts of hundreds of Pandesian soldiers, suddenly upside down, sliding down the deck, falling into the waters. The ship nearly vertical, there was little to stop their fall, and those holding weapons dropped them, sending them falling harmlessly straight down into the waters. Men shrieked as some fell a hundred feet, from the stern to the bow, breaking ribs, then landing in water. They flailed like ants as they splashed in their armor, their great ship shattering to pieces all around them.

The people of Ur, realizing, let out a jubilant shout of joy, as they all rushed forward toward the canal's edge.

"ATTACK!" her father yelled.

His men rushed forward, leaned over the edge, and threw spears down into the water at the Pandesians, who grabbed onto the sides of the canal and tried to scramble up. Dierdre rushed forward, too, as did all the girls that were with her. She kicked a Pandesian in the face as he reached the surface, sending him backward into the water, while the girls beside her fired arrows. Her father and his men hurled spears, and Dierdre watched as men cried out and the waters turned red.

Dierdre grabbed her spear, tightened her grip, and took aim for the Pandesian commander, bobbing in the water amidst his men, not so proud anymore. She stepped forward, raised her spear, took aim, and threw it. She watched, heart pounding, as it sailed through the air—then had a great feeling of satisfaction as it hit him in the chest. He raised his hands to the sky, fell back, and sank into the waters.

Citizens up and down the harbor grabbed rocks and anything they could find and hurled them down into the water, hitting the hundreds of floating men. One at a time, Pandesians sank, their lifeless bodies filling the canal.

Soon, all was quiet, all that remained the wreckage of the ship and the corpses of hundreds of once-proud soldiers, floating, dead.

A new horn sounded, and it was no longer a horn of danger. This time, it was a horn that had not been sounded in Ur for in Dierdre's lifetime: a horn of victory.

A great shout of jubilation filled the air, and as people embraced her from every side, all embracing each other, jumping up and down on the streets, Dierdre, still stunned, began to process what had just happened. Against all odds, they had managed to destroy a Pandesian warship. Whatever should come, for this one moment in time, they had stood up to them. They had not backed down in the face of the much larger enemy, and they had been rewarded. Victory, for this day, at least, was theirs.

CHAPTER TWENTY SEVEN

Aidan sat amidst the rowdy crowd in the capital square, jostled every which way amidst the masses, so many torches lighting up the walls, it was hard to tell it was night. Beside him sat White, and the two watched, rapt with attention, as they looked up at the stage. The entire crowd was riveted as Motley and his actors kept them laughing. Shouts and laughter filled the air as the joyous crowd pressed close to the stage, Motley standing at the edge of the stage, front and center, his big belly hanging over the edge, eyes wide as he stared out.

"So you want to take our women?" Motley boomed, facing an actor opposite him.

The actor, a head taller than all of them, dressed in golden robes, holding a golden staff, was playing Ra, the ruler of Pandesia, and he played him well as he looked down haughtily at Motley.

"I DECLARE IT!" boomed the actor.

The crowd booed, and Motley stepped closer to him, defiant.

"And why do you want to take them?" Motley countered. "To make them Pandesian women? And what is the virtue in being a Pandesian woman? There is no virtue in Pandesian women!"

The crowd laughed and cheered Motley on, as he stepped even closer.

"WE CAN DO AS WE WISH!" Ra boomed. "ESCALON IS OURS! IT WILL ALWAYS BE OURS!"

The crowd booed, and a few of them, Aidan noticed, threw tomatoes at the stage.

"Well," Motley countered, "for a land to be yours, I think you have to hold its capital. And the last time I checked, this capital was free."

A great roar and cheer rose up from the thousands of crowd members, as they all jumped to their feet. A bunch of actors rushed forward from the wings, circled Ur, and stabbed him, and the crowd stomped its feet as the actor collapsed to the stage.

The masses hooted and could not clap loudly enough as the curtain fell. The entire cast came to the edge of the stage and took a bow, to encore after encore. Finally this play, which had gone on for hours, came to a close. Aidan rubbed his eyes, exhausted, while people all around him threw coins onto the stage, the platform filling with gold and silver and bronze from all directions. The players reached down and snatched them up as quickly as they could.

Aidan enjoyed the play, though he didn't fully understand it all, and the parts he did understand he found too simplistic. It was as if they were dumbing it down to appease the masses, and as he looked around at the crude faces and garb, he realized most of these people could likely not read or write. They had not been as lucky as he, to have private tutors all his life, and to be schooled in the ancient scripts. He had hoped for something more complex from this play.

Beside him, White whined, and Aidan draped an arm around him.

"I know, boy," he said. "I'm hungry, too. Let's find Motley."

Aidan, impatient to finally talk to Motley and get help in finding his father, pushed his way through the throng, trying to near the stage. The crowd thickened, but he shoved and weaved his way through until finally he reached the actors, laughing and embracing the crowd, hundreds of people crowding them. He found Motley, sweating, in the center, his cheeks flushed red, taking a swig from a sack of wine and laughing.

Motley spotted Aidan and shoved people out of the way, making room for him.

"Young Aidan!" he called out, reaching out and draping an arm around his shoulder. Aidan was self-conscious as all eyes turned to him, and surprised that Motley cared about him, or even remembered him.

"I need help finding my father," Aidan said. "He's in Southern Square."

Motley laughed.

"Always in a rush, are you!? Always so serious! Your father can wait. You're joining us in the taverns!"

The actors cheered, but Aidan shook his head.

"I haven't time," he insisted. "Besides, I'm too young for the taverns."

Motley laughed.

"I had a sack in my hand when I was half your age!"

The crowd laughed.

163

"Besides," Motley added, "Southern Square is on the far side of Andros. You'd never reach him tonight. This city is too big, and the night too thick. You'll stay with us tonight and I'll bring you there in the morning."

Aidan hesitated, unsure, but as Motley laid a big beefy hand on his shoulder and prodded him on, he found himself ushered through the thick crowd, falling in with the actors. They made their way for the taverns, and Aidan soon entered a low stone building, its doors wide open.

Cheers and shouts met them as they entered the crowded room, all raising a sack toward Motley and the actors. This place was well lit, filled with torches. Aidan was crammed into the tavern, the room perhaps a hundred feet long yet shoulder to shoulder with men, White whining, clearly unhappy. The crowd made way and they soon reached the bar.

***"Two for myself," Motley boomed to the bartender, "two for each of my actor friends, and one for the young lad here."

Aidan held up a hand.

"I do not drink," he replied. "But White is hungry."

"Tonight you do," replied Motley, refusing to take no for an answer.

The bartender threw a slab of meat over the counter and onto the floor, and Aidan was pleased to see White snatch it up and gulp it down. Three overflowing, frothing mugs of ale were then set before them, and Motley took two for himself and placed one in Aidan's hand.

"Take a sip and you'll come to like the taste," Motley said. "Maybe not today, or tomorrow, but one of these years!"

Motley laughed heartily as he chugged both mugs, then slid the empty ones down the bar. Soon, two more came right back at him.

Aidan, feeling all the eyes of the actors on him, was embarrassed to not drink. The froth ran down his hand, and he lifted the mug to his nose and smelled it. He recoiled.

"Smells rotten," he said.

Motley and the actors laughed, and Aidan reddened.

"That is a smell you will come to cherish one day," Motley replied. "Ale is not for smelling, anyway, but for drinking. Go on, now!"

Aidan put the mug to his lips and took a small sip, to appease them all. He swallowed it, gulped, and then ended up in a coughing fit. He wanted to spit it out, it tasted so horrible, but he knew they were all watching.

They all laughed hysterically as Aidan set down the mug, feeling embarrassed, and at the same time feeling light-headed. He did not like the feeling at all.

"Well," Motley said, clapping him on the back. "We all have to start somewhere."

"Enough of this," Aidan demanded, feeling a growing impatience. "I don't want to waste any time here. I need to see my father."

Motley shook his head.

"Daybreak is still hours away, my boy," he replied, "and Andros is vast and wide. If you don't know your way, it could take days to cross one end to the other. You won't find your father at night. Be patient; in the morning, I'll take you to him. This city is no place for a boy to be roaming alone at night anyway. Stay here, and you'll be safe with us."

Aidan sighed, impatient, but realizing Motley had a point. Besides, he was exhausted from the long day; his legs ached, and he could barely keep his eyes open. He wouldn't mind a few hours' rest, and since there was nothing he could do now anyway, he didn't see the harm.

"So tell me," Motley said, turning to him, having finished two more mugs of ale, "what did you think of our play?"

Aidan shrugged, unsure how to respond.

"It was all right," he said.

Motley furrowed his brow.

"Just all right?" he asked, sounding puzzled, and a bit hurt. "Did you not like my performance?"

"Your performance was fine," Aidan replied, unfamiliar with actors and unsure what to say.

"Then what didn't you like?" Motley demanded.

"It's not that I didn't like it," Aidan said, struggling to come up with the words. "It was just that…"

He trailed off, thinking.

"What, then?" Motley prodded.

"Well," Aidan began, "it wasn't…real."

"Real!?" Motley asked. "It was a play!"

"What I mean to say is…I prefer for a play to be about serious things," Aidan replied. "About battle, for instance. And I also prefer to watch a real battle than to watch a play. And I would prefer, most of all, to be *in* that battle. Why waste time with make pretend?"

Motley smiled and shook his head.

"Have you been in many battles, then?" he asked.

Aidan flushed, embarrassed.

"I have heard all the details of all my father's great battles," Aidan replied proudly, "and I can recite them all."

Motley laughed.

"And does that mean you were in battle yourself?" he asked.

Aidan reddened, unsure how to respond. Hearing his father's tales of valor and courage had certainly made him feel as if he had been a part of them; yet as Motley put it that way, he realized he had not.

"One day I will be," Aidan insisted. "One day I will lead an army to battle. I will lead *many* armies into battle!"

Motley smiled wide and shook his head.

"You trade in reality," Motley said, "while we trade in fantasy. Our trade is stronger. More pure. More attainable. Your trade is short, confusing, messy, and lacks resolution. It is also fleeting. Our fantasy, though, lasts forever."

Aidan, between his exhaustion and the ale, had a hard time thinking straight. He yawned again, his eyes closing on him, and felt overwhelmed by all the noise and activity.

"Go upstairs," Motley instructed. "Find a room. Take your dog. Stay the night. At daybreak, I will help you. If I am still sleeping, or too drunk, just wake me."

"But I have no coin," Aidan replied, remembering how he'd given away his sack of gold.

Motley threw a coin on the counter and the barkeep took it and nodded.

"You're taken care of," he replied.

Aidan felt a rush of gratitude toward Motley; despite their opposing views, he had come to like him, and perhaps even to respect him, in his own odd way.

"Is there a chamber pot up there?" he asked, feeling the ale rush to his bladder.

"Not in here," the barkeep said. "Use the alley. That's what we all do."

"Take that dog with you," Motley added. "There are more cutthroats out there than in here—and that's saying much."

Aidan, exhausted, feeling disoriented still from the ale, made his way through the throng and back out the tavern.

He took a deep breath in the fresh night air, quiet out here, the shouting from the tavern now distant behind him. The alleyway was dark, barely lit by torches, and wanting privacy, Aidan headed down it, White at his side.

He turned down another alley, and this one, too, was filled with men peeing. So Aidan continued on, turning down yet another alley, until he found one that was dark and empty.

As Aidan stood against the wall, he suddenly tensed as he heard muffled voices. He looked down the alley and saw two dark figures, about ten feet away in the blackness, and he quickly realized he was witnessing something he was not supposed to. He retreated deeper into the darkness, crouched down, and watched.

There, at the edge of the torchlight, were two men. One looked very distinguishable, a tall man dressed in finery, with a long vertical scar down his left ear, a face was shifty eyes that was hard to forget, a man Aidan had heard the other one refer to as Enis. The other, dressed in royal yellow and blue, could only be a Pandesian lord.

Aidan's heart quickened.

"Show me," Enis demanded.

The Pandesian stepped aside and rolled forward a wheelbarrow. He pulled back a blanket, and Aidan gasped as he saw it filled with glistening gold—more gold than he had ever seen in one place.

Enis stepped forward and ran his hands through it, the gold clinking as it rained down in the torchlight. He finally turned and nodded to the Pandesian.

"He's yours," Enis said.

The Pandesian smiled.

"No mistakes," the Pandesian said. "Duncan dies. He and all his men."

Aidan's heart pounded as he heard his father's name.

Enis smiled back.

167

"We share the same goal," he replied. "You needn't worry."

"Good," Enis replied. "Then here's to the new King."

Enis smiled wide.

Aidan, aghast, suddenly stepped back—and as he did, he knocked over a piece of metal and it clanged in the alley. They both turned and looked his way.

"You, boy, stop!" Enis called out.

Aidan turned and ran, White beside him, and he immediately heard footsteps pursuing him.

He turned down alleyway after alleyway, running as fast as his little legs could take him, and as he ducked through a small stone arch he knew they couldn't pass through, finally he felt relieved. He turned and continued to run, knowing he had lost them.

Yet still, he was frantic. He thought of his father, of the death coming for him, and he knew he could not wait one more minute. He kept running, and running, and he knew, no matter what, he could not stop. Somehow, he had to find his father, had to warn him. He would run all through the night if he had to, all through this city, until he found his father and saved him—before it was too late.

CHAPTER TWENTY EIGHT

Kyra stared back at the boy's face, mesmerized, the face from which she could not look away. She felt lost in his crystal blue eyes, the long, light blond hair framing it, the perfect chiseled features, the boy not entirely of this world, staring back as if he had known her forever. She felt those eyes penetrating her soul, felt the earth shifting beneath her, and she looked down to see that she was floating at sea, standing on a wide raft, the boy standing on the other end. She couldn't understand what was happening, where she was, where they were floating to. But she knew they were floating together, the two of them in the midst of a vast sea, with nothing but each other.

"Kyra," he said.

His voice penetrated her heart, a voice which she somehow recognized, a voice she knew she had always been longing to hear.

"Who are you?" she asked, breathless.

He stared back, expressionless, the intensity in his gaze overwhelming her as he held out a single hand. He reached for her face, and more than anything, she craved for that hand to touch her face, yearned to feel the touch of his fingertips on her skin.

But suddenly, he fell backwards, straight into the water, stiff as a board, landing with a quiet splash and disappearing beneath the waves.

She rushed forward, horrified.

"No!" she cried.

She dove into the water to save him—yet no sooner had she jumped when she felt claws on her back, grabbing her shirt, hoisting her into the air. She heard a screech behind her, and suddenly, she was flying, being carried, she realized, by something greater than herself.

Kyra glanced up, and her heart quickened to see Theos above her, holding her as he flew, his great wings flapping. He flew her over the sea, and as she looked down, she was shocked to see a sea of black. Beneath her was a fleet of ships, greater than any she could imagine; they were flying so close her feet grazed the top of the masts. It was a fleet meant for an invasion, and flying the royal blue and yellow of Pandesia.

Kyra passed over one ship after another, and the fleet seemed to stretch to the end of the world. She knew in her heart where they were heading, and the thought pained her. They were going to destroy Escalon. She watched as the ships launched flaming boulders from catapults, raining fire for her land. Explosions shook the ground as massive boulders, aflame, rocked Escalon, and the entire land turned to flame.

There, she was amazed to see, in the midst of the flames, stood a single boy, with his long hair and blue eyes. He stood there, so noble, so unafraid, staring up at her even as the fire fell all around him. He was, she knew, the last man left in Escalon, and as the dragon dropped Kyra, she suddenly shrieking as she flailed through the air. She found herself falling, reaching right for him.

"NO!" Kyra shrieked.

Kyra woke with a start, breathing hard, disoriented. She felt a tongue on her cheek and sat up to find Leo, beside her. She looked out her hut and saw Andor chewing grass, lit up in the rays of the early morning sun, and she remembered. The woods. Ur. She was still training.

She rubbed her head. It had all been a dream, one long, horrific dream. And yet it had felt so real. Who was that boy? She remembered the day before, in the forest glen, when he had saved her, and she felt it had been more than a chance meeting—there had been something special between them, something beyond her understanding. And the dream—it had felt too real. Had the boy visited her in her dreams? Was disaster coming for Escalon?

Kyra jumped to her feet, agitated, and burst out of her hut, into the forest clearing, determined to find out.

"Kyra!" a strong voice called.

Kyra turned and was startled to see, standing there in the early morning dawn, her uncle Kolva. He stood tall and proud, a serious expression on his face, and she stared back, wondering. He had not visited her since he had led her to this place, and he was the last person she had expected to find here.

"Where is Alva? Has he left?" she asked, alarmed as she looked about the clearing and could not find him. She felt a sudden pit in her stomach. "Did I fail him? Was he disappointed in me?"

"I do not know the ways of Alva," Kolva replied. "I never understood him, even when I trained with him. *Disappointed*...I do not think that is a term which would apply to him. There is always a reason for his departure—and it is always part of the training."

Kyra felt a sense of dread.

"Will he return?" she asked, hesitant.

"I do not know," he replied. "Sometimes he is challenging you to look within; sometimes he feels his presence is a distraction; sometimes he demands you train yourself."

Kyra stared back, wondering, sensing that Kolva was withholding something from her.

"Yet you haven't come here to discuss Alva," she said, realizing. "I sense there is something else."

Kolva slowly nodded, grim.

"Yes," he said flatly. Then he fell silent.

"I had an encounter yesterday," she recalled. "I was nearly killed by a Pandesian. A boy saved me, a boy I do not know. A boy with long golden hair."

She watched a flicker of disapproval cross her uncle's face, and her heart raced.

"You know him," she said, realizing. Then, in a rush, she asked, "What is his name?"

"Kyle," he answered flatly.

Kyle. Somehow, Kyra already knew.

"Who is he?" she pressed, sensing her uncle didn't want to discuss it, but needing to know.

"He is a Watcher," he finally replied, reluctant. "He lives in the tower."

Kyra's eyes widened.

"The Tower of Ur?" she asked. "I wish to see him."

Her uncle's face hardened as he shook his head.

"You may not," he said, the firmness in his voice surprising her.

"Why?" she demanded.

"He is not of your race," he said. "It is forbidden. He was never supposed to see you. I do not know why this happened. He shall be reprimanded upon my return."

Kyra was aghast.

"Reprimanded?" she asked. "He saved my life. Does that count for nothing?"

"It counts for a great deal. But there are laws which cannot be broken. Ancient laws. Sacred laws."

"What laws, Uncle?" she snapped, impatient.

He sighed, impatient too.

"I have not come here to talk of Kyle," he said. "Do not speak of him again."

There came a long, tense silence as Kyra stared back, fuming.

"You are not my father," she finally replied, seething.

"And yet I have come here on his business."

She stared back, wondering.

"I have come to end your training," he said.

She raised her eyebrows, shocked.

"End it? It has not even begun!"

He shook his head.

"It matters not," he replied. "There is no time. Pandesia comes. Scouts close in. That is why you were spotted and attacked. You were lucky; behind that soldier lie a thousand more—all looking for you. It will only be a matter of days until they overrun Escalon and we are surrounded. You must retreat with me, at once, into the tower. We prepare a defense."

Kyra wondered if that meant she would see Kyle.

"Kyle will be on a different floor," Kolva continued uncannily, reading her mind. "Do not worry, you will never see him. Come at once."

Kyra stood there, facing her uncle head on, and felt a strength welling within her, the same strength that had driven her to want to become a warrior, to cross Escalon alone.

"No," she finally replied, defiant.

He stood there, looking stunned.

"I am your uncle," he said firmly.

"There are many authorities in my life," she replied. "And I've learned that I don't need to answer to any of them. I have not completed my training, and I don't quit. Not with my father out there needing me."

"Kyra," he said, his tone softening. "I am trying to protect you, don't you see?"

"I don't seek your protection, or anyone else's. I seek only to train, and to learn how to protect myself."

Her uncle stood, seeming unsure what to do.

"Your mother would not approve of this," he finally said.

Kyra felt her heart beat faster at the word. *Mother*. She could not help but be curious.

"When the time is right," he added, "I will tell you everything about her."

"I don't believe you," she finally replied.

"Kyra, we have no time," he said, exasperated. "Come with me now."

But she stood her ground and shook her head.

"Don't you see, Uncle?" she asked. "Death has never frightened me. Only not living with valor."

Kolva stared at her for a long time, then finally, seeing the resolve in her eyes, he turned and disappeared back into the trees, leaving Kyra all alone in this vast wood. She felt more alone than she'd ever had in her life.

Theos, she thought. *Where are you?*

CHAPTER TWENTY NINE

Vesuvius sprinted across the countryside, amazed to feel Escalon grass beneath his feet, amazed that he was actually standing on this ground he had dreamt of his entire life. Here he was, in the promised land, south of The Flames, the land his ancestors had only dreamt of, the land they had sung songs of, had planned raids for—the land that had always been just out of reach.

And now, here he was, the most triumphant of all his ancestors, the only one who had been able to achieve the dream. He was the one, as the prophecies had declared, who was destined to rule. Never in his life had he stepped foot in a land other than Marda, and he was enjoying himself beyond his wildest dreams. Already, he had led his army through the first village he'd found, murdering and torturing everyone in sight.

As he ran across the plains, Vesuvius delighted in the memory. He was still covered in fresh blood, and he smiled wide as he thought back to all the women and children and animals he had murdered. Torturing them, these humans who had deprived him of his dream all these years, had given him a pleasure he would never forget. Burning that village to the ground, seeing it as a pile of ashes, warmed his heart. He thought of all the other villages and towns and cities left to ransack in Escalon, and he knew it was just the beginning. Soon all of Escalon would be at his feet.

Vesuvius's initial impulse, after emerging from the tunnel, was to turn and head for the Tower of Ur, to steal the Sword of Fire; but first, he had another, more pressing, desire. He had always dreamt of seeing The Flames from the other side. He wanted to stand there and see what it felt like to be looking north, toward Marda. More than that, he wanted vengeance. He wanted each and every human who stood watch at The Flames, who had killed so many of his people, to pay. He wanted them dead first. He knew they would never expect an attack from behind, and he could not wait to see the look on their faces when he surprised them, pinned between an army of trolls and a wall of fire. He smiled wide, seeing it now: he would stab them in the backs as they ran face-first into fire. He might not be able to lower The Flames—at least not until he reached the Tower of Ur and stole the Sword of Flames—but in the meantime, at least, he could slaughter every last man that dared stand watch before them. That would teach them to dare guard the borders of Marda.

Vesuvius increased his speed, his legs burning as he ran up and down hills, his army of trolls on his heels. He held his halberd tightly as he ran, hardly even winded, as he, like most of the troll race, had enough strength to run for miles, to never lose his breath. He would use that natural strength to his advantage. Soon enough, his trolls would spread across every last corner of Escalon. As he ran, Vesuvius took note of places and decided where he would build new cities, how he would rename them, where he would raise statues to himself. He would enslave this human race, build mining factories, create great pits of fire where he could torture men and women for his pleasure. He could hardly wait.

Hours passed, and as Vesuvius finally crested a hill, emerging from a long stretch of woods, he stopped, amazed at the sight before him. There, but a hundred yards away, stood the roaring Flames, so bright, so tall, so magnificent that they nearly blinded him. He could feel their heat from here, could hear them crackling. He had never anticipated what they would look like from this perspective. It was awe-inspiring.

And there below, unsuspecting, were the human guards, spread out, standing guard at the flames, facing north. Never could they have suspected that their enemy was, after all, to the south.

"TROLLS OF MARDA!" he cried. "ATTACK!"

There came a great shout behind him as the troll nation cried out. They raised their halberds and their shouts echoed over the hills.

Vesuvius waited and watched, savoring the moment, as the hundreds of humans standing guard at The Flames slowly turned and looked up. He watched their expressions change to bewilderment—and then, to terror. Their backs to The Flames, these humans had nowhere to run.

Vesuvius shouted and charged. Leading his nation, he ran down the hill with delight, the flames growing brighter, their heat stronger. His heart pounded with glee as he raised his halberd high and set his sights on an unsuspecting boy, hardly eighteen, who gaped and dropped his sword in terror. Vesuvius reached him, brought his hatchet down across his chest, and hacked him in two.

All around him there came the delightful sound of blades puncturing flesh, of humans shrieking in terror as the trolls slaughtered them. Most were too panic-stricken to even put up a fight, and the few who tried were murdered instantly. As his army overcame them like a wave of death, the remaining humans turned and actually ran for The Flames, preferring death by fire to death by the trolls. The air filled with the shouts of humans, the smell of their burning flesh, as one by one, they all, these Keepers of the Flames, the elite of the human warriors, were killed.

Vesuvius leaned back and looked to the sky, grinning wide, relishing this greatest moment of his life. Covered in blood, holding his halberd, itching for more death, he shouted up with joy to the skies. This was all, he knew, just the beginning. There was nothing left to stop him.

Finally, Escalon would be his.

CHAPTER THIRTY

Theos flew above Escalon, breathing fire and never ceasing as he left a scar across Escalon that would last forever. His rage was unending, and he was determined not to stop until this land that had stolen his egg had been destroyed.

As he laced the land with flame again and again, flying back and forth, taking out entire swaths of wood at once, suddenly, he heard it. It was a noise, audible to him even amidst his destruction, so primal, so close to his soul, that it made him lift up into the skies, cease his flames, and listen.

It came again.

And again.

Vesuvius felt a thrill as he recognized the cry. There was no mistaking it: it was a dragon's cry. A baby dragon. He knew he was hearing, for the first time, the cry of his son.

Theos turned and flew with urgency, the sound unmistakable, filling his heart with hope. He flew low, peering down, determined, his entire body electrified. His child was screaming for help. Screaming for him.

Theos increased his speed, flying faster than he'd ever had in his life, covering miles of Escalon in a single flap. He flew over hills, rivers, forests. His child, he could sense, was close. So close.

Slowly, far below, Theos began to see it. There was the outline of a sprawling stone building, a fort, flying a flag of blue and yellow. Inside it scurried thousands of Pandesian soldiers, like ants, and there, in the center of the fort, was a sight that tore his heart to pieces.

His baby.

There was his baby dragon, tied to a stake in the center of the stone courtyard, bound by ropes and shrieking. Crying for him. All around him were Pandesian soldiers, wielding long pikes, jabbing at him, piercing his tiny flesh. With each poke, Theos's child shrieked in agony, and with each jab, Theos's fury deepened. It built inside him like a volcano, until his rage crossed a tipping point. He was ready to destroy the world.

Theos felt a rage unlike he'd ever felt, a rage that blinded him. He dove down with blinding speed, barely thinking as he opened his mouth and prepared to breathe fire, to incinerate these humans. He knew even as he did that he could not risk breathing fire onto his own child.

Theos breathed fire in a great circle, scorching the periphery of the courtyard, burning alive dozens of soldiers at once. He dove lower, his great wings flapping, knocking off chunks of wall, debris falling and crushing more men. He flew right past his child, nearly grazing him, and then circled around again, wanting to kill all the men around him before rescuing him.

Theos dove again, claws extended, and swiped and killed the fleeing soldiers, clawing them to death as they ran from his child. He snatched their pikes from their hands and snapped them in two, then he dove even lower and sank his great teeth into men's backs as they ran. He bit one soldier, flew up in the air with him, and shook his head until he fell to the ground in pieces.

Theos circled again, coming even lower this time, low enough to rescue his son. He smashed through more chunks of wall, destroying the fort, and it felt good. He flew lower than he ever had, lower than he was accustomed to, aiming right for his child. He would free him from the stake, and then, with his son on his back, circle around and kill any remaining soldiers.

As Theos neared, already anticipating the joy of having his child on his back, suddenly, he felt an unfamiliar feeling. He felt a tug at his wings, and he suddenly felt them constrained. He looked over, confused, and he saw, wrapping around his wings, thick ropes of reinforced steel, suddenly descending upon him from every direction. He looked up and saw more ropes, and he realized, too late, that he was flying into a net. Hundreds of Pandesians suddenly rushed forward and cast the net upon him, and he realized that they had been waiting for him to fly lower.

It had been a trap.

Theos suddenly felt his wings constricted, collapsing in on his body; he felt his great claws entangled, restrained, and he was no longer able to fly, to keep control. Unable to stay airborne, he suddenly felt himself diving straight down—and a moment later he crashed headfirst into the rock and dirt, taking out a stone wall as he slid and tumbled and rolled, still entangled, until he finally came to a grinding stop.

Theos, in agony, tried to break free—but could not. He writhed but felt himself restrained on all sides by the steel rope, clinging to his flesh, held tight by hundreds of soldiers, who soon closed in on him. And then, a moment later, he felt it: agony. His skin being pierced.

He shrieked out in pain as soldiers encircled him, long, glistening pikes in hand, and punctured his flesh. First one. Then another.

Then another.

Theos felt himself being pierced hundreds of times, from every direction. He was bleeding heavily, and with each jab he felt himself growing weaker. His struggling was useless.

Soon, Theos felt the great light, the one that had burned within him for thousands of years, beginning to fade. He knew he was dying. Because of his love for his child, he had let down his guard—and he had made the greatest mistake of his life.

Another stab came. Then another. In too much pain to think, he felt his great eyes begin to close on him. And as he had his final thoughts, oddly enough, they were of Kyra. Of what had almost been. He thought of her destiny, of how close they had come. Now, she would be all alone.

Now, it was too late.

CHAPTER THIRTY ONE

Kyra sat alone at dawn, atop the highest ridge overlooking the forest, perched atop a boulder, Leo and Andor nearby, her legs crossed, her palms facing the sky, as Alva had taught her. She breathed, her attention on her breath, and tried to focus. Becoming very still, hearing the crash of the ocean waves in the distance, she tried to reach the place of an empty mind.

Kyra desperately tried to summon a power which she wanted so badly to summon. She craved to complete her training, to become more powerful than she'd ever been, to feel once again the power she'd tasted in brief flashes of her life. She tried to recall the time she summoned Theos, how it had felt.

Yet try as she did, nothing worked. Alva's words rang in her head.

You wish to control the universe. But the universe controls you. Just for one second, let go of wanting to control everything around you. Let yourself be engulfed by it. It is a great tide, greater than you.

Kyra closed her eyes, took a deep breath, and stopped trying. For just a second, she stopped trying to mold the universe to her wishes, stopped trying to achieve. Instead, she let go of wanting to summon her powers; she let go of wanting to complete her quest; she let go of wanting her father's approval, of wanting her own approval, of wanting to be the best. For just one single moment, she allowed herself to be good enough, exactly as she was. She let the universe take over her, like a flood, allowed it to control her.

As Kyra sat there in the silence, breathing in and out, paying attention to her breath, slowly, an odd thing began to happen: she began to find herself in a place of deep calm. She found herself traveling deeper, through layers of calm, a calm deeper than any she'd ever experienced. She realized Alva had been right: she had been trying so hard to get ahead, to gain approval, to be the best. And trying, she realized, meant *lacking*. People who achieved did not want or crave or try. They already had it. She had to reach the place, internally, where she already had it. Then it would materialize in the outside world.

Kyra realized she lived with an iron grip clenching her stomach, driving her to always want to be the best, to prove herself. She was too driven, and it ran her life. Perhaps it was because she was a girl in a fort full of men, or perhaps it was because she wanted her father's approval so badly. Yet in order to achieve all that she wanted, she realized, she had to finally stop craving it. She had to allow it to come to her. Most of all, she had to appreciate and accept herself *in this moment*. Appreciate and accept that regardless of what would come, she was good enough, at this very moment, *exactly as she was*.

Kyra, lost in her mind, did not know how much time had passed when she felt a warmth begin to course over her body. She felt the universe begin to melt around her, and she began to feel the universe embrace her, accept her. As she did, she felt all her tension release. She entered such a deep state of calm, of focus, that she began to sense a new feeling stir inside her. It was a sense of clarity. A sense of new doors opening. A sense of inhabiting a place she had never inhabited before. It was a new power, always just out of her reach, slowly coming to her.

Kyra opened her eyes very slowly, shocked to see that it was sunset, and as she did, she turned to see Leo and Andor begin to walk away from her, cautiously, as if afraid. It was as if they sensed something had shifted within her.

She opened her eyes more, and as she did, she knew she was no longer the same person. She knew she had summoned her innate power—and that it was stronger than it had ever been. Alva had been right all along. She had been wrong about him; despite her skepticism, he had been her greatest teacher of all.

Kyra looked down at the forest below, and, wanting to test her power, focused on a branch. She directed the power within her, and a moment later, the branch snapped off the tree and flew to the forest floor.

Emboldened, needing to test her power further, Kyra heard running water, looked over at a stream, and silently ordered it to stop. It suddenly ceased, its water stopping, its bed running dry. She could feel the pent-up energy of the water, rising high as she stopped it, creating a wall. She released it in her mind, and it began to flow again.

Kyra, feeling more powerful than ever, looked far below at a huge, fallen tree, lying on its side on the forest floor. She willed it to stand upright again. She watched, heart aflutter, as the tree slowly rose, creaking with a great noise. She felt its great strength within her as it rose, its leaves rustling. Birds and squirrels scurried out of the way as it finally reached its full height, standing tall once again.

Kyra felt an unbelievable, limitless power coursing through her, like a river she couldn't stop. She felt more powerful than a thousand men, felt as if there were nothing in this world she could not achieve. She closed her eyes, elated, taking a deep breath and letting it out, feeling a great sense of victory. She had reached the summit. She did not know if it was the highest summit, and she did not know if it would last forever, or ever come again. But for now, for this moment, her powers were undeniable. They were real.

She knew, finally, that she was special. She knew, finally, that the prophecies were true: she did have a special destiny.

Kyra closed her eyes and took a deep breath, wanting to go deeper. She needed to know more. She sensed that all the answers to her life lay right before her, secrets about her mother, her destiny, all of it lingering at the edge of her mind's eye. She felt her palms grow hotter and hotter, felt the tingling between her eyes, and she breathed for a long time in the silence, sensing it was coming.

Caressed by ocean breezes, Kyra became lost in the silence for she did not know how long, until finally a vision flashed before her. It was so vivid, it felt as if it were real.

Theos. She saw him, soaring high in the sky, circling Escalon. Then, suddenly, she felt a pain in her stomach as she watched him shriek and fall from the sky, entangled in a net of steel. Kyra watched with horror as she saw him land face-first in the dirt. She felt his pain as he lay there, immobile, and watched as soldiers approached and punctured him on all sides with pikes. She felt the pain within her own body, as if she were being punctured, too, and she cried out involuntarily as she watched him close his eyes, suffering, and die.

Kyra gasped. She wanted to turn it off, to open her eyes and run—but the universe had more to show her, and it would not let her go.

Another vision came to her. She saw her father, in the vast capital of Andros. He was in a courtyard, at dawn, surrounded by soldiers. Soldiers he did not know or trust. Thousands of them. They encircled him on all sides. She saw the yellow and blue of Pandesia, and she watched as their commander stepped forward and raised his sword to thrust it through her father's heart.

Kyra gasped and opened her eyes, unable to stand it anymore. She jumped off the boulder and took off at a sprint down the ridge, through the forest, followed by Leo and Andor, scratched by branches and not caring. She sprinted all the way back to the clearing, desperate for answers, desperate to shake these nightmares from her mind, desperate to find Alva.

Kyra finally stopped before his hut, gasping—but she looked up and saw it sat empty. She was crestfallen.

"Alva!" Kyra cried out, her voice echoing in the woods. "Where are you?"

"I am everywhere and nowhere," came a soft voice.

Kyra turned and was shocked to see Alva standing in the clearing behind her, holding a staff, staring back calmly.

She approached him, still breathing hard, frantic from her vision.

"Theos!" she cried out, her words stumbling out. "He's dead!"

She was looking for confirmation, wondering if she were crazy, and she expected Alva to be frantic, too. She hoped more than anything that he would tell her that she was mad.

But Alva remained calm and merely nodded back, expressionless.

"He is," he said matter-of-factly—and those two words were like two nails on her heart.

She let out an involuntary cry.

"How can it be!?" she demanded, feeling the world fall out from under her.

Theos, the dragon she could summon, the beast that was meant to give her and her father dominion over Escalon, dead.

"You stand there with no emotion!" she yelled. "What is wrong with you!? Theos! My dragon! He is dead! The beast that could not die is dead!"

Kyra felt more vulnerable than she'd ever had.

"He was never yours, Kyra," Alva replied calmly. "His company was a gift, bestowed upon you for only a short while."

She stood there, reeling, trying to process it all.

"But…I don't understand. I saved him. Was it all for nothing!?"

Alva stared back, his blue eyes piercing.

"Did you save him?" he asked calmly. "Or did he save you?"

She thought about that, struggling to understand.

"If he's dead…" she continued, "we have nothing. I…am nothing."

Alva shook his head.

"Quite wrong, Kyra," he replied. "In fact, you are something far greater."

She fought back tears as she tried to recall her entire vision. She tried to listen to Alva, but it was hard to focus, her vision still hanging over her like a cloud. She had pulled back the veil, and she had not liked what she had seen.

"My father," she added, remembering. "He is surrounded. Betrayed."

She stared at Alva, hoping, praying he would tell her her vision was false.

But he nodded back.

"He is," he confirmed.

Kyra closed her eyes, feeling herself collapsing inside. The thought of her father out there, betrayed, alone, surrounded, without her being able to help him, tore her to pieces.

"They will kill him," she said.

"They will," he replied.

Despite herself, she began to cry.

"I must save him!" she cried out.

Without thinking, Kyra rushed across the clearing and mounted Andor.

"If you go, you will die."

Alva's voice rang out from across the clearing, and she turned and stared back, wiping tears from her eyes, the gravity of his tone striking her heart.

"You are not ready," he added. "Your training is unfinished. Your powers you are just beginning to know. If you leave now, you will die, too."

Kyra shook her head, refusing to listen.

"I cannot remain here while I know my father is going to die," she insisted, her voice rising in determination. "If I stay, what kind of daughter would I be? I would be dead to myself."

He shook his head.

"You have no dominion over others' fate," he replied. "But you can control your power. That is what your father would want. If you leave now, before you're finished, you will have nothing."

"I may fail," she replied, steeling herself with resolve. "But if I fail, I will know that I have died in the only cause that matters."

She grabbed the reins and prepared to kick, when his voice rang out once again.

"You make a very profound choice, Kyra," he said. "A choice that will shape your destiny. A choice that will shape the future of Escalon for generations to come. Don't go, Kyra. You will die."

But she sat there, on Andor, her back to him, resolved.

"There are worse things than death," she replied. "Like living life a coward."

Without another word, Kyra galloped off into the woods, Leo at her side, heading south toward the capital, toward her father. She prayed only that it was not too late.

Father, she prayed silently. *Let us die together. Wait for me.*

CHAPTER THIRTY TWO

Alec walked through the forge, amazed at how many people had flocked here since the downing of the Pandesian warship. It seemed as if the entire city of Ur was out in force, had all come together to prepare for the coming war. With no room left in here, people even spilled out of the forge, onto the streets, filling the courtyards, the sounds of hammers striking filling the air, as more weapons and shields and armor were produced than Alec could even keep track of. It had become a factory of war.

Sparks flew everywhere as Alec walked through, inspecting it all, the sound of molten steel hissing in his ears as he passed the vats, passing through clouds of steam. He adjusted people's work as he went and most importantly, he overlooked the lengths of chain being forged, now laid out on all the tables, the spikes being affixed every few feet.

After his success, they were all in a mad rush to replicate his chains and create as many new ones as they could. The citizens of Ur were now determined to lace their canals with traps, to stop the invasion, and to take out as many ships as they could. The entire Pandesian fleet would arrive soon, forcing them to finish several months' worth of work in a few days. Rows of entire tables were devoted to assembling chains, hundreds of feet of chain-link being dragged through the doors, forged into iron spikes, and dragged out again.

Alec was elated, still buzzing from the thrill of taking down that ship. His contraption had energized the entire city, and as he worked, he could feel his family smiling down, urging him to work harder. Since the death of his family, Alec finally felt a reason to go on living. There were still, after all, many more Pandesians left to kill.

Alec reached Dierdre's table, and he paused and watched. She pounded away at a sword, surrounded by her girls, all working equally hard, hammering relentlessly, as if hammering a Pandesian. Clearly, she had a vendetta to fulfill.

He was mesmerized by her. He thought back to her defiant stand against Pandesia, and his heart welled with pride. He reached over and gently touched her hand, guiding it, and she stopped and

186

withdrew it as if she'd been touched by a snake. He felt embarrassed, having forgotten how guarded she was.

"I meant no offense," he said, raising his palms. "I'm just adjusting your blow. You see the blade there? You must turn it just so. Otherwise it shall be dull."

She examined it, turned it, and pounded again, sparks flying. She did not thank him or look back at him again.

Alec, wanting to know more about her, to create a connection, did not give up. He took a seat beside her, wanting to try again.

"You do fine work," he said. "Better than most of the boys here."

She did not look up, but kept her eyes fixed angrily at the sword beneath her.

He did not think she would respond, but finally, she spoke:

"It's easy when you have a cause," she replied.

He wondered about the depths of what she had been through.

"And what is your cause?" he asked.

"To kill them all."

Alec understood; yet he also was taken aback by the depth of anger.

"I admire the stand you took for our people in the harbor," he said.

"I didn't do it for them," she replied, her voice hard. "I did it for me."

"Even so," he persisted, "it was your courage that gave our city courage."

She continued to hammer, not looking at him.

"I would have gladly died before they took me," she replied. "It was no ploy."

"I have no doubt," he replied. "I can see it in your eyes."

She still ignored him, and he was beginning to get the message that she did not like him. She stayed silent for so long that he was about to get up and leave, when suddenly she spoke again.

"I admire what you did," she replied. "With the chain and spikes. It was a fine thing for our city."

He smiled, his heart beating faster that she took an interest in him.

"Nothing gave me greater pleasure," he replied.

She turned and looked at him for the first time, and she seemed to soften a bit.

"And where are you from?"

He paused, looking away, suddenly feeling a pang of homesickness, unsure how to answer.

"I'm from here now," he said.

She studied him, seeming interested for the first time.

"And before?" she pressed.

"A small village," he replied, unable to disguise his remorse. "I am sure you have never heard of it. And now it is no more."

She seemed to sense something, and she asked: "And your family?"

Alec slowly shook his head, fighting back tears, and for the first time Dierdre's expression took on a look of compassion.

"I am sorry," she finally said.

A long, shared silence fell between them, each of them understanding.

"And you?" he asked. "Where are you from?"

"Right here."

"Ur?" he asked, surprised.

She nodded.

"Until my father gave me away. The Pandesians took me away, and I journeyed back."

"Journeyed?" he asked, shocked, his awe of her deepening. "If you managed to escape from the Pandesians, I suspect it was no mere journey."

Alec felt a growing sense of compassion for her, as he began to realize what she had been through. So many questions rushed to his mind, but he fell silent, not wanting to pry. He wasn't sure what to say.

"Well, that's all behind us now, isn't it?" he said.

"In some ways," she replied, returning to her pounding.

He watched her hammering away and wondered what to say to her; after all, he felt the same tragedy which she did, and he did not know what to say to himself.

"We can't fix the past," he admitted, thinking. "But maybe...we can change the future."

"I *will* change the future," she replied, and he was surprised by the fierce determination in her voice. "I will kill every last one of them."

"I don't doubt that you will," he replied. "But have you asked yourself, when all the killing is done, then what?"

That question had been nagging at him, too. He kept wondering to himself: after he killed them all, then what? It would never bring back his family. Would his suffering ever go away?

"Do you think it will take away your pain?" Alec asked.

She shook her head.

"No," she said. "But maybe, if I can change the future enough, maybe it can help the past. It won't make it disappear. But maybe it can make it…morph to something else."

"Maybe," he said. "Besides, the future is all we have, isn't it?" He paused. "Maybe it's better to have suffered," he added, "better to have tragedy than to never have any at all. It gives you strength, strength that you need. That's what my father used to say."

"Do you believe that?" she asked, setting down her hammer.

He shrugged.

"I don't know. Tragedy sucks. But I am stronger. More than that—I am changed. I am a different person than I was. Not just older. But deeper. Deeper inside. I have become something more, something I never would have become. I can't explain it, really."

The door to the forge suddenly opened and in walked a tall man dressed in a foreign, elegant garb, scarlet silks draped over his shoulder despite the heat, wearing a cape with an insignia and from a country which Alec did not recognize. He looked different from the others, with an elongated faced, flashing green eyes, a short, brown beard, a scar across his ear, and a mysterious, aristocratic countenance. He scanned the room and stopped and stared at Alec.

Alec had no idea who he could be. Was he another volunteer? His dress seemed too elegant.

The wooden floor creaked beneath his large boots as he crossed the room and stopped before him. He reached out and laid a surprisingly firm hand on his shoulder.

"I've come in search of a sword," the man said, his voice thick with a foreign accent Alec had never heard before.

"You wish to fight the Pandesians?" Alec asked him.

The man nodded.

"That, I do."

Alec reached over, took one of his freshly forged swords off the table, and handed it to him.

The man held it up and examined it, weighing it in both hands.

"Fine work," he said in his thick accent. But then, to Alec's surprise, he set it down disapprovingly.

"I need more than this."

"More?" Alec asked, puzzled.

"Come," he replied. "I will show you."

The man suddenly turned and, as quickly as he had entered, exited the forge.

Alec watched him go, baffled, and he turned and looked at Dierdre, hoping she would shed some light. But she had her head down, busy with her work. Alec knew he had much work to do here, but the mystery of the man tugged at him, and he had to know more.

Alec followed the man the forge, leaving it to be tended by the others. He emerged into the packed street, sunlight temporarily blinding him, and, as he spotted the man walking quickly into the crowd, he went after him.

Alec followed him through the bustling streets, barely keeping pace. Luckily this man was a head taller than the others—otherwise, he would have lost him.

"Who are you?" Alec called, rushing to catch up. "Where are you going?"

The man did not slow, but twisted and turned through the bustling streets until he headed toward one of the massive watchtowers that towered over Ur, facing the sea.

Alec hurried to catch up as the man headed inside.

"Where are you going?" Alec called out, puzzled. "I haven't time!"

"Follow me and you shall know," he called back, then disappeared inside.

Alec glanced back toward the forge, debating, annoyed. Then, curiosity getting the better of him, he realized he had come all this way and wanted to know what this was about. He sensed there was something special about this man, and he needed to know more.

Alec followed. He stepped inside the dim, cool watchtower, made entirely of stone, and as his eyes adjusted he looked up and spotted the man ascending a circular stone staircase. Alec followed, hurrying up flight after flight, his legs burning, trying to catch up with him. The stranger was surprisingly fast for such a tall man, and it was not until he finally reached the top that Alec, breathless, caught up with him.

Alec emerged to a rooftop and as he looked past the man, who stood with his back to him, he was in awe of the sight. From up here he could see all of Ur, stretched out beneath him, and beyond that, the limitless horizon and ocean. A strong gale hit him, and he felt as if he were on top of the world.

He looked around, saw nothing up here but this man, and he started to wonder if this were all some sort of trick.

"What am I doing up here?" Alec demanded, still catching his breath.

"Come here and see what I see," the man said, his back still to him.

Alec followed as the man walked to the edge, and as he stood beside him, laying his hands on the short stone wall, and studied the horizon, Alec gasped. The sight made his heart plummet. There, before him, the Sea of Sorrow was filled with black. The entire Pandesian fleet filled the horizon, a line of black which stretched as far as he could see. It seemed to cover the entire world.

"A million ships strong," the man observed flatly. "All sailing for Ur."

He turned and faced Alec, grim.

"And you think a few chains and spikes will stop them all?" he asked.

Alec felt a pit in his stomach as he studied the horizon and knew the man was right. He felt helpless, as if death were coming for them all and there was nothing he could do about it.

"They will stop enough of them," Alec responded, unconvincingly.

"Will a few swords and shields hold back an army that has conquered the world?" the man asked.

Alec sighed, exasperated.

"What would you have us do?" he snapped. "Fold our hands and give up?"

The man turned and fixed his flashing green eyes upon him, so intense that it gave Alec a chill. He seemed other-worldly.

"I have not come all the way here for your steel," the man said. "I have come for you."

"*Me*?" Alec asked, baffled. "Why?"

The man stared back at him.

"You are the last hope," he replied. "Your destiny is written."

Alec was so stunned, he hardly knew what to say. *Destiny?*

"I think you have the wrong person," he finally said, not understanding. "I'm just another boy from a small village. I have no destiny. I have nothing."

The man slowly shook his head.

"You are quite wrong," he replied. "You have far more than that—and you don't even know it."

The man studied him, and Alec did not know what to think.

"You can remain here," the man continued, "with your shields and swords and chains. You can wait and be murdered with all the others. Or you can come with me, and have a true chance to defeat Pandesia."

"Come with you!?" Alec asked, flabbergasted. "Where!?"

The man looked down and Alec saw a lone ship, with a red and green sail, docked by the canals. Alec looked back at the man, but he had already turned and walked away, heading back to the stairs.

"I don't even know who you are!" Alec called out after him.

But the man, disappearing into the staircase, did not even reply.

Alec stood there, numb. He looked out at the horizon, saw the black ships creeping inevitably closer, and his life, he sensed, was about to change. There was no escaping it, whether he stayed or left. He knew that leaving, crossing the sea with a man he barely knew, would be the craziest, most illogical thing he could do.

And yet, despite all that, the man's words rang in his head. Destiny. That was a big word, and no one had ever used it with Alec before, not once in his life. Could it be true? Was he someone special?

Without fully knowing what he was doing, Alec felt his feet leading him, felt himself walking, leaving the tower, heading for the staircase. He did not know what he would choose to do. But he knew that by the time he reached the bottom, the choice would be clear.

One destiny.

Or another.

CHAPTER THIRTY THREE

Kyle stood in the predawn blackness, high on the upper floors of the Tower of Ur, looking out the window, and felt a chill in his heart. He knew something was wrong. He watched as the sky began to light and listened as he heard nothing but the stillness of the universe, the sounds of insects rising, the distant crashing of the ocean waves. With all of his fellow Watchers asleep, this was his shift. On the surface, all was as it should be.

Yet his gut told him something else. Down below stretched the countryside of Ur, the plains barren, the forest a silhouette, the silence eerie. He knew he should be sleeping, should be preparing for the morning's shift—but his dreams had awakened him, and had kept him awake. They were dreams unlike any he had ever had, something profound shifting within him ever since his encounter with that girl.

Kyra.

When he had laid eyes upon her for the first time, he had known, unmistakably, that she was the one. The one from the prophecies. The one destined to change everything. And the one and only girl he would ever be with.

Yet he also knew that his laying eyes upon her, a human, was forbidden, she not being of his race, and had been a grave risk to take. He had suffered the consequences, confined here to the upper floors of the tower as a punishment. He knew that worse punishment would follow. But he did not care; it had been worth it to save her life, and even more so, just to see her. He could still feel the touch of her skin on his fingertips. It sustained him.

And yet his dreams, too vivid, had awakened him again and again. It was the same dream, repeating itself, like someone knocking on his soul: a disturbing nightmare, in which Kyra was riding alone, into the forest, and killed. He could not tell what killed her, but he knew it was not of this earth.

Could she really die now, he wondered, after all this? Anything, he knew, was possible.

Kyle paced before his window, his palms damp, a cold sweat running down his back. His heart slammed as he scoured the countryside, wondering. Had it all just been a dream? Or was it something else? Was Kyra in danger? Did she need him?

Kyle paced, agonized, knowing that if he fled the tower now, they would banish him. They would never let him back inside, ever, at any cost, and he would turn his back on centuries of training, centuries of guarding the sacred code. And yet he also felt that if he stayed here, Kyra, the one true love of his life, would die. And that was something he just could not allow.

Kyle closed his eyes and tuned into his special power, the one he tapped rarely, only when life and death were at stake. He became very still, and he waited.

Soon, it came to him. He began to hear it. It was a distant sound, miles off. He heard a horse galloping. He heard Kyra, breathing hard. He heard branches breaking. He heard the wolf beside them, running, breathing.

He tuned in, deeper, and he sensed danger. Kyra racing through the woods. Her being surrounded. Ambushed.

Kyle opened his eyes with a start and looked out at the countryside, his eyes aglow. He could not let her die.

Even though his next move would determine his fate, Kyle didn't think twice. He jumped up on the ledge, and without another thought, he leapt.

He fell a hundred feet through the air—until he landed, like a cat, on the grass below.

He began to walk. Then to run.

Within moments, Kyle was sprinting into the breaking dawn, toward the forest of Ur, turning his back on all that he had ever known for a girl he barely knew. He only hoped it was not too late.

*

Merk, unable to sleep, paced the lower floors of the Tower of Ur, his mind still reeling from his encounter with the trolls, from his near death on the roof from one of his own. Danger, it seemed, lurked everywhere. Busy securing the tower with the other Watchers, preparing for battle, he had lost himself in the work, determined to defend this place which felt like home. He knew he should feel a sense of peace, at least, in that.

Yet peace eluded him, and some inner sense kept gnawing at him, kept him awake. At first he thought it was his urge to protect; yet the more he dwelled on it, the more he realized it was something else, some sense of foreboding that had guided him his entire life. It had nothing to do with the coming army. It was something else, some other danger. He did not know what, but his instincts never failed him.

Merk paced, walking past dozens of other Watchers in the long, stone chamber. He looked out the windows as the dawn light slowly lit the place, making his way from window to window, even though it was not his shift. He was watching—but for what, he did not know.

He finally sat beside one window in particular, leaned against it, the stone cool on his hands, and searched the countryside as dawn broke.

All was still, nothing out of place. He watched and watched, and nothing changed, except for the slight rising of the sun, the quieting of the night birds. He knew there was nothing he should be worried about.

Merk rubbed his eyes, wondering if he should just go back to sleep—when suddenly, movement caught his eye. Something glistened across the clearing in the early morning light. It was a figure, running. It disappeared as quickly as it had appeared, and Merk blinked and for a moment wondered if he had seen anything at all. He reflected, and felt sure he saw the long golden hair, moving so fast, like lightning. It moved too fast to be human. And he suddenly knew without a doubt it could only be one person: Kyle.

Merk realized, with a chill, what he had witnessed: Kyle had somehow descended from the tower and had fled into the woods. But why? Merk knew Kyle had been punished, detained, transferred to the upper floors, forbidden to leave the tower. Everyone had been talking about it. Why would Kyle risk leaving when that meant he could never return?

Merk then had another thought, equally disturbing: Kyle's unannounced departure would leave the upper floors unattended. Vulnerable.

Merk knew he had to do something. All the others were sleeping, and he alone had witnessed it. He couldn't just stay here and act as if he had seen nothing. He had to, at the very least, go upstairs and find out for himself if the tower was truly left vulnerable.

Slipping across the room, quietly so as not to wake the others, many of whom he did not trust anyway, Merk opened the heavy wooden door and closed it quietly behind him. He stood in the stone hallway of the tower, cool and dim and circular, the huge spiral staircase sitting in its center. It sat like a work of art, leading up and down, like a warning to go in either direction, both forbidden.

Merk looked up and saw the early morning light filtering down through the golden dome, illuminating the stairs. He knew that ascending would mean being banished from the tower. And yet, he felt he had to go. It was the only way to protect the tower. Merk had to fulfill Kyle's watch.

He took a deep breath, debating, then finally took the first fateful step on the staircase, knowing it would change everything— and yet also knowing that, come what may, it was his sacred duty.

Merk climbed, heart pounding, knowing he was heading into forbidden territory, knowing he was risking everything. He quickly ascended flight after flight, each story engraved with different insignias on the wall, gleaming in different-colored jewels, with strange signs he could not understand, and different-shaped doorways. This tower was endlessly mysterious.

Finally, Merk reached the top floor, and breathing hard, he paused. The stone looked different up here, the doors a weathered oak, crossed with iron bars, doors meant to be sealed. And yet one, he saw with a jolt of fear, was ajar, light streaming out from the other side. Something was wrong. Someone clearly had taken advantage of Kyle's absence and had used the opportunity to enter this floor. Someone from inside the tower.

There was a traitor from inside.

Heart pounding, Merk stepped forward and slowly pushed open the door he knew he was not allowed to touch. On guard, he stepped inside, and was shocked to find himself in a chamber carved entirely of rubies, a glowing red light reflected by flickering torches on all sides. He peered into the dim light, disoriented, and saw at the far end of the room, another door, carved of gold, with intricate markings across it. Merk felt a rush as he sensed immediately that

that was *the* door. The door behind which no one could enter, not even a Watcher. The legendary door.

The door to the Sword of Flames.

As Merk squinted into the light he saw something else, something even more shocking: a figure, moving stealthily in the darkness, heading for the door.

The man spun, startled, as Merk entered, and Merk saw surprise and fear on his face, as if he were caught in the act.

"Pult?" Merk asked, recognizing his fellow Watcher, unable to forget the man after the way he had treated him on the roof. "But why?"

Merk looked down as Pult tried to hide something in his hand, and he saw a flat metal tool, clearly meant to pry open a door. Merk realized, in a flood of rage, that there was a traitor in their midst.

Pult let out a cry and suddenly charged across the room, right for him. He drew a dagger and swung for Merk's gut, a slash that would have sliced Merk in two.

Merk, though, let his instinct take over from years of fighting, and he dodged without thinking. The dagger flew by, slicing his arm, but not killing him.

Merk reacted without even thinking. He spun around and elbowed the man across the face. It was a hard blow, one meant to kill a man, and Pult dropped to his knees. But to Merk's surprise, Pult immediately jumped back up and swung with his dagger, slicing Merk.

Merk, reeling in pain, stared back at his adversary, realizing he had underestimated him. Pult charged and slashed again, and this time Merk wheeled around and kicked him in the stomach, sending him to his knees. He then kicked his chin, then his wrist, sending his dagger clattering across the floor.

But Pult, apparently undefeatable, spun and tackled Merk, wrapping his head and shoulders around his waist and driving backwards.

Merk was driven back until his back slammed into the golden door. There came a crack, as the door opened and Merk landed on the floor before it, winded. Merk could feel the cool draft from the open room on his neck.

Merk looked up to see Pult on top of him, dagger raised, lowering it for his face. Merk shifted his head at the last moment and the dagger clanged and sparked as it impacted stone. In the same motion Merk reached up, grabbed the man's face with both hands, and twisted. It was a crude move, but one that had served him well his entire life. The inevitable crack came, and a moment later the man slumped down on top of him, neck broken, dead.

Merk realized, too late, it had been a foolish move. He should have kept the man alive, to interrogate him, to understand why he had betrayed them, who had sent him. But with the man lying on top of him, dead, there was nothing for Merk to do but shove his dead weight off.

Merk slowly made it to his hands and knees, breathing hard, reeling from the pain, and collected himself. He felt the draft on his neck again, saw the unnatural light flooding the room, and he hesitated, realizing he sat at the entrance to the sacred room, its door ajar. His back was to it, and he knew he shouldn't turn around, shouldn't look inside, this forbidden room on a forbidden floor, the most sacred of the sacred places of Escalon. He knew he had no right to look upon the ancient Sword of Flames, the sacred object that protected all of Escalon. If it was even there.

He tried to will himself to just walk out. To not turn back. To close the door behind him.

But as he stood there, inside the sacred chamber, he burned with curiosity. He could not walk away. Not now. Not being so close.

Despite everything inside him screaming not to, Merk, despite all his efforts, slowly turned around. He had to lay his own eyes upon the legend that had haunted him his entire life.

As he slowly turned, the light grew brighter, and he soon found himself squinting, peering into the inner sanctum, the most sacred place in Escalon.

He gasped, and his eyes widened.

He stood there, breathless.

He could not believe what he saw.

CHAPTER THIRTY FOUR

Vidar stood atop the battlements of Volis in the falling snow, studying the countryside, sensing something was wrong. He had awakened early, before dawn, and had been standing here for hours, watching. All his men stood beside him, waiting.

They had asked what it was that had woken him, that had led him up here on this quiet dawn, but he had been unable to respond. It was some instinct, from years of battle, that death was coming. An instinct that had led him to survive. The same instinct that had led Duncan to put him in charge of Volis in his absence.

Vidar watched the horizon as day broke cold and gray, and saw nothing but snow. He had stood there so long, frigid, his hands numb, his men pacing, clearly wanting to return to the warmth of the fort, that he was beginning to doubt himself.

And then, suddenly, he saw it: a small plume of black smoke, wafting up on the horizon, barely visible in the snow. At the same time, he smelled it: a smell in the air of something burning. Something more than pine.

And then, he felt it: a tremor, the slightest tremor beneath his feet, not recognizable to others—but recognizable to him. It was, he knew in every bone of his body, the advance of an army.

But what army? he wondered. The Pandesians were nowhere close, the northeast of Escalon liberated. The dragon, too, had flown far away, and had not been seen since; nor would a dragon be marching on the ground. It made no sense. It was as if Escalon were under attack—but who could be attacking from within?

Vidar studied the horizon, pondering the skeleton force of men that Duncan had left him with to guard Volis, the force that Duncan had been sure he would never have to employ. Now Vidar wondered, with dread, if he would need it, if he would truly have to defend this remote fort with these few men. It was a defense, he knew, he could not sustain. Against a band of brigands, yes—but not against an army.

Vidar turned to his men, these loyal men, posted here in the midst of nowhere with him, staring back with their solemn faces, as frozen as the landscape, and he could see in their eyes that they would stand beside him anywhere. He loved them for that.

"Close the gates," he commanded to his lieutenant, his voice calm and cold as steel. It was a serious tone, and his men looked back with surprise.

"All women and children indoors. Bar the windows, lock the doors, and lower the portcullis."

His men hesitated just a moment, then nodded back with equal solemnity. One nodded to the other, a horn was sounded, a great, long horn, its sound feeling as if it were reaching the heavens, and Vidar closed his eyes and took a deep breath, the sound vibrating through him, hardly believing this was really happening.

Vidar hurried down the stone spiral staircase, his men close behind, as he descended from the parapets and marched quickly across the inner courtyard of Volis. All about him villagers scurried, vendors closing booths, women and children and the elderly hurrying in disarray to get indoors. Doors slammed and shutters were bolted. Vidar could feel the chaos and panic about him, and he prayed to all the gods he knew that he could protect these people he had been sworn to protect.

As his men began to close the massive gates, to turn the cranks for the portcullis, Vidar gestured for them to wait. He wanted to go out there, to see with his own eyes what it was.

Vidar walked through the gates, out into the danger zone, expecting to go alone, but he heard a few of his loyal brothers behind him, joining him. They crossed the drawbridge together, hollow wood creaking beneath their boots, and as they reached the far side, snow beneath their feet, Vidar stood there, watching.

He felt the cool breeze on his face, heavy with snow, and he still could see nothing but plains of snow and, in the distance, the dark treeline of the Wood of Thorns.

The rumbling noise grew, though, louder and louder, the vibration beneath his feet more intense, until finally his men exchanged a baffled look. Now, they felt it, too, and all were clearly wondering.

As Vidar studied the woodline, he saw it begin to move. Then there burst forth a sight which he could never have anticipated in his wildest dreams, a sight which he would never forget.

Vidar blinked, wondering if his eyes were playing tricks on him. Soon enough, he realized they were not. It was a nightmare, coming to life.

There, racing for Volis, was an army of trolls. *Thousands* of them. They spread across the countryside with their huge, misshapen bodies, their grotesque faces, wielding massive halberds, shouting and covered in blood. It was an army of death. And it was heading right for them.

Vidar stared back with a cold dread. He could not understand it. How had Marda breached The Flames?

Vidar felt a deep foreboding overcome him as he suddenly knew with certainty that on this day, he would die. They would all die. They had no possible chance of victory, not even if he had a thousand fine soldiers at his back. And he had but a dozen.

And yet, the idea of his own death did not pain him the most. What hurt him was the thought of those women and children inside. The idea that he would be unable to defend them. That he would let them all down.

Vidar locked his jaw, feeling a wave of indignation. He wanted to give them all time, all those women and children, a little bit more time in this world. And a slim chance, however bleak it was, of survival. Maybe, just maybe, if the portcullis held, the stone walls stood, maybe they could withstand a siege. Though deep down, Vidar already knew they could not.

"We cannot defend," came the too grave voice of one of his men, staring, too, at the horizon. Vidar was proud to hear no panic in the soldier's voice—just resolve.

"No," Vidar answered honestly. After all, dying men deserved to know the truth. "We cannot."

Vidar took a deep breath.

"But we can go down fighting," he added, his voice filled with a rising resolve, "and maybe, take a few with us."

Vidar turned and looked up at his men on the battlements. They were all staring down, looking to him for direction. This was the fateful moment in time, Vidar knew, for which he had been born.

"Man the battlements!" he shouted. "Prepare the oil and fire! Tighten the catapults! Upon my command, fire!"

Vidar turned to his squire, a young boy who had always been at his side, staring back now with fear in his eyes.

"Seal the portcullis behind me," he commanded.

His squire looked back at him, stunned.

"And you remain outside?" he asked. "Alone? You'll be killed!"

Vidar lay a reassuring hand on his shoulder.

"We shall all die, boy," he said. "The only question is how. Now, go.

"And you men," he added, turning to the loyal soldiers beside him. "Inside."

But they shook their heads.

"As you said," one replied, "the only question is how."

They all drew their swords and stood beside him, and turned and bravely faced the incoming army. Vidar nodded back in respect, admiring these men more than he'd ever thought possible. It would be good to die in company such as this.

The boy did as he was told. Soon, Vidar heard the great iron portcullis slam closed behind him, sealing him out of the fort for good. Vidar drew his sword as he stood there, appreciating the finality. It gave him strength.

He watched the army come closer, now hardly a few hundred yards away.

"CATAPULTS!" he commanded. "NOW!"

Vidar watched as overhead there soared a dozen flaming boulders, arcing high through the sky and landing in the midst of the troll army as they neared. Shouts filled the air as hundreds of trolls shrieked and fell.

And yet, thousands more followed. Too fast, and too close, for more boulders to reach.

Vidar drew his sword and waited. He felt the ground shaking beneath him now as they charged. He stood there, gripping his sword, and he knew he would not kill many of them. But the ones he would kill would matter. That was all he needed. He wanted to kill the first casualty of this battle himself, wanted to go down swinging.

They neared. Thirty yards, then twenty, then ten, so close that Vidar could make out the face of their leader, the troll he had heard was named Vesuvius, dripping with blood, grotesque, wielding two halberds as if they were toothpicks.

With the army just feet away, Vidar could no longer wait. He let out a battle cry and charged.

"MEN!" he shouted. "FOR HONOR!"

His men shouted, too, and they all raced forward beside him, swords drawn. A few of them against a thousand.

Vidar ran right for their leader, and as Vesuvius brought down his halberds, Vidar blocked them, sparks flying, their weight so powerful they shattered his blade.

A moment later, Vidar gasped as he felt Vesuvius plunge the point of his halberd through his gut. He had never had such exquisite pain, pain so intense that he couldn't breathe, couldn't think. This, he knew now, was what death felt like.

Any other soldier would have caved. But not Vidar . He thought of Duncan. He thought of his vow. Of the women and children inside Volis. And he refused to go down. Not until he had inflicted death himself.

Vidar thought of every battle he'd ever fought, of fighting by Duncan's side. And he was not ready to die. Not yet.

Somehow, Vidar mustered the strength. The strength for one last blow.

Then, even while dying, he raised the jagged end of his shattered sword and plunged it into Vesuvius's chest.

And as Vidar fell, dying, he had at least one final piece of satisfaction: Vesuvius, the shattered sword in his chest, was falling with him, two limp bodies on the battlefield, in the snow, falling on top of each other, trampled by an army racing for the gates, racing to destroy everything Vidar had ever known and loved.

CHAPTER THIRTY FIVE

The baby dragon stood tied to the stake, bound by ropes, in the courtyard of the Pandesian fort, in horrific agony from his wounds—and now, also, in despair. He ached in every part of his body, where the ropes dug into his scales, where his back met the pole, in so much agony he wished he had never emerged from his shell. Life, he was realizing, was cruel.

Even so, that was not what hurt him the most. What hurt him far more than any of his wounds was the sight before him: his father, lying there before him, dead.

He recalled his sense of pride in watching his father fly over the fort, killing his captors, his father's wings so massive, blotting out the sun. He still recalled the heat of his flames, flames that he hoped to breathe himself one day, waves of flame shooting down like rain. He had felt justice, vindication, knowing his father would kill all of these men. Most touching of all, he knew his father was doing it all for him, to rescue *him*. It had instilled in him a sense of love, of pride, beyond which he knew was possible. For the first time, he had not felt alone since being born in the universe. He had screeched, trying to join in and to make his father proud.

His father had been so close to saving him, his claws outstretched; he had anticipated the feeling of his father freeing him, grabbing him and flying away. He was just a few feet from freedom, from the two of them being far away from here, safe.

Instead, he had been forced to watch helplessly as the soldiers led his father into a trap, lured him lower and entangled him in that net. His heart broke as he watched his father plummeting, diving headfirst into the dirt. The final knife in his heart was watching those cowardly soldiers rush forward, all at once, surround his father, and stab him to death. He had sensed his father's great life force disappear, and it had torn him to bits.

The baby let out a screech, as loud as his small lungs would allow, a screech of agony, of despair, of a creature with nothing left to lose. As he screeched, his little lungs grew louder and louder, and the soldiers, still stabbing his father, began to take notice and turn his way. As he screeched, the feelings inside him began to morph:

despair was replaced with anger; sadness with rage. His agony over his father's death gave him strength, made him forget his wounds, his pain. It blinded him, and he felt stronger than he ever would otherwise.

As he leaned back and writhed, suddenly, to his surprise, he heard a snap.

Then another.

He did not need to look to know what was happening: he was breaking his ropes. One at a time they snapped, as the baby dragon slowly became infused with a strength he had never known. The remaining ropes loosened, and he leaned over and, with his sharp teeth, bit through one.

Then another.

Finally, he leaned forward, pulled back his wings, and in one great motion, snapped all the remaining ropes.

The soldiers turned his way, realizing, now directing their attention toward him. They slowly closed in, guardedly raising their weapons, with a look that belied their uncertainty. As they neared, he leaned back, opened his mouth, and breathed, praying for fire.

To his surprise, this time it came—a stream of fire. Molten hot, it was a fire unlike any he had yet breathed, a fire which came from deep within his soul. It stretched farther this time, and farther, rolling out in waves. It killed a dozen Pandesian soldiers instantly, all too shocked to get out of the way in time.

The dragon leapt from the platform, into the air, and as he started to free-fall toward the ground, he flapped his wings with all his might—and this time, he was happily surprised to find that they had grown, and that he now had control. He flapped harder and harder, and soon his free fall leveled out. And then he began to fly.

At first his flight was slow, awkward. But soon he gained strength and speed and found himself flying straight, then soaring. He was really flying. It was exhilarating.

He flew higher and higher, out of reach of the stunned soldiers below, and he was elated. He was free. Before him was an open horizon, clouds, freedom. He had survived. He could go anywhere in the world he wanted. He could control his movements, dive and rise, turn from side to side; his claws felt stronger, too, and he expanded and contracted them, feeling invincible—and needing to claw something.

He looked down below and saw the soldiers milling about, and vengeance summoned him. After all, his father's body still lay down there, and he was his father's son.

He turned and dove back toward the fort where he had been imprisoned, tortured, knowing the risks but no longer caring. He flapped his wings and let out a screech—no longer a baby screech, but now a dragon's screech—and he dove down impossibly fast. As the soldiers looked up, he opened his mouth and breathed, and out came hot flame, waves of fire unrolling below, killing hundreds at once.

Panic ensued as the men's shrieks filled the air. They ran for cover, but there was none to be had. He was too fast, too dexterous, small enough to weave in and out of tight spaces, and their little trick with the net had already been exhausted. A few soldiers lamely threw spears at him, but these merely bounced off his scales. He dove and breathed flame in return, and any soldier he missed with his fire, he clawed to death in a single swipe. One soldier, a man he remembered had tortured him, he snatched and hoisted into the air, higher and higher, until he was straight over the stake. He then dropped him.

He watched with satisfaction as the man plummeted, shrieking, then landed on the stake, impaled.

He screeched with all his might, and soon, it was a sound even he did not recognize. It was the sound of a dragon maturing too fast.

Of a dragon ready to take over the world.

CHAPTER THIRTY SIX

Duncan crossed the capital courtyard in the breaking dawn, filled with a sense of optimism he had not had in a long time. Finally, it was a new day in Escalon, a day which would change his life, and the fate of his homeland, forever. He had not slept since his encounter with Tarnis, filled with a sense of triumph, of anticipation. He thought of the imminent truce, the pact he was about to accept with Pandesia, and he realized he had achieved all he had ever hoped to achieve for his people and more. He felt as if he were walking into history. Once and for all, Escalon would be free.

Duncan marched quickly, Kavos, Bramthos, Seavig, Arthfael, his sons Brandon and Braxton and all his commanders beside him, his hundreds of warriors marching behind him, all of them filling the city in the early dawn, through the empty streets, the sound of their clanging armor echoing off the walls, off the courtyards and plazas, their boots marching on cobblestone to perfect rhythm. They were one, a unified force, the already legendary men who had liberated Escalon against all odds. This would be a great day for them all.

Duncan glanced over at Tarnis, marching with them, prepared to help broker the truce, and he could see from his earnest expression that he was eager to make up for past wrongs, for allowing Pandesia in, and that he wanted to set wrongs right. Duncan had always known that he would, that deep down, Tarnis was a good man.

They passed beneath a massive stone arch and finally, the city square opened up, and as it did, Duncan looked out before him and was thrilled at the sight. There, as Tarnis had promised, stood the Pandesian governor, alone, awaiting him, the ceremonial black and white sword of surrender in his hands, palms up. Duncan's heart quickened. Everything Tarnis had promised was true.

Emboldened, Duncan marched into the courtyard, Kavos on one side, his two sons beside him, and Seavig and Tarnis on the other side, ready to accept Pandesia's surrender, to negotiate a truce for all time.

They all finally came to a stop, Duncan but ten feet away from the Pandesian governor. The square was dead silent, almost too silent. The governor glared back at him, this representative of Pandesia, who had invaded his country, who had made their lives hell, and Duncan, face to face with the enemy, forced himself to contain his anger.

Duncan waited in the silence. It was the Pandesians, after all, who had offered the truce, and it was they who must speak first.

Finally, after a long, uncomfortable silence, the governor, a prim man in an elegant dress who was sweating despite the cool morning, stepped forward. His eyes darted nervously in his head, and Duncan expected him to reach out and hand him the ceremonial sword; but instead, to Duncan's surprise, the governor turned the blade and dropped it to the ground.

Duncan reddened.

"That is an insult," Duncan said, baffled.

The governor smiled back.

"Good," he replied.

Suddenly, the courtyard filled with the sound of armor rattling, of boots marching from all directions. Duncan spun and was stunned to see himself entirely surrounded by a division of Pandesian soldiers, thousands of men marching in a coordinated fashion from all sides of the courtyard, entering through the open-aired arches, emerging from every possible crevice. He heard the sound of arrows being drawn, and he looked up to see thousands more soldiers perched atop the battlements, arrows trained down on him. Even more shocking, they were dressed in the colors of Escalon. Duncan narrowed his eyes and realized they bore the red and black insignia of Baris. Yet he did not see Bant amongst them.

Duncan tightened his grip on his sword and clenched his jaws with fury, beginning to realize the depth of the betrayal. He was dumfounded that his own countrymen could turn on him, and astounded that he had led his men into a trap.

Duncan's men shifted nervously in every direction, realizing, too, that they were surrounded, and Duncan turned to Tarnis, furious that he had sold him out. Yet Duncan was surprised to see from his face that Tarnis was shocked, too. Duncan followed his glance and turned to see Enis emerge from the Pandesian side, standing beside the governor, and it all became clear: Enis had orchestrated this all. He had sold out not only Duncan and his men, but his own father.

Duncan froze, realizing that, for the first time in his life, he had been outmaneuvered. They could perhaps fight the men surrounding them, even against the greater numbers, but with all those bows aimed down at them, they couldn't even risk drawing their swords.

Enis stepped forward, a satisfied sneer on his face, came close to Duncan and stared him down.

"Well," Enis finally said, breaking the tense silence, "you had your chance. Now I have made myself King."

Duncan frowned back, repulsed by this boy.

"My boy, what have you done?" Tarnis asked, his voice pained, sounding much older.

Duncan saw the genuine horror, the sense of betrayal, on Tarnis's face, and he realized that, at least, Tarnis had not collaborated with his son. He clearly had no knowledge of this.

"I did no worse than you, Father," Enis replied, "when you let them in through the gates. I am merely finishing the job which you began. Your time has passed—it is my time now. You have your way of bartering, and I have mine. Mine is much more efficient, it seems. All I had to do was trade one man and his men to secure our borders. Quite the deal, don't you think?"

Duncan glowered.

"You are worse than your father," he seethed. "Tarnis, at least, sought to help our country. But you—you make a pact with your own countrymen to ambush your own people. And not for any sake of peace, but all for your own position. Your father did it for security—but you do it for power."

Kavos, clenching his jaw, tightened his grip on his spear.

"I warned you, Duncan," he said, his voice filled with rage. "I warned you to kill them all."

"The time for words has passed," Enis snapped, turning to Duncan. "Lay down your weapons now, and I will spare your men. Resist, and look up: you will all be dead before you draw a sword. There is no way out."

Duncan looked around, fuming, knowing he was right. As a soldier, he craved to fight anyway, even with arrows protruding from his body, to fight to the death; yet as the commander of these men, and now as their King, he felt a responsibility. He could not sacrifice all these men's lives. They would follow him anywhere, would fight anywhere for him, and he could not betray that sacred trust.

Duncan slowly laid down his sword, and one at a time, the air filled with the sound of men drawing swords slowly and laying them down on the stone. The courtyard filled with the clatter of a thousand pieces of steel hitting stone.

Only Kavos stood there, gripping his weapon, trembling with anger.

"Kavos," Duncan said softly.

He gave Duncan a long, hard look, then finally, reluctantly, he laid it down, too.

Enis's smile widened in satisfaction.

"Son, you cannot do this," Tarnis said in a fatherly tone, stepping forward and laying a hand on his shoulder. "It is dishonorable. I negotiated a truce, in my name. You disgrace it."

"Your name was already disgraced, Father," Enis replied. "But mine, on the other hand," he said, and stepped forward, pulled out a hidden dagger, and stabbed his father in the heart. "Mine will live forever."

Tarnis gasped as he collapsed to the ground at Duncan's feet.

Duncan stood there, horrified, disbelieving what he had just seen. A father killed by his own son, all for the sake of power. As much as he disapproved of Tarnis, he did not deserve to die that way.

Duncan, irate, rushed forward to grab him, but suddenly, he felt himself grabbed and yanked backwards from behind, as Pandesian soldiers from all sides closed in and restrained him. Duncan writhed with all his might, but he could not break free as he watched the nightmare unfolding before him. He was furious, most of all, at himself. Kavos had been right all along. Why had he trusted them?

"You will pay for this!" Duncan shouted.

"I think not," Enis smiled.

Suddenly, from the Pandesian side, Bant emerged. He stepped forward and sneered at Duncan.

"It looks like you can't protect your little birds any longer," he seethed.

Bant then stepped toward Brandon and Braxton, each restrained by Pandesian soldiers, and sneered at them, but a few feet away.

"Not so big now without your father to protect you?" he asked them.

And then, before Duncan could react, Bant raised a sword, stabbed Brandon, then stabbed Braxton, in the chest.

Duncan felt as if he himself were stabbed as he watched his boys collapse at his feet.

"NO!" Duncan shrieked.

He writhed with all he had, dying inside, unable to break free, and suddenly he felt a metal gauntlet smashing him across the face, knocking him unconscious. And as his face hit stone, landing beside his two dead sons, his world turning black, he had one final thought:

Kyra? Where are you?

CHAPTER THIRTY SEVEN

Aidan sprinted through the back streets of Andros in the breaking dawn, White at his side, gasping for air as he ran, refusing to stop. He turned down street after street, criss-crossing the sprawling city, his lungs bursting, his legs burning, and not caring. After witnessing those men in that back alley arranging to betray his father, he was more desperate than ever to find him, to warn him before it was too late. But with dawn breaking, Aidan's heart fell as he knew his time was running out. He ran even faster, ignoring the pain.

Aidan ran and ran, crossing through small squares, entering alleys, then emerging into squares again. He tried to follow the directions those people had given him, hours before, asking everyone he could. He followed street signs, etched into the stone the walls, illuminated by torchlight, hard to read. The city was so still in the early morning light, so quiet, so peaceful, it was hard to believe that any chaos could be imminent.

Aidan stopped and rested as he emerged from an alley, grabbing onto a wall, heaving. He wiped sweat from the back of his hand, unsure if he could go on, unsure if he was even heading in the right direction—when suddenly, he heard it. It was the unmistakable sound of boots, marching. Of armor, clanging. It was an army. His father's army. And it lay just beyond those walls.

Aidan burst across the square, sprinting again, determined, running so fast he could barely breathe, White keeping pace beside him. Finally, after passing through a series of arches, he turned down an alleyway and emerged to see a huge open arch—and the sight on the other side of it dazzled him. There was a great square, the greatest of the capital, and assembling inside it, he saw with a thrill, was his father, standing there proudly, leading hundreds of men.

Aidan rushed forward, about to pass through, when something made him stop himself. He stood there, at the edge, in the shadows, as he noticed something else: thousands of other soldiers, dressed in blue and yellow, surrounding his father. Aidan's heart lurched as he realized who they were: Pandesians.

His father, he realized with a shock, had already been betrayed.

Aidan watched in horror as he saw his father and his men lay down their weapons; as he saw his father detained; and, most of all, as he watched his two older brothers, standing beside his father, suddenly get stabbed in the heart.

"NO!" Aidan cried out.

He began to run, to race out into the square, to help his father, his brothers, to grab whatever sword he could find and kill any Pandesians he could.

But a strong palm suddenly smothered his face, closing his mouth, silencing him. It pulled him back, stopping him in his tracks. The palm was fat, meaty, slick with sweat, the palm of an overweight man, and yet still it had strength, enough strength to detain him. Aidan was surprised that White didn't snarl, didn't help him—but then he looked over and realized, with a shock, why: it was Motley.

Aidan, anguished, desperate to aid his family, struggled to free himself.

"Let me go!" he tried to yell, between Motley's fingers.

But Motley tightened his grip and shook his head.

"If I do, you'll end up like them," he replied firmly, yanking him back into the shadows.

Aidan tried to resist with all his might, but Motley was too strong.

"That is not the way," Motley urged. "Be silent. You'll get us both killed, and you'll be of no help to your father or his men."

Aidan tried to resist, but it was no use. Despite himself, he felt tears pour down his cheeks as he relived in his mind's eye the image of his brothers being murdered.

"There is another way," Motley urged, his voice earnest for the first time since Aidan had met him. "A far wiser way. Don't die here. Live to fight another day. I will help you."

But Aidan thought of his family out there, on the other side of that wall, needing him, thought of how far he had journeyed, only to be stopped so close, and he writhed to break free, even if he knew, deep down, that Motley spoke the truth.

"I'm sorry," Motley said. "I don't want to do this. But if I don't, it will mean your death."

Motley stuffed a rag in Aidan's mouth, gagging him, and tossed him over his shoulder. Aidan tried to cry out, but it was no use; he kicked and flailed, but Motley was too strong.

Before he knew what was happening, Aidan was bouncing up and down, slung like a sack of potatoes over Motley's shoulder as Motley ran away from the square, through the dark alleyways, White at their side. Motley, badly overweight, heaved from the effort, but to his credit, he never stopped running. He managed to take them far from the square, far from the death of his brothers, the ambush of his father, far from all the misery, from all the events that Aidan knew would change his life forever, and off somewhere to another world.

CHAPTER THIRTY EIGHT

Anvin stood guard before the Southern Gate, Thebus and his men behind him, and as the sun rose high in the sky, the heat relentless off this patch of desert, he clenched and unclenched his grip on his sword. It was an old habit, one he always fell back on when danger was coming. And as he watched the horizon nervously, he saw looming the greatest danger of his life.

The rumble was growing louder, as it had been for hours, the horizon filled with a sea of black, infantry marching, hoisting the yellow and blue banners of Pandesia. Behind them came rows of cavalry, and behind these, rows of elephants, rhinos, and other beasts he did not recognize, all ridden by soldiers. The infantry bore all manner of weaponry, and they marched in perfect and terrifying discipline. The clip-clap of their boots sounded consistently, like a heartbeat, minute after minute, hour after hour, never breaking rank, never slowing, never speeding. That was what terrified him the most: the discipline. He'd never witnessed such exacting discipline in his life—especially amongst an army that size—and he knew that didn't bode well. Discipline like that, combined with numbers like that, could destroy anything. He could only imagine the exacting and cruel standards the Pandesian commanders must have employed to maintain it.

It was as if half the world were marching his way. The rows and rows of soldiers marched across the Fields of Ore, their boots now stomping on the hard, black rock, their armor clanging, each step like a small earthquake. There was no mistaking it: they were all, the weight of the world, marching for the Southern Gate. Right for him.

Anvin turned and looked out at the Sea of Sorrow on his one side, and the Sea of Tears on his other, and he took no solace in the sight. The oceans, too, were full of black, all closing in on him. Escalon was being squeezed, surrounded on all sides. There was no doubt: the great invasion had begun.

Anvin had expected this; yet he had also expected Duncan and his men to be at his back when it happened. The Southern Gate could hold them all back—but he couldn't do it alone, and he couldn't protect their flanks without support. He needed Duncan and his men. And while Duncan had vowed to be here, he was nowhere in sight.

"And where is your Duncan now?"

Anvin turned to see Durge glowering back, his eyes cold and hard, stung by betrayal. His men, too, stared back at Anvin with the same dark expression. Anvin turned and glanced over his shoulder for the thousandth time, searching the horizon, the barren plains of Thebus, expecting to see Duncan appear at any moment, with his army, to back them up as he had vowed.

Yet as he stared, Anvin was shocked and crestfallen to see nothing. He had been watching since dawn, convinced that Duncan would not let him down. Never once, in all their years together, had Duncan broken a vow, had he abandoned him. Yet now the sun reached high noon, and no reinforcements had arrived. If they had not come by now, Anvin knew, they would not come. Duncan had abandoned them all to die.

"You vowed," Thebus said, his voice trembling with anger. "You vowed the men of Thebus would not be betrayed again."

"Duncan will come," Anvin insisted, wishing he could believe it.

Durge stared back angrily.

"You cling to dreams," Durge replied. "The time has passed. We are alone now, left to be killed."

Anvin hardly knew what to say. Duncan's not arriving meant his death, too.

"He would not abandon us," Anvin insisted. "If he does not come, that could only mean one thing: he was captured or killed himself."

Thebus shrugged, uncaring.

"And a lot of good that does me," he replied.

Despite the death he saw marching for him, Anvin felt more concerned for Duncan, who was like a brother to him. For Duncan not to be here, he was either betrayed, captured, or dead. And if that had happened, then all of Escalon was lost. They had gambled—and failed.

The reality began to sink for Anvin that Duncan would not come. He would be alone out here, with these few men, to defend the Southern Gate against the hordes of the world.

And yet somehow, as the realization sank in, he felt no fear. No remorse. Instead, he felt gratitude. Gratitude that he could be allowed to make such a final stand in life, that he could die with a sword in his hand, outnumbered, facing the enemy bravely, a just cause behind him. It was all a warrior could wish for. Honor sometimes exacted a price, and this, indeed, was the precious weight of honor.

The marching grew louder. A series of horns sounded, deafening, and Anvin watched as the infantry broke into a jog—and then a sprint. The gap was narrowing; they were now but several hundred yards away.

"I won't die cowering behind this gate," Durge said.

Anvin saw his sneer and understood at once, feeling the same sentiment at the same time.

"Open the gates?" Anvin asked.

For the first time since they had met, Durge smiled wide.

"Open the gates," he echoed.

They turned to their men and nodded, and to their credit, their men opened the gates without hesitation, all apparently thinking the same thing, none showing any fear. They turned the heavy cranks, one turn at a time, and slowly but surely the chains rattled, and the massive gates rose higher and higher.

As it opened high enough, Anvin walked through it, Thebus by his side, two veteran warlords, two men who had seen it all, who had devoted their lives to Escalon. Two men who could command armies in their own right. They stood there, on the other side of the gate, unprotected, side by side, facing off against the hordes charging for them, thundering, deafening. They stood proudly, unflinching, neither looking back.

Anvin heard boots crunching in gravel, and he was proud to see, one at a time, all of his men step forward beside them, on this side of the gate. All unflinching. All doing what they had been born to do.

As Anvin squinted into the sunlight, into the rising clouds of dust, he thought of his life, of his family, of Volis. He thought of his friends, his children. He thought of Duncan. He thought of Kyra, how much he admired her, how he had always been a mentor to her. And for some reason, of all his final thoughts, he wished that she, above all, would survive. Would live to avenge him.

217

The hordes neared, hardly a hundred yards away now, the ground shaking, and Anvin drew his sword, the distinctive sound still able to be heard above the din, while Thebus and the others drew theirs, too. Not one of them looked back. They all stood there in the open, no gate before them, unprotected. Welcoming. Ready to embrace their fate.

"MEN OF ESCALON!" Anvin shouted. "FOR FREEDOM!"

They all let out a great shout, as suddenly, Anvin broke into a sprint. He would not wait for the enemy—instead, he would rush out to greet them. His men followed close behind, a few men against a million, racing toward battle, toward death, and toward the glorious ecstasy of honor.

CHAPTER THIRTY NINE

Kyra, riding Andor, Leo at her side, galloped through the thick forest of Ur in the morning light, haunted by her visions and determined to reach her father in time. She saw her father's face as she recalled her vision of his getting killed, and she closed her eyes and tried to blot it out. She saw Theos, too, lying dead, and she hoped and prayed that somehow it was all just an illusion, all just another test. Yet somehow, deep down, she knew it was not.

Kyra rode on and on, as she had for hours, knowing the capital was still far away yet determined to cross Escalon. She would not stop until she reached him. She heard Alva's warning ringing in her mind, urging her not to leave, and she tried to shake that, too. But she could not shake her own premonition that she was heading into danger. She did not care; if her father was dead, then she had no reason to live, either.

Kyra galloped, head down, increasing her speed, pushing herself as hard as she could, when something caught her attention in the early morning light. Out of the corner of her eye, she saw something glisten in the woods, and as she looked over, she saw a pond, reflecting light. Standing over it, in beautiful silver chain mail, she was shocked to see, was Kyle, his long golden hair down to his waist, staring back at her with his mesmerizing gray eyes. The boy who had saved her. The boy she had been unable to stop thinking about.

He held out a hand, looking right at her.

"Kyra," he called out. "Help me."

Kyra, entranced by the voice, by his eyes, had no choice. Without thinking she pulled on the reins, stopped Andor. She quickly dismounted and ran through the forest clearing, to the pond, to help him.

Kyra stopped a few feet away from him, the morning sun catching his eyes, radiating such beauty and love that she could hardly breathe.

"Are you hurt?" she asked.

"I need you," he replied.

She sensed something different about him, his voice. There was something different in his mannerisms, his expression, something she could not quite process.

She took a step closer, puzzled.

"What has happened to you?" she asked, concerned. She owed him her life, and she would do anything to help him.

Kyle removed a hand from his chest and as he did, Kyra was horrified to see it was covered in blood.

"Who did this to you?" she asked, breathless, wondering if he were dying.

She quickly tore a strip of cloth from her shirt and held it to his chest with both hands, pressing it into the wound. She examined it, expecting it to fill with blood, and was baffled to find no blood on the bandage. She looked up at the wound, and it was now entirely healed.

Kyra looked at Kyle, baffled, and to her shock, she no longer saw the boy's face. Instead, it was the face of an old, haggard woman, dressed in armor, in the blue and yellow of Pandesia. She sneered back at Kyra with a hateful smile, and as she reached up with a glistening object, and as Leo snarled, Kyra realized, too late, that she had been tricked. It was not Kyle after all, but a powerful shapeshifter.

At the same moment, Leo and Andor rushed forward, to protect her and, snarling, leapt for the woman; but the woman merely raised a wrinkled hand, and as she did, they both collapsed to the forest floor, immobile.

Kyra was too stunned to react as she saw something flashing, and a moment later, before she could fully process it all, she felt the agony of a sharp blade puncturing her skin, entering her stomach, deeper and deeper, until she could no longer breathe. She had never felt pain like that in her life.

Kyra gasped, gushing blood, unable to think, the pain so intense.

"Greetings," the woman said, "from Pandesia."

The woman cackled as Kyra fell to the ground, limp. She lay there, getting weaker by the moment, only dimly aware of her surroundings. As blood dripped from her mouth, as she felt herself leaving this world, one final thought swirled in her mind:

Forgive me, Father.

COMING SOON!

Book #4 in Kings and Sorcerers

Books by Morgan Rice

KINGS AND SORCERERS
RISE OF THE DRAGONS
RISE OF THE VALIANT
THE WEIGHT OF HONOR

THE SORCERER'S RING
A QUEST OF HEROES
A MARCH OF KINGS
A FATE OF DRAGONS
A CRY OF HONOR
A VOW OF GLORY
A CHARGE OF VALOR
A RITE OF SWORDS
A GRANT OF ARMS
A SKY OF SPELLS
A SEA OF SHIELDS
A REIGN OF STEEL
A LAND OF FIRE
A RULE OF QUEENS
AN OATH OF BROTHERS
A DREAM OF MORTALS

THE SURVIVAL TRILOGY
ARENA ONE (Book #1)
ARENA TWO (Book #2)

the Vampire Journals
turned (book #1)
loved (book #2)
betrayed (book #3)
destined (book #4)
desired (book #5)
betrothed (book #6)
vowed (book #7)
found (book #8)
resurrected (book #9)
craved (book #10)
fated (book #11)

About Morgan Rice

Morgan Rice is the #1 bestselling and USA Today bestselling author of the epic fantasy series THE SORCERER'S RING, comprising seventeen books; of the #1 bestselling series THE VAMPIRE JOURNALS, comprising eleven books (and counting); of the #1 bestselling series THE SURVIVAL TRILOGY, a post-apocalyptic thriller comprising two books (and counting); and of the new epic fantasy series KINGS AND SORCERERS. Morgan's books are available in audio and print editions, and translations are available in over 25 languages.

Morgan loves to hear from you, so please feel free to visit www.morganricebooks.com to join the email list, receive a free book, receive free giveaways, download the free app, get the latest exclusive news, connect on Facebook and Twitter, and stay in touch!

CPSIA information can be obtained
at www.ICGtesting.com
Printed in the USA
BVOW10s0707140417
481098BV00008B/83/P